Secrets of Zynpagua

Secrets of Zynpagua

Search of *Soul* Mates

Ilika Ranjan

PARTRIDGE

Cover Page Designing: Nideep Varghese.
Sketches: Nideep Varghese
Edited by: Swati Kapoor Malhotra

ISBN: Softcover 978-1-4828-8667-2
eBook 978-1-4828-8666-5

Print information available on the last page.

To order additional copies of this book, contact
Partridge India
000 800 10062 62
orders.india@partridgepublishing.com

www.partridgepublishing.com/india

Contents

Secrets of Zynpagua: Search of *Soul* Mates

The book Secret of Zynpagua: Search of *Soul* mates is the sequel of the first book Secret of Zynpagua: Return of the Princess

Book 1: Secrets of Zynpagua: Return of the Princess (Summary of Part one enclosed with this book)

Book 2: Secret of Zynpagua: Search of *Soul* mates

To my lovely parents, my angels, my soul
Thank you for making my life so magical

Acknowledgement

I extend my gratitude to Mr. Sawal Das Jethani, founder and managing trustee of Chrysalis schools Bangalore for encouraging the spirit of reading and creative writing among students. I immensely appreciate his enlightening communication with me.

I thank Mr.George Ivan Gregory Mann, Principal of Carman School Dehradun and Bhowik Sir, the English teacher at Carman School.

A big thank you to all the lovely children. Thank you for being my light and constantly motivating me. Thank you for the love and affection showered on Secrets of Zynpagua. Thank you for constantly writing to me.

Many Angels extended their hand to help me and encourage me in this difficult journey of being an author.

The journey of the book ***Secrets of Zynpagua*** started from Delhi Public School Sarjapur, Bangalore. I extend my heartfelt gratitude to the Principal of Delhi Public School, Sarjapur Bangalore, Ms Manila Carvalho for her progressive outlook and helping the book reach children.

When I was a child, I wish I had a librarian like Ms. Beenu Garg of DPS Sarjapur who is so passionate about making reading interesting. Her warmth and help in reaching out to children is a memory I will cherish for life.

A big thank you to Dr. S. Sujatha, the Principal of BVM Global School, Chennai for her encouragement, warmth and passion for promoting reading.

I extend my gratitude to the Principal of Hopetown Girls School, Dehradun, Ms Maya Norula.

A big thank you to Ms Anita Bohra, the passionate and caring librarian of Hopetown Girls school, Dehradun.

I am grateful to Ms Chitra Venkateswaran for a very warm welcome at DPS, Coimbatore.

I humbly thank the Principals, librarians and teachers of the following schools for their support, encouragement and guidance.

Sherwood Nainital, Birla Vidya Mandir Nainital, Delhi Public School (all branches)Bangalore, School of India Bangalore, Army Public School Bangalore, BVM Chennai, Lotus Valley school and KR Mangalam school Gurgaon, Arya Cambridge School Mumbai, Vaidehi school Bangalore, Chrysalis School Marathahalli and Yelahanka Bangalore, Victoria Educares Pune. Ebenezer International school Bangalore, Mt. Carmel school Dehradun, Mussoorie International girls school, Hopetown girls school Dehradun, Gear International Bangalore, Delhi Public School Coimbatore.

I thank Mr. Parmil Mittal, head of D.K publishers and distributors for his guidance and support.

I thank Mr Kailash Thakare of India Book Distributors for ensuring the book reaches the children online.

A big thank you to Sunny Devatwal and Harshil Shah from Crossword Bookstores Ltd, for ensuring the book reaches its target and for their patient listening and help.

Crossword Aundh Pune team: This team taught me the power of selling, registering record sales of Secrets of Zynpagua. A big thank you to Mr Akash Gupta, owner of Crossword bookstores Pune and his Aundh store team -Ajay Gupta, Narendra Patil, Priyanka Mohan, Vijay Yadav, and Anil Yadav.

My sisters Malvika and Geetika, friends and family members for being a pillar of strength, always!

Character line up

Characters from Left to Right

Sussaina, Frederick, Anika, Drudan, Vivian, Leo, Femina

Summary of Book 1

Secrets of Zynpagua: Return of the Princess

Zynpagua was once a region on the Earth, ruled by Queen Sussaina and King Soto. Drudan the evil scientist of Zynpagua secretly created a fatal light called *Violet* to oust the King. This violet light generates such catastrophic movements and separates Zynpagua from the Earth, carrying with it all the people on that land. King Soto vanishes in the universe while Drudan imprisons Queen Sussaina behind the shadow of the Moon. The Sun and the stars witness this debacle and blame Queen Sussaina for the mishap. The stars withdraw all the favours from this land. Thus Zynpagua becomes a dark planet, lost in the universe.

Drudan's wife Pajaro, who had taught him magic, opposes him. She saves Sussaina's five year old son Vivian from Drudan. But Drudan hits her and she dies. Before dying, she transfers her magical powers to Vivian. After killing Pajaro, Drudan hides his own four years old son Leo somewhere. Leo had taken traits of his mother. He was a gifted child in whose presence no evil could function.

While locked behind the shadow of the Moon, Sussaina discovers she is pregnant. She prays to the Moon to save this child. The Moon grants Sussaina's wish and sends this infant to the Earth. The child lands at the doorstep of an Indian family. They adopt her immediately and name her Anika. This child has the power to influence the stars and save Zynpagua.

The story commences in the city of Shillong in India. Anika a ten year old girl, is running in the woods and her elder sister Radhika is chasing her. Something strange happens to Anika. She gapes at the Moon and in a state of trance, says 'the Moon is calling, I have to read the stars!' and faints.

Her sister Radhika brings her back home. When Anika is alone in her room, she meets a strange boy who comes out from the pomegranate juice. He speaks in an unknown language and disappears. This boy introduces himself as Frederick. He tells Anika that her brother Vivian from Zynpagua is coming to take her.

Vivian, who is now fifteen years, comes to take Anika to Zynpagua. He tells Anika that the only way to save Zynpagua from Drudan is to win the favours of the stars and request them to send their special rays and oust Drudan from Zynpagua. Vivian, who knows magic, puts Anika's family to sleep till she returns. Anika reaches Zynpagua and gradually impresses the stars and saves her land from Drudan. Drudan Leaves Zynpagua, pledging revenge!

(The book is available on flipkart and amazon and as e-book. Do read part one to enjoy Secrets of Zynpagua: Search of *Soul* mates.)

Secrets of Zynpagua: Search of *Soul* Mates

Prologue

'Lifc will ebb out from her soul
That is my mission my goal
My head burns and smoulders like coal
Seek revenge!
My heart cajoles.'

Drudan sat beside the coconut tree which was overlooking the foaming sea. It was an eerie night and the Moon had a strange halo around it. Drudan was angry and weak but an undercurrent of revenge kept his blood boiling and his heart beating. His marvelous creation, the violet light had been destroyed.

Before leaving Zynpagua, Drudan had declared that he knew where Soto was, but in reality, he knew nothing. Using his magical abilities he had sensed that Soto was somewhere near the confluence of Arabian Sea, Bay of Bengal and Indian Ocean and thus had landed in the city of Kanyakumari, in India.

Now, sitting on the banks of the Indian Ocean, he murmured 'Vile Anika, I detest you and will kill you. You impressed the stars and rescued Sussaina. You caused the Sun to rise in Zynpagua and destroy my violet light. Oh! Violet, my wonderful creation, my soul, my heart. I am so dead without you, so dead indeed.'

He held his head and pulled his hair. 'Ah! It is painful being without you my Violet, so painful. I feel lifeless, lifeless, lifeless... but I promise, this pain will give me strength. I will nurture this pain and create something as fatal as Violet. Oh my weeping soul, I promise I will extract Anika's soul out from her body.'

He looked up at the Moon and yelled **'You gave life to Anika and now it will be you who will take away her life.'**

For some time, he continued to look spitefully at the Moon and then turned his gaze towards the fierce sea. The waves looked eerie now, something Drudan had not noticed a while ago. They seemed to be dancing to the tune of the Moon.

'Does the Moonlight have a mystic effect on the sea?' he murmured.

Drudan fixed his gaze where the water of Arabian Sea, the Bay of Bengal and the Indian Ocean united, three shades of water mixing uniformly to lose their identity.

Then he thought, 'Leo's soul split and gave life to Anika; if I unite the souls, they can lose their identity. Then it will be farewell time for both. The Moon gave you life Anika; I promise I will use the Moonlight to take life away from you.'

Though Drudan failed to locate Soto here, this discovery had made his hopes rise high. He had been observing the movement of the tides in the moonlight for several days. The full Moon definitely had a magical effect on the waters of the confluence of the Bay of Bengal, the Arabian Sea and the Indian Ocean. This point seemed to him a power generating point, capable of uniting anything. Drudan had been pondering if he could collect a sample of this water and test it scientifically.

He tried reaching the point of confluence, on his magically created bee, but as he approached closer, his magic stopped working and his bee changed to crimson handkerchief and was swallowed by the sea. Had he not been an adept swimmer, he too would have been drowned in the sea. This experience made Drudan even more convinced about the strange effect of the Moonlight.

Drudan promised himself 'Let the sun rise and the stars

protect that wretched land. I will dissolve their Princess's soul.' Laughing aloud he yelled 'Yes, I will dissolve Anika's soul.'

The beach was almost deserted now except for a few fishermen, who were winding up for the day. He walked towards a fisherman who was tying nets on the boat.

'Friend, I need your help' said Drudan to the fisherman.

The fisherman looked at Drudan intently but did not answer and continued tying the nets.

Drudan repeated 'Friend I need your help'

The fisherman ignored Drudan once again.

His insouciance made Drudan livid and he yelled, 'You insect. How dare you turn your back on me'

Pointing his finger towards the fisherman, he roared 'Blaze!'

The fisherman instantly caught fire and was reduced to ashes. Other fishermen around were so petrified by this site, that they began to run. Drudan blew air towards them and trapped everyone with a magical spell.

'Please don't kill us. We will do whatever you command' pleaded one of the fishermen.

Drudan laughed and said, 'That is like a good man! I am your commander from today. I will rule you. Give me a house to stay.'

The fisherman said, 'Sir, we are poor people. We do not have a house to give you. We live in huts.' Pointing towards a building, he said, 'there is an old palace vacant at the shore of the sea.'

Drudan narrowed his eyes to locate the palace at a distance. It was a massive heritage building in ruins. Drudan pointed his fingers towards the citadel and said, 'New I want you to be!'

The palace instantly became new and glittering.

The fishermen were awestruck. Drudan realized that and decided to take advantage of their fear. 'Now you will live with me in the palace or else I will kill you' he commanded.

One of them braced courage and asked Drudan, 'Sir, what do you want from us? We are underprivileged people who catch fish and sell them to earn a living.'

Drudan pointed towards the point where Moonlight was falling on the confluence of the Arabian Sea, Bay of Bengal and the Indian Ocean and said 'Get me seawater from there and free yourself.'

The fisherman gasped 'No Sir, It is impossible. The sea is cavernous, we will die. You know magic then why can you not get water yourself.'

'You fool, if magic worked, I would not have bothered to talk to you' said Drudan absolutely exasperated.

He raised his hand and pointing it towards the fishermen, said 'Trap them in a net'.

A huge fishing net appeared which covered the fishermen. Soon they were taken in the captivity of the net. The fishermen began to yell 'Help Help!'

Drudan then rubbed his palms vigorously and blew air towards the net. When it began to rise, he calmly instructed the net, 'Head towards the heritage palace while these insects are trapped in.' The net soared higher and disappeared from the view.

'I need a vehicle to travel. What should I create? Something as slimy as me?' thought Drudan, as he prepared to leave the shores.

'Yes, it should be a flying snake' This idea made him smirk viciously. He picked a pebble from the bank and blowing air on it, he said 'Oh sea snake, let us escape!'

A yellow coloured snake with big black spots appeared in front of Drudan. It was so long and huge, that even Drudan gasped in surprise. In no time the snake curled itself around Drudan. He began to yell 'No, No, you are choking me!"

Chapter 1

The Premonition

It was a bright and sunny day. The tall mountains, the apple laden trees, the chirping birds, the trotting horses and the silently flowing river, were glistening in the heavenly rays of the Sun. The cool breeze was adding spice to the milieu and spreading joy everywhere. Zynpagua looked heavenly.

From a distance, a black stallion could be seen approaching the trees. It galloped steadily as its rider aimed the arrow and pulled the string of the bow. The arrow dashed forth, splitting a falling apple.

'Halt' Vivian yelled. The apple, pierced by the arrow, stopped mid air.

'Well done' Exclaimed Sussaina clapping.

The rider jumped off the horse removing her helmet. It was Anika; her twinkling eyes lit her face as she smiled.

'My daughter you can defeat anyone with this bow and arrow.' said Sussaina, as she hugged Anika.

By then Vivian grabbed the apple suspended mid air and with the force of both his palms, split it into pieces. He raced back towards Sussaina and Anika and while offering the apple to them, he said, 'I am proud of Femina. She is the one who trained Anika'.

The memory of Femina saddened him and his face fell. With a tone of deep agony, he said 'Alas! She has been reduced to a statue.'

Sussaina saw Vivian's expression and became tense. Her son was suffering silently.

Femina was Vivian's childhood friend and the only companion he had for years. Drudan turned her into a statue by combining a scientific formula with an evil spell. Vivian tried various magical spells to rescue Femina but failed. While the people of Zynpagua had begun to live in bliss, Sussaina and her family remained worried and sad. Anika's eleventh birthday came and went, but neither anyone remembered it, nor Anika mentioned it.

Anika gently placed her hand on Vivian's shoulder and said 'Brother, I promise, we will bring Femina back to life one day.'

'How?' asked Vivian. 'We are bound by the spell of her life and cannot leave Zynpagua. How will we save her?'

'Brother, I had a premonition before Femina was turned into a statue. A girl holding a gadget was standing with Femina and was trying to save her. I am confident we will find that girl soon.'

'Vivian, have patience my son' said Sussaina. 'Frederick is going to the Earth to meet Anika's family. I am sure he will be able to find that girl with the gadget.'

Vivian hugged Sussaina and said 'Yes mother, I trust you completely.'

'It took Frederick almost six months to recover from Violet's wound, but now he is healthy and ready to leave. Let us return to the palace, he must be waiting for us', said Sussaina.

Vivian noticed Anika's despondent face and tried cheering her up. 'Anika have the apple, it is delicious!'

Then he coughed a little and said 'Dear Sister, I have a confession to make. I had lied to you about thirty minutes on Earth are equal to thirty days in Zynpagua. I am sorry sister but when I had come to the Earth to take you, this was the only way I could convince you to accompany me to Zynpagua'

Anika was taken aback but simply said 'No problem brother. I am glad you came'

'Thank God!' said Vivian, heaving a sigh of relief.

'Please have the apple' he continued.

Anika smiled and took the apple. As she noticed the colour red, she shivered again. She had been feeling jittery seeing the red colour for a long time now.

'What happened Anika? Mount your horse. Mother has already left' said Vivian.

Anika came back from her reverie and smiled.

While mounting her horse, Anika noticed the apples hanging from the trees yet again. *They are so round and red*, she thought.

'Hurry up Anika' yelled Vivian while mounting his favourite brown horse.

'Not all round and red things spread happiness. Some send misery' murmured Anika.

'What are you saying Anika?' asked Vivian, taken aback by Anika's words.

Anika looked perplexed. She didn't know why she made that statement.

Seeing Vivian leave, she mounted the horse, wore the helmet and followed him. While riding back, her gaze kept falling on all red and round things- red berries, red tomatoes, red pomegranates....

When they reached the palace, they were greeted by the head cook. His chubby face and pink cheeks beamed with excitement. He bowed to the Queen and secretly moved towards Anika and whispered, 'I have made chocolate cake for you!'

Anika was overjoyed. She loved cakes. Calling everyone to meet at the dining table, she rushed in with the cook. The head cook refused to show her the cake and told Anika to sit with everyone. Anika did as she was told and joined Sussaina and Vivian at the dining table.

'¡Hola! ' Frederick greeted everyone while hurrying down the flight of stairs and approaching the dining table.

'Hello!' he repeated, when he realized that they did not understand his greetings in Spanish.

'Uncle, come join us for a cake treat' said Vivian.

Frederick sprinted towards Vivian and sat beside him.

Soon they heard the bugle being played and trumpets being blown.

Sussaina laughed 'Our head cook makes everything eventful and melodramatic!'

The others laughed as well.

The head cook announced, 'Introducing our new dish- the universe of cakes'.

Drums were beaten as the head cook walked in with a huge tray, veiled with a white cloth.

When he placed the dish on the table, the aroma of freshly baked chocolate cake enticed everyone. Seeing their expression, he slowly unveiled the dish.

Sussaina exclaimed and complimented the cook 'How wonderful- a cake representing each planet!' Then looking closer she said, 'But why is the Moon red and not white? You could have used white chocolate'.

The head cook looked puzzled 'Good point my queen. I am so dumb. I have made a Red Moon!'

Sussaina smiled and said 'Never mind, let us taste it.'

The head cook cut slices from the cake and commenced serving it to everyone.

Others clapped but Anika's heart sank. Did the head cook unintentionally design an ominous future?

Sussaina tapped on Anika's shoulder and handed her a piece. 'It is delectable, have it'.

As Anika bit in, flashes of future began to appear in front of her eyes. She could see Moon turning evil. As she blinked, she saw images of shadow on Mars, Venus and Sun. Tears rolled out from her eyes and she shut them.

'What's wrong Anika? Why are you crying?'

Anika hesitated for a moment and then pretended to smile 'Mother, the cake is so delicious that my tears are trickling down to taste it.'

The head cook guffawed while the others helped themselves with several pieces of cake.

Post an appetizing cake session, Anika excused herself and went to her room. There, she sat on the bed, and held her throbbing head. *Why did the cook make a red Moon? Why was she fearing round and red things?* These thoughts kept flooding her mind as she sat still on the bed.

All of a sudden, she began to murmur,

'As Venus gets closer to the Moon
A red shadow will catch her soon
Mars too will get covered by its rays
This shadow will turn Moon evil for seven days
A huge storm will come that day
And make me a prey.'

Anika was terrified at this revelation. What was this red shadow which would cover the planets and the Moon and why will it make her a prey? She sat in her room for some time, but was unable to control her nerves.

Then she ran out to get some answers from Sussaina, who was sitting in the main hall, speaking to the helpers.

Composing herself, Anika asked Sussaina, 'Mother, are there times when the Moon and the planets get covered by an evil shadow?'

Sussaina was taken aback by Anika's question. She requested the helpers to leave and asked 'Anika, why are you asking these questions? What happened?'

Anika concealed her fear. Her mother had been much stressed and a prediction of disaster would shatter her hopes. She cleared her throat and said, 'Nothing mother, I just generally asked.'

Sussaina began to get concerned. Anika was asking questions which were related to deep secrets of the universe. 'Is there something bothering you Anika?'

Anika smiled and said, 'Mother, I am just trying to know how the Universe functions, to be able to read the stars better'.

Though Sussaina was not convinced with Anika's answer, she ignored the doubt rising in her mind and told her, 'Anika there are two shadow planets in the universe. These are called demon planets and they function negatively. This is all I know'.

Anika was unable to understand the connection with the demon planets. ***Why would these planets turn evil to make her a prey?*** She thought.

Thanking Sussaina, she left the palace, to find the answer to this thought. She mounted her horse and rode to the river. On reaching the river, she left the horse near the trees and began to walk towards the bank.

Anika sits near the bank of the river in Zynpagua, thinking about the stormy sea.

As she moved closer, she felt the river turn into a stormy sea. She rubbed her eyes and looked again. There was no sea and the river was flowing peacefully. **Why did she see the vision of a stormy sea?**

She looked around yet again to discover anything strange. There was nothing around except trees. Her head began to throb and thoughts poured in, one after the other. **What was the connection between the planets turning evil and the stormy sea?**

She looked up at the sky. There was no sign of danger. Then why was she feeling so low?

Anika was tense. She continued to sit near the banks of the river till the evening, watching the Sun set and the Moon appear. As the Sun began to sink in the west, the horizon was lit by an orange glow. The Moon appeared at dusk, from somewhere behind the trees. It was the usual evening scene, but Anika was petrified seeing the scene. These symbols seemed to point towards an eerie future. She could see doom!

Her lips turned dry as she murmured,

'When the Red Evil Moon will shine behind the tree
And its light will fall on water of stormy sea
A drop will rise from a hole
To unite our soul
Taking away my power
I will become a shrunken flower'.

As she interpreted the meaning of the symbols, her mind got flooded with frightening thoughts. There would be a day when the Moon will turn red over a stormy sea. That day a drop will rise from the depth of the ocean. This drop will harm her. But she could not interpret how her soul would unite with somebody else's.

Chapter 2

Drudan and Romeo

'Help help...Nooooooooo!' cried Drudan as the yellow spotted serpent began to wound itself around him and tighten its grip on him. Struggling for breath, Drudan spat out, 'You snake, I am your master, loosen your grip on me or vanish'.

The snake raised his big stippled head and touched Drudan's nose with his tongue. Drudan cried aloud as the venom of the snake burnt his nose.

He yelled 'Vanish you............'

The snake brought his face very close to that of Drudan's and said, 'I have been rescued now and will never vanish. I have come from the depth of the ocean with deep secrets in my heart. Secrets that will help you win.'

'You are choking me to death and my nose burns like charcoal. How will you help me if I die of suffocation?'

The snake chuckled and said, 'I will get you close to death but never let you die.'

'What the hell is this? I thought I created you to help me, not to kill me. Am I not your creator?'

The snake wounds himself around Drudan.

The snake laughed and said, 'No, you have not created me. I was trapped in the pebble. You have rescued me. Nevertheless, you are my saviour and I will follow your command, but....'

'But what?' asked Drudan desperately

The snake smiled and said, 'Give me a name.'

Drudan instantly responded, 'I will call you Serpie.'

'What a horrible name! Nay, I don't like it. Give me a human hero's name.'

'What?' exclaimed Drudan totally disgusted.

'Yes give me a good name and I will be as slimy as you want me to be.'

Drudan said, 'Ok, what about Alexander?'

'No'

'Julius Caesar?'

'No, he was assassinated!'

'What the hell. I don't know of any hero?'

'Hmm... said the snake. 'You are a villain, how will you know of heroes?'

This statement of the snake uplifted Drudan's mood. 'Yes, I am a powerful evil man. But how did you know that?'

The snake chuckled and said, 'You look evil.'

Drudan laughed aloud, 'Yes, I am an evil scientist. My creation, the violet light was so powerful, that it separated Zynpagua from the Earth.'

The snake stared at him and said 'Are you dreaming? I have never heard of this land called Zynpagua.'

'None on Earth has heard of this land. It has vanished in the Universe. My creation, the violet light had separated it from the Earth', said Drudan.

'I am much impressed' said the snake observing Drudan.

He continued, 'You are a scientist but you look like a vampire to me with that black gown. Should you not be more humanly dressed? I mean a pair of pants and a shirt. In fact, I suggest, you wear spectacles. Even if you are evil, no one can deny that you are intelligent. But you don't look sharp. The pair of spectacles can give you a sharp look. And this dirty plait of yours. Please get your hair chopped. I can't travel with people who are unhygienic.'

Drudan's face turned blue with wrath 'How dare you? I will kill you!'

'Don't dare me. I am free now and no one can kill me. I will help you because you rescued me.'

Drudan cooled down. He knew he needed this snake. If his secrets of the sea could help him get control on Zynpagua and take revenge from Sussaina, it was worth tolerating his nonsense. He said, 'Fine Serpie, I am sorry.'

'That's like my bad evil man! Can you please take bath and chop your hair. It seems you haven't bathed for years. I cannot tolerate your dirty smell.'

Drudan controlled his temper. No one ever dared to speak to him this way. 'Alright Serpie, I will change my look with a magic spell.'

'Wait, hang on! I mean real bath. No magic and all. What if magic fails? I will be shocked to see a naked you.'

'Stop insulting me' growled Drudan.

The snake continued, totally ignoring what Drudan had just said 'I want you to dip your dirty self in this sea.'

Drudan did not want to argue. He had actually not bathed for years. Reluctantly he said, 'Fine Serpie!'

'And don't call me Serpie!' fumed the snake.

Drudan panicked seeing the snake's furious eyes which popped out from the socket and hung loosely on his face. 'Please suggest a name' he stammered.

'What about Romeo?' asked the snake, smiling. His eyeballs receded to their sockets.

'Excellent' said Drudan. 'Who is he?'

The snake spat out venom and said, 'He is the hero of a tragedy written by William Shakespeare, the great author. While in the play both Romeo and his beloved Juliet die, in my life I will rescue my wife Juliet and live happily ever after.'

Drudan responded repulsively, 'I don't care whether you meet your Juliet or not.'

'You should care because my Juliet is locked in the deep sea, where the moonlight is falling on the confluence of the Indian Ocean, Bay of Bengal and Arabian sea. She is bound by a magical spell. I will take you there and you will rescue her. I know you can do magic. I will collect the water in my mouth and get it for you. You are right, the water where moonlight falls on the confluence of the three seas, is magical, capable of uniting anything. I have been observing you since last two days. While I was locked in the pebble, I could read your thoughts'

Drudan's face brightened 'That is wonderful. Then why don't you take me there?'

'Going there would require preparation. Besides, the water becomes magical on a particular day. That day cannot be predicted, I have to observe the movement of planets to decipher that. That particular day the sea becomes raw and waves rise as high as mountains. I need strength to swim in such magical waters' Romeo responded.

'Even you would need special training to swim in such waters' He continued.

'You can read the movement of planets? Wow! That's wonderful' said Drudan.

'Of course, all snakes can do that 'replied Romeo arrogantly.

'Really?' said Drudan with his eyes blinking in astonishment.

'Drudan, my stomach is making noises. I am very hungry' continued Romeo.

Drudan immediately responded, 'I have captured some fishermen, eat them all and gain strength.'

Romeo once again spat venom on Drudan's face.

'What the hell is this!' reacted Drudan.

'You are such a rotten man. Why should you kill fellow humans? I am a pescetarian, and eat fishes', Romeo responded.

Drudan pointed towards a heritage palace situated at some distance. 'Take me to the heritage palace. I have tied the fishermen in a net there. We can ask them to get you fishes.'

Romeo nodded and instructed Drudan to stand still. Then he wound himself around Drudan and lifting him, flew towards the palace.

'Ahhhhhhhhhh!' wailed Drudan. 'Can you not fly straight and make me sit on your back. This way I will get strangulated.'

'I will make you sit on my back only once you take bath' said Romeo.

'Aaaweee!' cried Drudan again as the snake flew high, carrying Drudan wrapped in his confines.

'Fine, then let me bathe first and travel on you' said Drudan.

'No, I will eat first and then I will take you to the depths of the ocean, where my family lives. You will have to take bath there. Once you bathe in our waters, we will ensure all your ill intentions for us are washed away. You can then safely stay with us.' said Romeo.

'And how will I breathe in the deep sea?' asked Drudan skeptically.

'Mystery' said Romeo, laughing.

'Here comes the palace', said Romeo. Where do you want to land?

'I am the king of the palace. I should have a grand entry' said Drudan.

'Sure, why not' said Romeo with mischief playing in his eyes.

He flew towards the entrance gate and when they were still hovering at a considerable height, Romeo straightened himself instantly thus releasing Drudan and making him fall straight on the sand. Drudan cried aloud as his head hit the ground and his face got smeared with sand.

Romeo chuckled seeing Drudan who was fuming with rage. He turned towards Romeo and spelt out an evil curse with his magic 'Hang in the sky forever!'

Within seconds, Romeo could be seen hanging limply in the sky.

'Ahhh Drudan, please help me, I am stuck in the sky' howled Romeo.

'Stay there and die!' said Drudan

'Oh please Drudan, release me' beseeched Romeo.

Drudan looked venomously at the snake and laughed aloud.

Romeo also began to chuckle and began to dance in the sky. He then dashed straight towards Drudan and wound himself around his neck.

Drudan was petrified and screamed 'Oh no.......................!'

'Remember you evil man. Magic doesn't work on me. I have Lord Shiva's blessing. There are only few special days when I get trapped by magic, otherwise I am invincible', responded Romeo furiously, tightening himself around Drudan's neck.

'I am s..o..r..r..y, v..e..r..y s..o..r..r..y' implored Drudan coughing.

Romeo released him and commenced his concertina movement, wriggling towards the palace to locate the fishermen.

They were tightly tied in nets and were breathless and weeping. Seeing Romeo, they began to scream 'God, save us from this huge snake!'

Drudan came behind Romeo and on seeing the fishermen roared, 'This is Romeo, my friend. I am releasing you creeps so that you can go and get fishes to feed him.'

Once the nets were released, one of the fishermen came forward and bowed in front of Romeo. 'Sarpraj*, we will fetch as many fishes as you want. But please protect us from this evil man.'

'You insect, what did you say?' fumed Drudan.

'Shhhhhhhhhhhh..' said Romeo 'Did you call me Sarpraj?' he asked the fisherman.

'I am sorry, if I have hurt you' apologized the fisherman.

'No, you have not hurt me' said Romeo emotionally. 'Sarpraj means king of snakes. No one has ever given me such respect. I will do justice with you as a king would for his people. I will save you from this man and hunt my own fishes. Go enjoy life, you are free now!'

The fishermen were overjoyed and touched Romeo's tail. Romeo too basked in the glory of a king and elevated his face to give his blessings.

'You are an emotional fool. I am capturing them back' shouted Drudan.

'No' fumed Romeo. 'Don't you dare touch them or play your magic on them. I will swallow you for this impudence.'

'What?' Drudan was shocked.

'Yes,' said Romeo, pretending to be a king.

Drudan cursed Romeo under his breath. He thought that once he learns the secrets of the sea from Romeo and procures magical water from the confluence, he would find a way to kill him. Romeo's mischievous voice brought him back from his thoughts.

Romeo was asking the fishermen, 'Can you please make this evil man take bath and arrange for a pair of pants and shirt for him? Who will crop his dirty hair and give him a decent haircut?'

Many volunteered instantly.

Romeo instructed Drudan, 'Can you please get a pair of scissors by magic.'

Drudan fumed but did as he was told. As soon as the scissors appeared, one fisherman dashed towards him, pulled his plait and chopped it. Then he rapidly cut his hair.

Romeo was much pleased and said, 'Now gentlemen, can someone arrange for a pair of pants and shirt?

'Use magic', suggested a fisherman.

'I don't trust his magic. What if it stops working mid way, then we will witness a Drudan without clothes. I get very embarrassed seeing nude humans' chuckled Romeo.

'Will you stop it' rebuffed Drudan.

Romeo winked and said 'Dear fishermen, behave yourselves.'

Drudan cursed himself for rescuing Romeo. In the meanwhile, two fishermen left the palace to fetch a pair of pants and shirt from a small market at the seashore. The others lifted Drudan till the shore, to give him a bath. Drudan yelled and Romeo chortled as the fishermen scrubbed his body with sand and seawater.

Chapter 3

Frederick leaves for India

Anika was at the river bank, lost in her thoughts, when she heard someone call her name. It was a guard from the palace. He came galloping on a horse and informed Anika, 'Princess, Frederick is leaving for the Earth. Queen Sussaina wants you to hasten to the palace.'

When Anika reached the palace, she saw Frederick standing with Sussaina at the entrance, preparing to leave. He had worn his favourite frill shirt, feather cap and stockings with boots.

'Here comes Anika' waved Frederick. Anika got off the horse and ran towards him.

'Vivian and Anika, please take care of Mother Sussaina in my absence' saying this Fredrick hugged Sussaina.

'Frederick, you have to reach India and gently wake Anika's family. Tell them about her past and assure them that Anika is safe in Zynpagua. After that you will have to find a way to rescue

Femina. My intuitions tell me that the solution to rescue Femina lies in India. I wish I could send Vivian with you. Alas! We are bound by the spell of Femina's life.'

Anika added, 'Uncle Frederick, when the villagers had attacked us and Femina and her group of women were fighting for us, I had seen a vision that Femina had become a statue and a little girl named Aarna Malhotra had a gadget in her hand with which she was trying to cure Femina.'

'That's brilliant Anika! Frederick, in that case, once Anika's family is fine and protected, please find Aarna Malhotra. Lady Carol, the queen of clouds, has promised me that she would send Leo to India as soon as the kingdom of clouds is back in order.' said Sussaina

'Thank you Mother. How will I communicate with you from India?' asked Frederick.

'Good question son' voiced Sussaina and looking up at the sky, she called out, 'my angels, my protectors, my friends, I need your help. Please come my sweet little birds of heaven.'

A beautiful rainbow appeared in the sky, stretching from one end of the horizon to the other. From beyond the rainbow, seven tiny birds could be seen steadily flying towards Zynpagua. The little red bird descended first and sat on Sussaina's shoulders. She said 'My queen, we are eager to help you. Your wish is our command. Tell us my dear queen, what can we do for you?'

Frederick is surrounded by the Angel birds

Sussaina kissed the red bird. Then placing her on the palm, she said 'My angel, please travel with Frederick to India and save Anika's family there. Try casting a protective spell on them so that Drudan cannot harm them. Be with Frederick always.'

The red bird bowed and pecked Sussaina's hand in agreement.

'That's like my lovely angels' said Sussaina and then looking at the other six birds hovering around her head, she said 'My sweet birds, come closer. Are you angry with me?

Instantly the other six birds flew down and sat on Sussaina's head and shoulders, and began pecking her.

Sussaina laughed and said, 'that's enough, you are tickling me. Sorry... I am sorry. I shouldn't have asked whether you are angry with me. I know my angels can never be annoyed with me.'

The red bird suggested, 'Frederick can sit on our back and we can fly him to the Earth.'

Sussaina smiled and said, 'Thank you. I had not thought about this.'

Frederick nervously shouted, 'How am I going to travel on them? They will get crushed and die if I sit on them.'

The red bird chirped, ***'Chin chunaki chin chin'*** and tapped on his head. Frederick instantly diminished to the size of the bird.

Sussaina, Vivian and Anika exclaimed in surprise.

Frederick jumped high to reach Sussaina's height.

The red bird cried out 'Noooooooo!'

In no time Frederick was floating in the air. His weight had become as light as feather. Fredrick screamed 'Mother Sussaina, I will be blown away by the wind. How am I going to survive like this?'

The red bird dashed forth and sat on Frederick's head. Then she tapped his hair with her foot. Frederick felt his body become heavy. The red bird said 'Now you have gained weight and no wind can blow you off '.

'Dear red bird, how will I regain my height?' asked Frederick

'By saying ***Chin chunaki chin chin'*** chirped the bird.

Sussaina smiled and instructed Frederick to leave instantly. Frederick sat on the red bird and waved, '¡Adiós!' to all. The red bird flew first, followed by the other six. Soon they were seen flying in one line, high up in the sky, till they crossed the horizon and vanished from the scene.

Chapter 4

Drudan meets the mermaid

'Now that's like a good boy' said Romeo, looking admiringly at Drudan.

The fishermen had cropped Drudan's hair and the black gown was replaced by a pair of pants and a shirt. After bathing, Drudan's skin became fresh and supple and he looked dashing.

'We can leave now, my handsome friend' chuckled Romeo.

Had it been Zynpagua none could have dared to mock Drudan this way. But times had changed and Drudan had no power except his magical abilities. He had to tolerate everything under his breath till he developed something as fatal as the violet light.

'Don't take my compliment so seriously. You still look evil! ' chuckled Romeo.

Drudan felt like throttling him that moment.

'No, No, don't ever think of throttling me' smirked Romeo.

'How does he know what I am thinking?' thought Drudan.

'I can read the mind, my friend' said Romeo haughtily.

Drudan thought again 'Wow, if only I could learn this art of reading the mind from Romeo...'

'Yes, I will teach you many things. The secrets of the sea; the art of reading the mind; and the science behind the movement of the stars.' said Romeo.

'Why will you do that?' asked Drudan cynically.

'Because you will rescue my Juliet' said Romeo

'Oh yes, of course' said Drudan.

'So will you leave me after that?' asked Drudan.

'You rescued me from the pebble and I can never forget that. Honestly, I don't like you but gratitude binds me to you.'

Drudan smiled maliciously. This was such a win- win situation. This snake would teach him the secrets of the sea and also be subservient to him.

'We are leaving now,' saying this Romeo began to wound himself around Drudan.

Drudan yelled 'Nooo... Romeo, you promised that once I take bath, you will carry me on your back.'

'Once I clean you with the water of deep sea will I allow you to place your bum on me. As of now, you have no choice but to travel like this' asserted Romeo.

Drudan frowned but remained silent.

Romeo wound himself around him and bringing his head very close to Drudan's face, licked him.

Are you mad? 'asked Drudan crying aloud in pain as the venom burnt his cheeks.'

'No.....' and saying this Romeo rose high up in the sky, carrying Drudan along. Accelerating with great speed, he flew parallel to the sea, and without warning, dived in. Drudan yelled with fear as Romeo pulled him deeper in the sea. He was feeling breathless and his body shuddered as he struggled to inhale oxygen. 'I will die' he whispered in Romeo's ears'.

'Just focus on your breath, you won't die' assured Romeo as he accelerated further.

Drudan struggled for breath initially but gradually felt better. There were bubbles of air enveloping his face throughout, which surprised him greatly. He touched his nose and realized that he wasn't inhaling or exhaling. Then how was he breathing?

Drudan tried voicing this question, but his voice got swallowed in the gushing water. He felt numb within the confines of Romeo's grip.

After sometime, Drudan felt Romeo had reduced his speed and was descending towards a reef. As they neared the reef, Drudan heard a melodious voice singing a mysterious song. He struggled to locate the source of the voice, when he saw two bluish green eyes peeping from behind the leaves. He felt they were human eyes. *How can a human being stay in such deep sea?* He thought.

Romeo changed his direction by then and pulled Drudan away.

'Who was singing the song?' asked Drudan

'Shhh.....don't question now, just be quiet'

'Was it a human?' asked Drudan, nudging Romeo.

'She is the mermaid of the sea. She is like our queen, who rules us. Don't look at her. She is evil and might kill you' said Romeo.

'What makes her so powerful? The king has a huge army?' asked Drudan.

'Which king?' asked Romeo.

'Her husband' said Drudan.

Romeo silenced Drudan instantly. Drudan had never seen Romeo so petrified. *This mermaid was so powerful that she ruled the entire sea*? Thought Drudan.

'Stop thinking about her' warned Romeo.

Drudan instantly realized that Romeo was reading his mind. Thus changing the topic, he said,

'Romeo, it's a miracle that I am managing to breathe in this sea.'

'You are not managing to breathe, I am making you breathe. I had licked your cheeks so that your skin functions like gills. If you want to learn the secrets of the sea, you will have to live in the sea 'said Romeo.

'My head feels heavy and I want to vomit' said Drudan.

'Don't! Vomiting is a punishable offence in the sea. We live here. You are not allowed to litter our environment' said Romeo, heading towards a mushroom.

On reaching there, he tapped it. A voice resonated from the mushroom 'Welcome to the ocean world. Who is it?'

'It is Philip.'

'Philip, is that you?' The mushroom asked.

'Yes, it is me. Mashy my dear friend, how are you?'

Drudan was wondering who Philip was when the mushroom jumped high in the sea and transformed into a giant cobra.

Drudan gasped for breath.

'Who the hell is Philip' he thought.

Romeo immediately turned to Drudan and said 'I am Philip and I can give you hell.'

'Damn! Why does he have to read my mind always' murmured Drudan.

Romeo missed listening to this sentence as his attention had drifted towards Mashy.

'Call me Romeo, Mashy. The name Philip did not suit me and brought disaster for me and my wife.'

'As you say my friend' beamed Mashy. He continued looking at Romeo with excitcment.

'Where are my parents?' asked Romeo.

'They stay with me and have been miserable for the last two years, since you disappeared' said Mashy.

'The callous mermaid tricked my wife Juliet and captured her in the magical waters of the confluence. She had locked me in a pebble. This man saved me' said Romeo, pointing towards Drudan.

Before Drudan could realize, Mashy jumped high in the sea and then landed on Drudan's shoulders. He licked his cheeks and smiled while Drudan froze.

'Don't worry my friend' said Romeo 'This is Mashy's way of showing affection.'

'My face is on fire' revolted Drudan.

'Mashy doesn't lick everyone. He has licked you and now you can live in the sea forever. Check for yourself, are you still feeling giddy?'

That's when Drudan realized he was as comfortable in the sea as he was on land. The feeling of giddiness was replaced by an elating experience as if Drudan was the king of the sea.

'Mashy, I have to meet my parents. I have to gain strength to swim in the magical waters and save Juliet, my wife. I have to kill the mermaid.'

'Shhh..., don't say that Romeo. You know she eavesdrops' alerted Mashy.

'I don't care about her anymore. What else can she do? How can a mermaid be so vicious and jealous?'

'Romeo, we cannot displease her. You know she rules the sea.'

'Mashy, I have decided that we will wage a war against her' said Romeo.

'No one, absolutely no one will support you' said Mashy.

'This man will. He knows magic. We will teach him the secrets of the sea and he will use magic to make us win' said Romeo.

'Romeo, why will he do so much for us?'

'He needs the magical waters to seek revenge from someone. I will fulfill all his wishes and in turn he will help me save Juliet and capture the mermaid.'

'What a shrewd snake? He wants me to capture the mermaid. I will do that but then I will rule the sea. Drudan will rule the sea' thought Drudan.

'No wicked fellow, you cannot rule the sea. Your magic will not work on me. If I see you doing any monkey business, I swear I will wrap myself around you and strangulate you' warned Romeo.

'I don't think it is wise to teach him anything regarding the sea. His intentions are ill' said Mashy, looking angrily at Drudan.

'Oh, please don't say that. I am only interested in procuring the magical waters and seeking revenge from Sussaina. Why would I want to rule the sea?' said Drudan.

'Don't let mischief play in your mind, or else I will swallow you alive' said Mashy.

'Hey Mashy, forget this man. He poses no real threat. Let us make haste. The mermaid has seen me. Before she ousts me from the sea, I have to meet my parents.' Said Romeo.

Drudan meets the Mermaid

Just then, Drudan heard the melodious and enchanting voice of the mermaid.

It was saying,

'Handsome human of the land

What are you doing with the snake clan?

Come to me I have a plan

To get back your land'

'Did you hear that voice?' asked Drudan.

'Which Voice?' asked Romeo.

'The same melodious voice' said Drudan.

'Don't listen to her. She is vicious' rebuffed Romeo.

'How is she vicious' asked Drudan.

'Only she has the power to use magic in the sea. Only she has the power to transform into a human form. She is the one who has been torturing the inmates of the sea' said Romeo.

'But why did she let us pass. She could have captured us' asked Drudan.

'She quietly observes the activity in the sea and makes evil plans. Then one fine day, when others are unaware, she attacks the person who is revolting against her and captures him. We get no time to retaliate. She has a human brain and therefore her plans are beyond sea creature's imagination.'

'Philip my son' a voice called out.

'Mother, my mother, how are you?' replied Romeo racing towards a huge snake. Romeo's mother saw Drudan and hesitated a little.

Romeo smiled and introduced Drudan. 'This is Drudan. He saved my life mother. He can do magic.'

Drudan thought it was a nice opportunity to impress everyone. Thus he raised his hand and murmured, 'I want a waterproof house here. Come house dear.'

In no time a yellow house appeared in the sea. Drudan laughed aloud and said, 'In I want to be'. In minutes he disappeared from Romeo's back and appeared inside the house. He then announced, 'Furniture, dining table, sofas, curtains, carpets and beds.' The house instantly got furnished.

The snakes entered the house and were aghast to see the grandeur of the place. Drudan caught their expression of bewilderment and said further 'Ringa Ringa roses, table full of dishes.' To everyone's surprise, the dining table got covered with beautiful red roses and delicious dishes. It had chicken, mutton, cakes, breads, milk, and some barbequed animals.

Romeo's mother whispered 'I am not getting a positive vibe from him. Can we not talk in privacy?'

Romeo nodded in agreement and said

'Drudan, I am going home with Mashy and mother. You can rest today. We will start our swimming practice tomorrow.'

'Sure' smiled Drudan.

This was a welcome break for Drudan. When the snakes wriggled away, he thought 'I wish the mermaid could hear me.'

'I can hear you, handsome human in the sea' the same melodious voice said.

Drudan concentrated and thought again 'If you can hear me, so can the snakes. I will be caught interacting with you.'

'Then don't interact with me' said the mermaid's voice.

Drudan felt a surge of pain in his head and he could not think anything further. A knock at the door alerted him and on turning around he saw the most beautiful woman in the world, standing at the door. She had dreamy sea green eyes with long eye lashes and pink lips.

She was human till the torso but instead of legs, she had the body of a fish.

The mermaid stared straight into Drudan's eyes and said, 'Look at me, I will block your thoughts from reaching the snake.'

Drudan looked intently at the mermaid. A happy and light feeling lifted his spirits. 'I feel great' he said.

The mermaid smiled innocently and said 'Yes, I have blocked the saliva connection of the snakes. When the snakes spit on humans, they start reading their thoughts. This makes the humans feel like slaves. A feeling of being tied in chains.'

'Thank you so much' said Drudan. 'They cannot read the mind without the saliva connection?'

'No, they cannot' smiled the mermaid.

'Thank you for coming' said Drudan.

The mermaid smiled and said 'I am uncomfortable here. My body needs water to swim'

'Oh!' said Drudan.

The mermaid chuckled and said 'That is why I will transform into a complete human'

Saying this, the mermaid changed to a human being. Drudan was awestruck. The mermaid walked in smartly and sat on the sofa.

Drudan clapped with excitement 'It is nice to see a human being in the sea' said he.

'It is nice to see a handsome man in the sea' smiled the mermaid.

'Why don't you join me for lunch?' asked Drudan

'Very well' smiled the mermaid.

The two dined together. Drudan did not know why the mermaid had come to meet him but he was totally mesmerized by her charm.

'You stay here with your family?' asked Drudan.

'No, I am alone. I don't have a family' said the mermaid.

'Oh, that's sad' said Drudan.

'Yes, my entire mermaid clan was swallowed by the sea' she continued.

'How did you survive?' asked Drudan.

'My mother threw me away from her lap. I was an infant then.'

'Was it a violent storm? I haven't seen any such storms!'

'These are sea storms, they come inside the sea' said the Mermaid.

'Oh, I see. Natural calamity in the sea' said Drudan.

'Not a natural calamity. The Moon did it. Our community had become very strong in the sea. The Moon governs the tides and caused the sea storm that swallowed my clan.'

'Oh! It is shocking', Drudan feigned concern. His mind was racing, trying to scheme a plan.

'Is there any way we can defeat the Moon?' asked Drudan.

'Why do you want to defeat the Moon?' asked the Mermaid.

Drudan then narrated a snapshot of his life to the mermaid. She patiently listened, with her eyes fixed on Drudan's expression.

When Drudan finished, the mermaid asked 'Where is this King Soto?'

He looked at the mermaid intently 'Why are you asking me about Soto?'

The mermaid laughed wickedly and said, 'What will you do if you find Soto?'

'Anything!' said Drudan.

The mermaid continued, 'I have a dream and that is to rule the world. I have overpowered all the sea creatures, but ruling this world is a totally different ball game. I want your help.'

'O...k' said Drudan.

Before Drudan could say anything, the mermaid said 'I know, even you share the same dream. I want to marry you. You can then become the King and me your Queen.'

'Marry me?' asked Drudan.

'Yes', smiled the mermaid.

Drudan laughed aloud and said, 'Which man would refuse to marry a beauty who rules the sea.'

The mermaid smiled and said, 'On the day of our wedding, I will give you a gift.'

Drudan smiled and asked 'And that is?'

'King Soto' said the mermaid mysteriously.

'Soto?' Drudan almost yelled with excitement.

'Yes, he is in my captivity. He fell in the sea some ten years back. I tried convincing him to marry me, but he refused.'

'Oh my God, I can't believe my luck. I am to get married to the most beautiful woman I have ever seen and what do I get as a gift?....King Soto, whom I have been searching for years.'

The mermaid blushed and said 'We can get married right now!' Saying this, the mermaid removed the ring from her ring finger and put it on Drudan's ring finger.

'That's wonderful. We are engaged' said Drudan.

'We are not engaged. We are married. As soon as I kiss the ring, we will be tied together for life. This is not an ordinary ring. It is ring of partnership which mermaids of Indian Ocean gift to their husbands. It is a mystic ring which will connect us. I will come to know whatever you experience through this ring.'

Saying this, the mermaid kissed the ring.

As soon as she did that, Drudan felt someone was pulling out the veins from his body. He shuddered with pain and screamed 'What have you done??'

Chapter 5

Radhika and Frederick

'Radhika wake up!' Frederick whispered.

'Wake up Radhika' he repeated, standing near Radhika's bed.

Radhika continued sleeping and murmuring 'Anika, finish your Mathematics homework. Miss Ruth had warned me, that she will report to ma and papa if the homework is not done.'

'¡Despierta Radhika!' (Wake up Radhika)

Frederick repeated in Spanish but she did not move.

'How should I wake her?' he thought.

The angel birds had left Frederick in Radhika's room where he had found her murmuring in her sleep. Anika had asked Frederick to explain everything to Radhika and let her wake their parents. Thus Frederick had been trying to wake Radhika first.

In the meanwhile, fatigued by the long journey, the angel birds went to sleep on the tree overlooking Radhika's house. They instructed Frederick that he had to call '*Chin chunaki chin chin*' to wake them or else they would continue sleeping.

Frederick kept trying to wake Radhika for another fifteen minutes but Radhika refused to stir. Vivian had put Radhika and her family to sleep when Anika had accompanied him to Zynpagua

Frederick murmured 'Vivian, what should I do?'

Memory of Vivian brought hope.

Before Frederick left for India, Vivian had shaken hands with Frederick and passed the touch of his hands to him. He had clearly instructed Frederick to touch Radhika's forehead in order to wake her.

Thus Frederick came close to Radhika's bed and gently stroked her forehead. Radhika moved a little. He softly called out her name 'Radhika!'

Radhika opened her eyes slowly. Her eyelids felt heavy and everything seemed blurred. Unable to see clearly, she closed her eyelids again and gradually got out of bed. Her bones ached and her body felt numb. *For how long have I been sleeping?* She thought. It seemed ages to her. She could not recollect anything. She rushed towards the washroom and splashed water on her face which made her feel better. As she came back to the room, she saw Frederick sitting on the chair. The site of a stranger made her yell. Frederick panicked. Radhika called for Anika and on not finding her on the bed, she yelled again. Frederick tried silencing her, but when she continued to scream, he placed his palm on her mouth and said 'Just be quiet for a while. I will explain everything'

'I am Frederick, Anika's uncle. I have come from a region called Zynpagua. Anika is your sister but she is the Princess of Zynpagua.

Vivian, her brother from Zynpagua had taken her there to defeat the evil scientist Drudan....'

Before Frederick could complete, Radhika bit his hand and ran screaming towards her parents' room. Frederick followed her. Radhika yelled on top of her voice, trying to wake them but her parents continued to sleep.

'They will not wake like this' said Frederick.

'Where is my sister Anika?' asked Radhika

'That is what I am trying to tell you. Your sister is in Zynpagua. She cannot come here due to some problem. She has sent me to wake you' Frederick tried explaining.

Radhika was trembling with rage and fear. She thought of a plan and gently told Frederick 'Sir, whoever you are, please wake my parents'

'Yes of course, I have travelled all the way–from Zynpagua to wake your family and to explain them where Anika is' said Frederick.

'You are a foreigner? Which country do you belong to?' asked Radhika, trying to be cool.

'Country? We belong to a land suspended in the universe' said Frederick.

'Suspended in the Universe? You are an alien?' asked Radhika, trying hard to conceal her fear.

'No, we are not aliens. Our land was once a part of the Earth, but now it is lost in the Universe' said Frederick.

'What is the name of this land which is now in the Universe?' asked Radhika

'Zynpagua' said Frederick.

'If this land was a part of the Earth, then why have we not heard about it?' asked Radhika.

'Zynpagua belonged to a group of regions which were closed by mountains. These regions traded with one another and had no contact with outside world. When the violet light hit this region, sudden catastrophic movements separated Zynpagua from the Earth. The other adjoining regions perished'

He has created such a fantastic story! Radhika thought.

She cleared her throat and said 'That is very sad. Could you please wake my parents?'

Frederick was glad he could convince Radhika. He believed her and gently touched her parents. Radhika secretly crept out of the room and ran towards the kitchen. She came back hurriedly, carrying a frying pan in her hand. As her parents stirred, she hit Frederick on the head with the Pan.

Frederick shrieked in pain and fainted. Radhika immediately brought two bed sheets and tied Frederick's hands and feet. She also tied his mouth with a stole. Radhika's parents gradually woke up and were flustered to see the scene. They assumed that Frederick had kidnapped Anika and immediately called the police.

When Frederick woke, he found himself in the jail, still gagged and tied up. The Police let him lose and asked him about Anika. Frederick tried explaining that he belonged to Zynpagua but they began to hit him. He was terribly wounded and fainted again.

Radhika and her parents went home, sad and anxious about Anika.

Chapter 6

Drudan and the Mermaid

'Ahh.........' howled Drudan in pain, as his body began to swell after the mermaid kissed the ring.

The mermaid was standing very close. She had a naughty smile on her face. Seeing that, Drudan said 'I trusted you but you cheated me!'

'If you trusted me, then why are you worried?' smiled the mermaid

She came forward and kissed Drudan on the forehead. His ache vanished, replaced by an inexplicable feeling of love and delight. The mermaid held his hand and said 'I truly love you and now we are connected for life'

Drudan was mesmerized by her charm and hugged her. He was totally in love with her!

'You will be able to hear my voice through this ring. If you are in trouble, I will be your guard' the mermaid said

'And I will protect you like my most prized possession' Drudan sat on his knees and vowed.

He reticently held his hand up.

Flowers began to shower in the room.

'My God what is this?' asked the mermaid.

'Magic!' said Drudan smiling.

Suddenly the mermaid hushed Drudan and said. 'Listen, the snake clan is coming. Do not tell them about me. You need Romeo to take you till the magical waters. I have the curse of the Moon and will not be able to help you. Use the snake and pretend that you are with him' the mermaid whispered.

'Sure' said Drudan.

'And now I am going to hide inside the house' saying this, the mermaid hastened in. Drudan magically set the dining table to show unattended food.

Just then, Romeo wriggled in from the main door, wearing a silken yellow scarf and a pair of black goggles. He looked at Drudan and asked 'You look haggard and weary. Did you not take rest?'

'No..oo' stammered Drudan.

Romeo looked at the dining table which still had unattended food

'Oh my God, you did not have your lunch! Why?' asked Romeo.

'Seasickness!' blurted out Drudan.

'Hmmm' said Romeo, with mischief playing on his lips. 'Just as poison kills poison, the sea will kill your sickness. Let us leave immediately for our practice session'

'What are you saying? Give me some time, I am famished and will start feeling weak if I don't eat'

'Ok, you have ten minutes. Have your meal'

Drudan rushed towards the table and sat on the main chair. He began to gulp food as fast as he could.

'Why can I not read your mind?' asked Romeo skeptically

'Can't you see I am stuffing food down my throat' Replied Drudan, feigning to be angry. Mentally, he was glad that the mermaid had ensured that his thoughts could not reach Romeo. He swallowed the food and stood up.

'Alright friend, let us leave' said Drudan walking towards the door. He rushed out in haste before Romeo could discover the mermaid

Chapter 7

Sussaina sends Leo

Back in Zynpagua, Sussaina saw what happened with Frederick. She was gifted with a special vision with which she could see anything on the Earth and in the Universe. She tried waking Frederick by making her voice reach him. Frederick was deeply injured and did not move. This worried Sussaina. She immediately focused towards the kingdom of clouds and called Leo. Since the Kingdom of clouds was settled now, Leo flew to Zynpagua. Sussaina told him what had transpired. She also told Leo to carry a crystal ball which could make Anika talk to her parents.

Leo placed the crystal ball in his pocket and immediately flew towards the Earth. He reached the Indian jail late in the night. As he entered the main room, he found the guards sleeping. There were empty prison cells in the corner of the main room, but Frederick was not there. Leo descended and walked around to locate the other cells. There was a staircase going down towards the basement. As he descended the steps, he saw Frederick locked in one of the cellars, tied with ropes and his mouth gagged. He noiselessly walked towards him.

'Frederick' voiced Leo, standing outside the cellar.

'Frederick, wake up!' repeated Leo, gently touching his legs.

Frederick could barely manage to open his eyes and look at Leo. He gave a feeble smile and then groaned in pain. His mouth was still gagged. Leo stretched his arm through the spaces in the cellar trying to reach his mouth 'Drag yourself closer towards me so that I can take the cloth off your mouth'

Frederick rolled towards Leo. As soon as Leo's hand reached Frederick's mouth, he pulled out the cloth that was stuffed in. Frederick began to cough and asked for water. Leo quickly flew towards the policemen, quietly picked their water bottle, returned to the basement and made Frederick drink it.

'Radhika is such an irrational and dim-witted girl.' Frederick fumed as he uttered these words in disgust.

Leo tried calming him but the pain emitting from his limbs enraged him. His face was bruised and sore. His eyes sank in the deep dark circles and his limbs were hurting. In some places, blood had trickled out and dried.

'Stupid girl!' said Frederick as he tried to move his hand.

'Calm down Frederick. Let us get out of this place first' said Leo.

'Yes, you are right' agreed Frederick.

'Let me try and extract the keys of this cellar from the policeman's pocket' said Leo.

'Yes' said Frederick but then immediately responded 'Wait! We can call the angel birds. They will get us out without even sourcing the keys'

Leo nodded and Frederick instantly muttered '***Chin chunaki chin chin***'.

Within minutes, seven rainbow birds came flying in the jail. The red bird entered the space between the bars of the cellar and sat on Frederick shoulder 'Oh my God, what happened to you?'

'Dear birds, I will tell you everything, please let me out'

The red angel bird chirped and flew out of the cellar while the other birds hovered outside the cellar and began chirping.

'Winds of North and South
Widen the space
With the air
Emitting from our mouth'

After this, the birds took a deep breath and sucked in all the air. Their stomachs swelled up ten times their size and then, together, they blew out the air. In no time, the space between the bars of the cellar widened. The birds continued to blow air till the gap was wide enough for Leo to enter. He immediately stepped in and untied Frederick's hands and legs. Frederick staggered to stand. Leo gave him a hand and helped him get out of the cellar.

Leo held Frederick's hand and holding him gently, flew up. He asked the angel birds to follow him.

'Where are we going?' asked Frederick.

'To Radhika's house' said Leo

'No point. She is an obstinate girl who would never understand' insisted Frederick.

'Frederick, aunt Sussaina has sent a crystal ball which will show Anika's Image to Radhika. She will understand' said Leo.

'I cannot tolerate Radhika anymore. You can leave me outside the house' said Frederick.

'Fine', said Leo.

They reached Radhika's house and descended on the roof. Frederick stayed back with the angel birds while Leo flew down to meet Radhika.

'Oh my God!' yelled Radhika as she saw Leo flying near the roof of her room.

She felt dizzy and fainted. Leo panicked and rushed to call the angel birds and Frederick.

They came back with Leo. Then the angel birds suggested that they would tell Radhika about Zynpagua in the form of a magical song.

The red bird sat above Radhika's head while the other birds sat on the sides of her bed. They commenced chirping and their voice gradually emitted a sweet magical song.

'This is the story of a cursed land called Zynpagua
Whose Princess Anika was sent to India.
But one day Anika heard the call of the Moon
Her mother's voice was telling her to come soon
To rescue her from the Shadow of the Moon
And free Zynpagua from Drudan the goon
Anika impressed the stars and victory was ours
But then the evil goon escaped
Binding everyone with the life of a brave girl
Femina is her name.
If Anika now leaves Zynpagua
Will it not be a shame?
To see a brave girl die
No, she can't leave the sky'

Radhika unconsciously heard the song and began to murmur

'Yes, it will be a shame
To kill a brave girl
Femina is her name'

The birds began to chirp in excitement as they had managed to convince Radhika with their story.

Radhika gradually opened her eyes and sat up. She looked at Frederick, Leo and the birds and spontaneously mumbled 'sorry!'

Her gaze was fixed on Frederick. She was petrified and guilt ridden

Leo instantly stepped in and placed his hand on Radhika's shoulder. Smiling, he said 'Just relax.'

'I am sorry for sending this man to jail' said Radhika

Frederick was furious and said 'I have a name. It is rude to call me -this man'

'He is Frederick' said Leo, trying to intervene.

'I am sorry Frederick' repeated Radhika.

Frederick shook his head, without saying a word.

Leo immediately pulled out the crystal ball and said. You can see Anika in the ball.

He blew air on the crystal ball, rubbed its surface and called 'Anika'

Anika's image appeared instantly. She looked around and saw Radhika.

Radhika and Anika's gazes met and tears rolled down Radhika's eyes 'Anika, my sweet little sister, you are not from my family, you are the Princess of Zynpagua. You are not my sister!'

Anika began to weep as well 'My dear Radhika, I am your sister. Please, please do not say that. I love you more than I can love my real sister. I love you so much'

'I love you too' said Radhika, weeping profusely

She continued 'Anika, take care of yourself. I am not in Zynpagua to look after you. And my sister, please tell me how can I help you to save Femina?'

Anika smiled and said 'Dear Sister, keep loving me. I miss you so much!'

Then a thought made Anika stand up and say 'By the way, do you know a girl by the name Aarna Malhotra?'

Chapter 8

Venus

Nostalgia engulfed Anika after seeing Radhika through the crystal ball. How much she missed the innocent and uncomplicated life in India. The only villain she then faced was the school homework.

The word 'Villain' brought back memories of Drudan and gave her goose bumps. Where was he now? An eerie feeling made Anika restless. This feeling foretold disaster. The same premonition began to haunt her

'When Red Evil Moon will shine behind the tree,
And its light will fall on water of stormy sea,
A drop will rise from a hole,
To unite our soul,
Taking away my power,
I will become a shrunken flower'

Why would the Moon become evil and turn her into a shrunken flower? Whose soul was going to unite with hers? These thoughts continued to bother her.

Anika was petrified but did not want to tell anything to Sussaina and Vivian. They were already troubled.

Then how am I going to get answers to these questions? She thought and secretly went to the palace garden to see the Moon. Looking at the Moon, she called out 'Oh Moon, our savior, why will you turn evil?

There was no answer. She repeated the question once more, hoping to get some clue from the sky but to no avail.

Unable to get an answer, she marched helplessly in the garden. When she looked up again, she was surprised to see Venus twinkling in close proximity to the Moon.

'Venus' murmured Anika.

A white beam emitted from Venus, hit the ground and transformed into a beautiful woman.

'Anika, why are you so distressed?' asked Venus.

'Oh Venus!' rejoiced Anika

'I am so glad to see you dear Venus. I am scared, so scared' she continued.

'What makes you so scared?' asked Venus

'I feel the Moon and the planets will turn evil and stop supporting me' said Anika wearily.

'Anika, my child, calm down.' Venus assured

'Please tell me. Is it true that the planets will turn evil?' insisted Anika

'No, planets can never be evil. But there are days when planets come under negative influence and they may not be able to stop evil. But nothing is stronger than the wish of a human being. He can defeat evil' said Venus.

A ray of hope lit Anika's face 'Wish of a human being?'

'Yes, if you want to defeat evil, put in effort and you will defeat evil' said Venus.

'Really!' asked Anika expectantly

'Yes, a person who wants to defeat evil can do it anytime but great effort is required.'

Anika muttered softly 'How can the Sun and stars allow evil to rule?'

Venus smiled, held Anika's hand and said 'Come sit with me'

Anika was mesmerized by Venus's charm and simply followed her. Venus gently sat on the bench, patted Anika's cheeks and said 'Sometimes it is important to see evil to value the good in us. That is the law of universe. Evil exists everywhere and it does trouble those who are good. When one faces evil, he struggles, gets pained. But when the person attempts to defeat evil, he becomes stronger and better'

Anika asked candidly 'How will the Moon turn red?'

Venus smiled and said 'There are two shadow evil planets in the universe called the demon planets. When their evil shadow falls on the Moon it turns red and becomes helpless, but only for some time.'

'When this will happen, I will shrink like a flower? ' asked Anika with a trembling voice.

Venus held Anika tightly and said 'Anika, the premonition of future events should not weaken you. Humans who base the future on stars are weak but those who are guided by their own wisdom are the ones who are strong. If a person wants, he can change his destiny'

Anika was not able to understand

Seeing Anika confused and shocked, Venus hugged her and said

'Anika, your future is in your hand. The only thing that can decide your future is your determination. The stars will support you in anything you decide to do ' said Venus.

'I decide?' asked Anika, absolutely confused.

'Yes, stars will be guided by your decision' smiled Venus.

'Will the planets be harmed?' asked Anika

Venus smiled and said 'Anika we will be fine. Don't worry about us. Just remember - Use your wisdom, be brave, put up a fight with destiny and............. ***learn to swim'***

'Learn to swim?' asked Anika, absolutely flummoxed.

'Take care darling and remember, the stars are with you' saying this, Venus disappeared.

Chapter 9

Romeo and Drudan

Drudan had been practicing in the deep sea for over four days. He had gradually gained strength to swim anywhere in the sea and face any kind of danger. Romeo was impressed with his progress but did not reveal any secret of the sea to him.

Drudan realized this and decided to consult the mermaid. The mermaid had promised him victory over Zynpagua. She would have a solution for sure.

His thoughts were broken by Romeo's voice giving him instructions.

'Move your hands faster Drudan. Your swimming speed is very slow. Your hands should work like blades cutting through the water.' Romeo was saying.

'Why can you not carry me on your back, at least while returning?' asked Drudan.

'No, the magical waters will be in my mouth when we return. I will have to manage my breath and keep my mouth closed to avoid spilling it over. Besides, Juliet, my wife will be too weak to swim. I will have to tag her along. In case you need help, I will be there, but you will have to swim on your own. Remember, your magic will not work on those waters. It will only work on breaking the mermaid's spell.'

Drudan nodded and began focusing on increasing his swimming speed. By the end of the session, he felt his shoulders had gone heavy and stiff as if they were carrying a mountain.

'Drudan, you will have to practice more. The full Moon is day after tomorrow. The water of the confluence becomes magical only on a Full Moon day' said Romeo

'Oh no!' reacted Drudan, taken aback.

'Romeo, you can leave me here. I will practice all night so that I am ready for the day' said Drudan nervously.

'No Drudan, you should take rest. Let us leave now. We will practice only for an hour tomorrow. Rest is very important'

'As you say my good friend' said Drudan.

'Why do you always look deceptive?' asked Romeo

This question startled Drudan. Was Romeo reading his mind?

'Why is your face turning pale?' Romeo asked again, screening his countenance.

'Why do you keep suspecting me?' revolted Drudan

'I feel you have devised a way to hide your thoughts from me' said Romeo, eyeing his expressions.

This made Drudan very nervous. In order to hide his fear, he screamed aloud 'Enough is enough. I have been following your instructions like a slave. If you cannot trust me, let us call it off.

Leave me from where you picked me and never show your face again'

'I owe my life to you and that is why I am with you, otherwise I would have dropped you back. Let us leave now' said Romeo, still not convinced by Drudan's reactions.

Romeo left Drudan outside his house in the sea and left. As soon Drudan entered the house, he heard the melodious song of the mermaid. She was dancing near the dining table. She looked so pretty and enigmatic that Drudan's heart skipped a beat. The mermaid took his hand and made him dance too. His body ache vanished as soon as the mermaid held his hand. Drudan felt he was floating in heaven. He had fallen in love for the first time in his life.

'I have to tell you about the demon planets and our chance to rule the world' the mermaid whispered in Drudan's ears.

'Please tell me about them' urged Drudan

The mermaid smiled and said 'Of course! The demon planets rule the universe for a week. They slowly cast their shadow on the Moon and other planets and make them helpless. When this happens, the universe begins to favour the evil and negative people. But the demon planets can cast their shadow only for a week. That week is a great chance for evil beings to rule the world'

'What will happen after that week? The stars will become powerful again and oust the evil man?' asked Drudan.

'No, the one who rules and is undefeated in this week, can rule forever. Once these evil planets bless him, it is very hard for anyone to defeat him. Even the stars cannot do much' the mermaid replied.

'Wow! This is superb. In other words if I defeat Sussaina in that week, I can rule Zynpagua forever?' asked Drudan

'Not only Zynpagua, you can rule the world. We can together rule the land and the sea'

'This is fantastic', said Drudan excitedly.

'I am watching the movement of the stars. The evil planets are becoming powerful and would cast their shadow on the other planets in a week or so'

'Oh my God, we have to plan very fast' said Drudan

'Don't worry, I have planned everything. First go and procure the magical waters. I will let you know about the rest'

'I have a question. Why did you lock Romeo's wife near the confluence' asked Drudan

'Romeo was instigating other sea creatures against me. I wanted to teach him a lesson 'said the Mermaid as she held Drudan's hand again and began to sing. Drudan got mesmerized by the song and dozed off to sleep.

'Drudan, wake up'

'I like melody, who's hoarse voice is this?' asked Drudan, his eyes still closed.

'Romeo!'

'What?' said Drudan as he panicked and woke up. Romeo was seated coiled up, just in front of him.

'It is late in the afternoon. Have you been sleeping throughout?' asked Romeo

Drudan was still in a state of trance. The dance with the mermaid seemed like a fairy tale to him. He looked around but could not find her. Assuming that she had hidden herself from Romeo, he said 'Yes.'

'Why do you smell like a woman?' asked Romeo, sniffing around him.

Drudan was shocked to hear the question. He sheepishly replied 'I like floral perfumes'

Romeo immediately changed the topic and said 'Hurry!, we have to practice for another hour to face the Moon tomorrow'

Drudan stepped out of bed, quickly got dressed and left with Romeo. The memory of the mermaid, her beauty and her melodious voice continued to distract Drudan during the session. While practicing, when Romeo swam a little farther, Drudan murmured to himself 'Love you my mermaid'

'Love you too' came a melodious reply.

'Where are you?' murmured Drudan. He heard a chuckle and then the same mesmerizing voice 'I am near you and my eyes are on you'.

Drudan looked around and could not find anyone. He murmured again 'Where are you?'

'Look around' came the melodious reply.

He looked around and saw a pair of beautiful eyes peeping from behind the leaves.

'You will drown like this' said an angry voice from behind.

Drudan looked back and saw Romeo. 'What the hell are you doing? Why are you not swimming?' asked Romeo

'Sorry, I was mentally planning for tomorrow's event' said Drudan

'Hello Uncle, if you do not practice now, tomorrow is your death day' said Romeo fuming. A fit of rage made Drudan out of control. He wanted to kill Romeo then and there, but the same melodious voice silenced him. 'My Hero Drudan, be patient. Once you collect the magical water, we can take care of the snake clan. I love you and can kill anyone who displeases you. Just have patience my hero.'

Drudan nodded and swallowed his temper

Chapter 10

Anika finds a teacher

'Learn how to swim?' Anika kept repeating even when Venus had left.

Her heart was sinking. What was this new danger she had to gear up to battle with?

Why was she being advised to learn to swim?

Anika was stressed and exhausted. She silently walked back to her room and slept. When she woke up in the morning, a feeling of helplessness and anxiety engulfed her yet again.

Anika took a deep breath and repeated 'I will be brave, I will fight my destiny'. With this determination she stood up and marched towards Sussaina's room. She had woken by then and was dressing up to go for the assembly. Anika knocked at her door and entered the room.

'My dear daughter looks stressed. What happened?' asked Sussaina

'Mother, I want to learn swimming. Who can teach me swimming?' asked Anika.

Sussaina was taken aback by Anika's question and asked 'May I ask why my daughter is keen on learning swimming?'

'Mother, when I was in India, I always wanted to learn swimming. Can someone teach me?' asked Anika.

Sussaina laughed 'There are no swimming pools in Zynpagua and the river is raw and dangerous' said Sussaina.

'Mother, Femina used to bathe in the stream' said Anika

'Anika, that stream is a tributary of the main river and is very shallow. You need deep waters for swimming' Sussaina said.

'Then I can learn swimming in the river' said Anika.

'Anika, the river is dangerous' insisted Sussaina.

Anika did not know how to explain the problem to Sussaina. Venus had instructed her to learn swimming, but who would teach her?

'Anika, is there a problem?' asked Sussaina suspiciously.

'No mother' said Anika, trying to hide her feelings.

'Queen, the ministers are waiting for you in the assembly' informed a guard as he knocked at the door.

'Will speak to you later', said Sussaina and left for the assembly.

Anika feigned a smile and nodded. When Sussaina had left, she decided to go to the banks of the river. Calling her horse, she mounted it and galloped towards the banks.

On reaching there, she jumped from the horse and walked towards the river.

The river was bustling with youthful energy. Its water was so clear that the undercurrents were visible. 'How will I swim in these currents?' thought Anika.

She sat on the bank of the river. It was raw, wild and huge. The undercurrents made a strange gurgling sound. Anika began to tremble seeing the expanse of the river. Exasperated, she picked a pebble and threw it in the river'

'Ouch! who is this?' came a voice from the river.

Anika panicked and jumped back. She looked around to locate the source of the sound, but there was no one. She tip toed and walked closer to the river and peeped in but could not find anyone.

Attempting to find the source of the voice, Anika threw another pebble in the river.

'What an impudent human!' came an angry voice from the depth of the river.

Anika tried straining her eyes, but could not see anyone. She widened her pupils and peeped again. She saw a huge boulder stuck between river weeds.

'Did the voice come from this boulder?' Anika asked aloud.

'I am not a boulder' replied the same angry voice.

'Hi, I am sorry if I hurt you. This is Anika, who is there in the water?'

'You mean you're princess Anika?' asked the voice.

Anika was surprised as no one called her princess. 'Well, yes, this is Princess Anika' she said.

Before she could complete her sentence, two legs ejected out from one side of the boulder followed by a tiny head on the other.

'Oh! It is a tortoise' murmured Anika.

The tortoise elegantly swam up towards the river bank, gradually crept out from the water and walked towards her. Anika sat down on seeing him.

'Hi, this is Mootu' said the tortoise.

'Hi Mootu, this is Anika. How do you know me?'

Anika meets her teacher Mootu

'I am a friend of the angel birds. They told me about you. I also know the birds have accompanied Frederick to the Earth'

'Really?' asked Anika excitedly.

'Yes, in fact I am their teacher' said Mootu proudly.

'Teacher? What did you teach them Sir' asked Anika.

'Swimming' said the tortoise.

Anika's face beamed with excitement 'Sir, you taught them swimming?'

'Yes' smiled Mootu.

'Sir, I too want to learn swimming. It is very important for me. Please teach me how to swim'

'Why do you want to learn swimming?' asked Mootu.

Anika hesitated and asked 'Mootu Sir, do you know I can read the stars and decipher the future?'

'Yes, I do' said Mootu.

'Then please help me. I feel I should learn swimming because I will need it in future.'

The tortoise looked at Anika's face intently and said 'Okay'.

A thought made Anika shudder. What if this tortoise was sent by Drudan to capture her? She hesitated and asked 'Mootu Sir, something is disturbing me. How can I trust you when I don't know you?'

Mootu laughed and said 'Do you recognize the birds that came to Siepra Nevada? While angel birds aren't here, the rest of them will stand testimony to my integrity'

'Of course I recognize them' said Anika.

Tortoise nodded and raising his head, looked at the sky. He clapped his hands and began to sing

'La La la la
Waiting for our gala,

Birds my friends are you far,
I have cherries in my jar,
Why don't you come soon?
Before walks in the Moon
It's time to party party
With this Princess who so sporty
But she has a whim
She wants to swim
Erase all her doubts
My brave scouts'

The song was so entertaining that Anika began to laugh and dance. The tortoise held her hand and danced with her, singing in both high and low notes. Soon thousands of birds could be seen flying in the sky and coming towards them. Once they descended and sat on the trees, they began to chirp gleefully.

These were the same birds who planted seeds in Siepra Nevada, where Frederick was sent when he was cursed.

'Hello friends, how have you been?' asked Anika excitedly.

'Wonderful Princess' chirped the birds.

'How do you know Mootu?' asked Anika

A multi coloured bird flew down and sat on Mootu's back. Jumping on it, she said 'He is our friend for many years'

'Hey, it hurts' said Mootu, a bit annoyed.

The bird pecked on his cheek and flew back towards the tree.

'You got your answer Princess, now let us party party' said Mootu.

Some birds flew down and circled around Anika while the others sat on trees. They began to chirp in unison

'Princess let us Party Party,

Mootu is very naughty,

Let us sing and dance

This is a brilliant chance'

Anika raced with Mootu and danced with the birds, forgetting all her worries.

After sometime, Mootu dived in the water and carried back a jar full of cherries. The birds cheerfully feasted on them.

Then Mootu declared 'Friends, from tomorrow, I will be teaching swimming to our Princess. Let us assemble every morning at 5 am and help her learn.'

The birds nodded and chirped willingly.

Anika jumped with excitement and thanked them. It was evening already. The birds bid farewell and flew away. Mootu instructed Anika 'You should wear clothes that cover your entire body, hands and legs. If you can, wear a dress which fits you perfectly and tightly.'

'Surely Sir, as you say' smiled Anika.

'See you tomorrow' saying this, Mootu walked back and stepped in the river. Anika waved goodbye to everyone and mounted her horse.

When she reached the Palace, Vivian was waiting for her. He rushed towards Anika and helped her dismount the horse. He hugged Anika and asked 'Anika, mother said you want to learn swimming'

'Yes brother' said Anika sheepishly.

'Why?' Vivian asked bluntly

'Generally brother' replied Anika

'Nothing is general in your life. Tell me now or else I will inform mother that you are hiding something from us' said Vivian.

'I am telling you the truth, there is no problem' assured Anika.

Vivian held her hand and said 'Anika, if anything happens to you, mother and I will die. We cannot live without you. Please tell me why you want to learn swimming'

Before Anika could say anything, Sussaina joined them. She asked 'Anika, please tell us if you have a premonition about future events.'

Anika cleared her throat and said 'Yes mother, I feel there will be a day when a red shadow will cover the Moon and the planets. Moon will turn evil. That day, my soul will unite with somebody else's and I will shrink like a flower'

'Oh my God!' exclaimed Sussaina as she sat on her knees. Vivian also got frightened listening to this revelation. He asked Sussaina 'Mother, how can the Moon turn evil?'

'I don't know son, but Anika's prediction states something unusual will happen in the universe.'

'What is this shadow that will cover the stars and the Moon?' asked Vivian.

'Son, I have only heard about this. My grandmother once told me that there are two demon planets in the universe. They are evil. When they cast their shadow on Moon and other planets, they are unable to do any good. But I have never seen this happen in my entire life!'

'Oh my God mother that means this is going to happen now. How is this related to Anika's soul?'

'When demon planets become powerful, evil starts ruling the world. The only evil man we know is Drudan. Maybe Drudan is about to get powerful and attack Anika. Since the planets will be under evil influence, they will not be able to help us.' Sussaina guessed.

Sussaina looked at Anika's stressed countenance and said, 'Don't worry Anika, we will be prepared to face Drudan. I assure you, nothing will happen to you' said Sussaina

'Yes mother, Venus said that my destiny lies in my hand'

'You spoke to Venus?' asked Vivian

'Yes, she descended last night when I was sitting in the garden. She told me that nothing is greater than a wish of a man. We can change our destiny. Venus advised me to learn swimming' said Anika.

'Learn swimming. Why?' asked Vivian, absolutely bewildered.

'Listen to Venus's advice. If she says you have to learn swimming, just do that' said Sussaina

'Yes mother, we wish to defeat Drudan and we will do that' said Vivian

'Yes Vivian, Drudan's return also means threat for Zynpagua and our people here. We cannot take destiny's decision as it is. We will fight our destiny' said Sussaina.

'Vivian, alert the army and the people of Zynpagua. We have to be prepared for a combat and we have to be prepared to save our people.' She continued.

'Mother if Drudan attacks, our people will be the victims first. Zynpagua has a meager population. Should we not build high walls around our palace and instruct all the citizens to stay within the palace?' asked Vivian

'Excellent idea Son but there is a problem. Zynpagua has close to 250 families. We need 250 rooms within the palace to accommodate them. The palace will not be able to accommodate so many houses' said Sussaina.

'I can use magic and build their houses, but Drudan will discover that' said Vivian.

After thinking for a while, he continued

'Mother, it is possible. We can build underground houses within the palace. Drudan would not know about it and even if we are captured, our people will be safe'

'Excellent idea Son' said Sussaina.

'In the meanwhile I will send a message to Leo and Frederick to hasten search for Aarna Malhotra. They have to find her soon. We have to rescue Femina before Drudan attacks. We are bound by the spell of her life.' She continued.

Chapter 11

Frederick and Leo

'¿Cómo estás?' (How are you?) Asked Frederick.

'¡Muy bien, gracias!' (Very fine, thank you) beamed Radhika

'Perfect' said Leo, clapping. The rainbow birds chirped as well.

Frederick and Leo had decided to stay in Radhika's house and find Aarna.

Radhika had to opt for a foreign language in class 8th and Frederick suggested Spanish. Radhika gladly agreed.

After a carefree Spanish learning session, Leo and Frederick decided to find details of Aarna on the internet. Radhika volunteered to teach them how to find information through the search engine.

In the meanwhile, the rainbow birds flew away to look for Aarna.

While searching on the internet Leo and Frederick did find plenty of girls with name Aarna but none were six or seven years old. Disappointed by the day's search, they decided to visit the city of Mumbai.

Radhika requested Leo if he could make her fly with him.

Thus Leo held Frederick and Radhika's hand and said

'We fly high, away from people's eye'

Within seconds Radhika and Frederick rose high with Leo.

Radhika laughed excitedly and directed Leo to head towards the Gateway of India.

While descending, a sprawling structure grabbed Leo's attention. He asked Radhika 'This is such an astonishing building. What is it?'

'This is the Taj Hotel' said Radhika with pride.

'Can we go inside and check the premises?' asked Frederick.

'Sure, why not. My uncle works here.' said Radhika.

Radhika's uncle gave them permission to see the hotel. They were cheerfully passing through a corridor when they heard a girl's voice from behind. 'Aarna, don't run so fast or else you will fall'. They turned in the direction of the voice and saw three girls, racing in the corridor. The eldest seemed to be around ten years old and was warning Aarna not to run.

Leo whispered in Frederick's ears 'Did she call her Aarna?'

Frederick nodded excitedly 'Yes!'

Radhika affirmed 'I am sure she said Aarna'

Radhika stepped forward and greeted the three children 'Hi, my name is Radhika. Did you just call out Aarna?'

The eldest girl looked at Radhika skeptically and said 'Yes, do you know her?'

'Is her name Aarna' Radhika asked again.

'Why do you want to know?' questioned the girl.

Radhika was taken aback. She said 'Oh, I am sorry; I am a stranger for you and should not be asking your names'

The eldest girl smiled and said 'Actually I know you. You are Radhika. Am I right?'

'Yes, that's true. How do you know me?'

'You had played the role of princess in the play ***the return of the thief***. I have seen the play' said the girl.

'Wow, you are very sharp. What is your name' asked Radhika.

'My name is Saanvi and I am Aarna's sister.'

'Hello Saanvi, glad to meet you. Are you from Mumbai?' asked Radhika.

'No, we are from Noida, but we often come to Mumbai' Saanvi replied.

'Glad to meet you Saanvi!' said Frederick and Leo as they joined Radhika.

Aarna and the other girl, who was youngest of the three, were quietly listening to the conversation.

She came closer and said 'Hi, I am Aarna and this is my sister Viti'

Frederick cleared his throat and asked 'Aarna, are you fond of playing with gadgets?'

Before Aarna could respond, Saanvi excitedly said 'Yes, she is. We call her the gadget girl'

'Really!' said Frederick in excitement.

Saanvi laughed and said 'Yes she loves to play with laptops, and other electronic gadgets'

'How old are you Aarna?' asked Radhika

'I am seven years old' she replied.

While they were excited to find Aarna, they wondered how such a young girl would rescue Femina.'

Leo asked Aarna 'Do you know how to solve formulas?'

'What are formulas?' asked Aarna.

'A combination of words or symbols to solve a problem' Radhika tried explaining.

Saanvi too looked confused. 'We have to leave now' said Saanvi.

'Yes, Ma and Papa are waiting for us' reiterated Aarna.

'Where are you staying?' asked Radhika.

'We are staying here' replied Saanvi

'I see' said Radhika

'Yes. We have come to attend a marriage in Mumbai and are returning to Delhi tomorrow evening,' saying this, the three little girls bid farewell and left.

Frederick wondered why Anika predicted Femina could be rescued by Aarna, when she did not even know what a formula meant.

Just then they heard Sussaina's voice reaching out to them 'Frederick and Leo, can you hear me?'

'Mother Sussaina, is that you?' asked Frederick.

'Yes son, this is Sussaina. How are you my children?' she asked.

'We are fine mother' said Frederick.

'Could you locate Aarna?' asked Sussaina

'Yes mother' said Frederick

'Superb' said Sussaina. 'Now we can rescue Femina soon' she rejoiced.

'No aunt, there is a problem. Aarna is very young and does not know any formula. Then how will she solve Drudan's formulas'

'Oh!' said Sussaina. 'Children, I suggest you observe her. Maybe her activities give us a clue to the formula. But please hasten'

'What happened Aunt? You sound stressed' asked Leo

'Leo my child, Anika has been experiencing strange feelings. She says there would be a day when an evil shadow will cover the Moon and the stars, stopping them from doing any good. We have to rescue Femina before this day arrives'

Leo and Frederick became worried. 'Yes mother we have to find the solution soon' said Frederick.

'Children take care' saying this Sussaina bid Goodbye.

After speaking to Sussaina, Frederick called the angel birds. The angel birds appeared and Leo narrated the entire episode to them. After pondering over the problem, they decided to stay in the hotel, to observe Aarna's activities. Leo volunteered to drop Radhika back.

When Leo returned after leaving Radhika, the red bird suggested 'I will reduce your size so that none can notice you'.

Both agreed with the plan. She pronounced '***Chin chunaki chin chin***' and reduced Leo and Frederick's height and size.

Chapter 12

Romeo and Drudan

Romeo and Drudan must have practiced for another half an hour, when Romeo noticed something and panicked 'Oh my God! There is a change in the movement of the Earth. I think Earth is quaking!'

'Ok, then what is the problem?' asked Drudan.

Romeo looked up and said 'Drudan, if the earthquake is strong, there will be a storm in the sea and the magical waters will get diluted. Instead of tomorrow, let us leave now. We will take six to seven hours to reach the point of confluence. By then, the Moon would be heading towards being full. We have to rescue Juliet before that. Once the first rays of Moon falls on the water of confluence, it will become magical and I will quickly collect it in my mouth. If there is an earthquake on a full Moon night, the tides will rise as high as heaven. No one can escape death in such volatile waters. We will have to move fast'

Drudan nodded nervously. First time in his life he wanted to escape from such dangers. Had it been any place on land or the air, he would have been very confident, but sea was a totally different ballgame.

He suggested 'Why can I not use magic now and reach there in minutes. Why do we have to swim for so long?'

'Your magic will fade as soon as we enter the zone of magical waters, and you will be sucked by the sea. Swimming towards these waters increases the strength ten times. The more you swim towards the waters, the more strength you will gain.'

'Really?' asked Drudan amazed.

'Yes' said Romeo with his attention on the change in weather

Drudan was mentally calling the Mermaid.

'Go with him Drudan. He is right; there will be an Earthquake soon 'replied the melodious voice of the mermaid.

Drudan whispered 'Ok' and focused on Romeo's instructions.

'Ok. Before we start, I will be taking you above the sea once. Suck in as much air as you can. Fill your lungs with oxygen. We will then fall back at a lightning speed so that all the oxygen gets locked in your lungs. Once in deep sea, I will spit on you to activate your skin to work like gills'.

Drudan nodded nervously. 'No magic and no oxygen' he whispered.

'Hurry up and sit on my back. We are going up' Instructed Romeo

Before Drudan knew, Romeo pulled him on his back and with the speed of lightening ascended the sea. Within seconds they were above the sea, floating in air. Drudan was in a state of shock, breathless and out of wits. He tried breathing, but could not. Water had entered his eyes, his nostrils and his mouth and he gasped for breath. Seeing him turn pale and blue, Romeo wound his tail around Drudan's legs and suspended him upside down in the air.

All the water that had entered his eyes, ears and nostrils, seeped out. Drudan was stunned and howled in pain.

He promised himself that once he gains some powers, he would take revenge from Romeo for these insults.

'Fast, take deep breath and fill your lungs with oxygen' said Romeo

Drudan quietly followed his instructions. Once he had inhaled enough air, Romeo placed Drudan on his back and with a speed of lightening, dived in the sea.

Once they had reached deep in the sea, Romeo asked Drudan to get off his back and swim with him. 'If we lose each other, you follow the ray of the Moon' instructed Romeo.

'I hate the Moon and shall never follow it' said Drudan

'Then get lost in this wild sea' said Romeo

'Why are you so rude?' asked Drudan

'Follow my instructions. While swimming, if there is an Earthquake, the tides will rise high and we may not find each other. Don't panic and just follow the rays of the Moon. This way, I will be able to locate you fast' instructed Romeo.

Drudan felt the sea was swelling.' My God, the sea looks wild!' he said fretfully.

'Just follow my instructions and you will be fine. Saying this, Romeo swam a little ahead and looking back told Drudan 'Now let the race begin!'

Within seconds he was wriggling ahead at a great speed. Drudan also forgot his inhibitions and followed him, slicing the water with his hands and pushing his legs to gain pace. He must have swum for an hour when a thunderous uproar and a loud cracking sound, pierced his ears. He looked ahead and was satisfied to see Romeo's tail still in the view. 'Come fast come fast, the Earth is cracking' yelled Romeo.

Just then, Drudan saw a huge tidal wave right in front of him. It was as high as a mountain. Drudan began to yell as the wave rose higher and then fell on him. He shrieked but his voice got subdued in the sound of the waves. The waves pushed him down deeper in the sea. The intensity of the fall of water was so great that Drudan felt as if thousand elephants had fallen on him and crushed him. He floated lifelessly in water for some time and then another splash of water hit his face and he woke up. He was drifting away at a very rapid speed, riding on a wave. With every rise, he would go up thousands of miles and then the fall was even more drastic. Water had entered his eyes and nose, only his skin could breathe.

With another rise of wave, he opened his eyes and was shocked to see a huge Moon at a distance. Before he realized, the waves dropped him back in the depths of sea. That is when Drudan saw another wave rising in front of him. It continued to gain height till it was so tall that it seemed to touch the Moon. Screaming, Drudan swam away from it moving his limbs vigorously, till he was far away from that wave. Just then, he felt he was rising again. The wave beneath him rose as tall as the one he had escaped, aiming high for the Moon. This time Drudan gaped at the Moon as he was riding the high tide.

The Moon seemed to be having a reddish hue to it, though the reddish tint was very subtle. Before Drudan could notice further, the tides threw him back in the depths of the sea. Drudan's head ached with the jerk of the fall. He felt dizzy and weak. 'How will

I locate Romeo?' he thought. He looked around and could only see high tidal waves and violent waters, nothing else. His hands and legs ached like never before and he wasn't even sure if he could continue swimming any longer. He tried calming his nerves and focusing on Romeo's Instructions. *He had to follow the rays of the Moon***.** Drudan tried straining his eyes but all he could see was the wild tide.

He was in deep sea and the only support he could get to escape the deep waters was to swim on the crest of the wave. Drudan decided to give his limbs some rest before he targeted to remain abreast on the wave. He became still, closed his eyes and let his limbs relax. The tyrant waters continued to lift him and throw him but he kept his eyes shut and calmly focused on finding Romeo. After sometime when he sensed the waters were lifting him high again, he opened his eyes and looked at the Moon. As he continued to gape, he saw the Moon was approaching its fullness. He panicked. Romeo had said that they had to rescue Juliet before the Full Moon. He continued to look at the Moon, but did not see any rays being emitted from it. After a deep thought, he decided to swim in the direction of the Moon. Maybe he could find Romeo on the way. Moon was towards the South western direction from where he was. The waves that were rising facing the south western direction would fall in that direction. These waves were rising many miles high and when they would throw him down, it would be many miles in the South western direction. Thus Drudan swam towards one such wave. It was gearing to rise and Drudan aggressively moved his limbs to climb up the wave and ride on its crest. The wave rose higher and higher and Drudan maintained a steady momentum, managing to float on the crest. It rose so high that even the sea began to look blur from that distance. Drudan's heart sank as the wave continued to rise. At that moment, the wave dropped down throwing Drudan far far away in the sea.

Drudan came screaming down and with a thud entered the depth of the sea. He could hear screams even though he had stopped yelling himself. On looking down he saw he had fallen on something hard.

'Where the hell have you been you buffalo? You almost crushed me by falling from such a great height'

'Who is talking to me?' asked Drudan, alarmed by the momentum of the fall.

'Who can call you a buffalo in this wild sea?"

'Romeo?' asked Drudan, both relieved and excited to find Romeo

'Yes it's me and now get off my back' spat Romeo.

'I cannot tell you how relieved I am to meet you' said Drudan, still holding onto Romeo.

'Yes, so am I 'said Romeo and continued 'Drudan, we have almost reached the point of confluence. Swim for another ten minutes in the North West direction and we will reach the point. First you will rescue my Juliet. The mermaid has used a magical spell on her. Once you rescue her, I will carry her on my back and wait for the Moon to approach its fullness. Then I will fill the magical waters in my mouth and we can swim back'

Drudan smirked and pulling out his golden chain wound around his neck, he said 'You needn't carry the magical water in your mouth. Look I have carried a tiny bottle to fill it' said Drudan, pulling out the little bottle that hung to the chain.

Romeo gave him a disgusted look and said 'I expected this stupidity from you'

Drudan's face flushed with fury. Controlling his temper, he asked 'Why, what is wrong in that?'

'These are magical waters. No one can capture them in any vessel' said Romeo

'Then how will you be able to carry them in your mouth?' asked Drudan.

'You have no idea of Indian mythologies?' asked Romeo

'Why should I know Indian mythology?' asked Drudan, cutting the water with his adept hand and moving forward with Romeo.

'Well, it is said that millions of years ago, the Gods and the Demons churned the ocean to dig out divine and magical water. Whenever such churning happens, the poison comes out first and then the divine and magical water. Thus logically, in order to carry divine water, one must carry poison as well. Snakes naturally have venoms and therefore are apt to carry these divine magical waters' explained Romeo

'Oh, I see' said Drudan.

'Yes, this is the reason the mermaid captured my wife, here. She had tricked her and got her here at the confluence to carry back the magical waters. Juliet being an idealist, refused because she thought the evil mermaid would bring disaster for sea creatures with magical waters. Thus the mermaid bound Juliet with a magical spell at the point of confluence. I tried to save her, but wasn't as strong then. The mermaid captured me inside the pebble and threw it out of the sea, where you found me.'

Drudan nodded. The mention of the mermaid made his heart beat faster. Her sea deep eyes, her floral fragrance, the magical dance, her memory.... made Drudan forget everything, his past, his mission.

'Hello uncle, do you wish to drown?' said Romeo, slapping Drudan's face with his tail.

The tail hit Drudan so hard on the face that he yelled aloud 'you scoundrel!'

'I saved you from committing suicide. Stop day dreaming or else these waves will swallow you alive. Now let us swim fast. It will be a Full Moon night in a matter of half an hour'

Chapter 13

Drudan and Romeo

Drudan controlled his temper once again and swam speedily with Romeo. He saw a bright broad beam falling on the sea and penetrating its depth. Just at that point he saw a multicolored snake suspended in the waters. It wasn't moving and looked frail and dying. 'That is my Juliet' said Romeo, traumatized by the condition of the snake.

'Please rescue her' he continued.

For a moment Drudan felt that this was the opportune time to take revenge from Romeo but the memory of carrying the magical waters back in Romeo's mouth, stopped him. Instead he focused on the way Juliet was captured and slowly commenced pronouncing spells that could rescue her.

Initially he tried some general life saving spells which did not work. Then he tried the one which could be used in deep waters. He went very close to Juliet and pointing his fingers towards her, said

'Droplets in the ocean as deep as the sea
Come together to break the spell
And set this snake free
Set this snake free'

A blue light emitted from his finger and began to swim in water. After sometime, small droplets of water began accumulating near the light and rotating with it. Romeo looked at his wife nervously. Soon these droplets began to sparkle with the blue light, formed a huge wave and with great velocity, dashed towards Juliet. As the light and the droplets went close to her, Romeo saw that his wife was actually enclosed in a glass like structure. The droplets hit the glass, with great force and broke it. Juliet was thrown high up in the sea. Romeo sprinted ahead and jumped high and wound himself around her.

'Romeo, you are alive? You saved me?'Juliet murmured on seeing Romeo

'Yes Juliet I am alive and have come to save you'

She heard Romeo's voice, feebly smiled and fainted.

'I have done your work, rescued your Juliet. Now it is your turn to fulfill the promise.'

Romeo nodded and said 'Thank you for saving her. Yes, I am waiting for the Full Moon. As soon as the rays of the Moon fall on the confluence of Arabian sea, Indian Ocean and Bay of Bengal, I will dive in and fill my mouth with the water. We can return then'

Both Drudan and Romeo patiently waited for the moment. Tall waves continued to play havoc and the sound of Earth quake sent tremors in Drudan's heart. Finally the Moon began to gain its fullness. It looked so huge and bright that Drudan's eyes felt blind and his skin felt parched and burnt. 'Hurry I can't stand the Moon' he told Romeo.

Romeo asked Drudan to hold Juliet while he dived in to fill his mouth with the magical water. Once he had done that, he wrapped himself around Juliet and gestured Drudan to swim ahead. They swam for more than eight hours non- stop. Drudan felt dizzy and weak in between but the voice of the mermaid kept giving him strength. She continued to call out to him 'My Hero, my King, don't lose hope. Keep moving your limbs.'

When they were still far away, the earth cracked with a deafening sound and the sea turned very violent. A huge tidal wave created a barrier between Drudan and Romeo. Drudan lost track and fell deep in the sea. He thought it was his last day as he had lost all his strength to fight the sea. That moment, a pair of tender hands pulled him up and dragged him to safety.

When he opened his eyes, he found himself in a palace of water. He was lying on a bed of corals and the mermaid was sitting beside him, singing the same melodious song. The mermaid helped him to sit and made him drink a juice made of herbs and salt.

Drudan felt energized after having the juice. 'Where is Romeo? He is carrying magical waters in his mouth!' asked Drudan

'He is still on his way. I deliberately sent the tide to distract him and get you here' said the mermaid

'But why did you do that?' asked Drudan flummoxed and tired.

'Don't ask so many questions. Relax!' smiled the mermaid

Drudan was mesmerized by her beauty and he calmed down.

Then the mermaid said 'I wanted to get you here to plan our next move. While you have the magical waters, it can only travel in a snake's mouth. Also do you know how you can unite the souls by using magical water? You have no plan in place!'

Drudan nodded in agreement.

The mermaid continued 'In a matter of two days, the demon planets will cast their full shadow on the Moon, the planets and the Sun. Such times are best for initiating anything negative and evil. If you capture Zynpagua during this time, victory will be yours and these planets will continue to support you throughout. It's a rule of the universe that anything captured during a week long reign of these demon planets will remain under the victor's rule unless within that week, someone defeats him and conquers the region back.'

Drudan's face brightened 'This is awesome. That means if I conquer Zynpagua in next two days, the stars will become helpless and will not save Sussaina or Anika?'

'Yes ' the mermaid affirmed.

'Then can I not kill them. Why bother with this whole uniting of souls bit?'

'No, don't take any chance. What if you are not able to capture them? How will you take revenge?'

Drudan nodded.

'Use the magical water and unite Leo and Anika's souls. The water is so powerful that no human can stand it'said the mermaid.

'And this will be my way of taking sweet revenge from my treacherous son Leo and that gifted girl Anika' said Drudan

'I have a brilliant plan to unite Leo's soul. It will leave Anika lifeless and Leo wreathing in pain!' the mermaid giggled. 'Anika borrowed Leo's soul to live. It is time to give it back!' she laughed aloud.

Chapter 14

Zynpagua

The soldiers of Zynpagua were playing drums and calling the people

'People of Zynpagua,
We have an announcement to make
Hey ladies, stop filling aqua
Come closer for God sake!
Our Queen has a wish
Which you cannot dismiss
Hey Gentleman
Lend you ears for God's sake
Our Queen has a wish
Which you cannot dismiss
You have to live in the palace
To escape a menace
Don't be scared

The villain will not be spared
We need volunteers to build houses
In the depths of the palace
Prince Vivian will be there too
To build houses for you'

The people of Zynpagua were petrified listening to the announcement. Drudan was the only threat for Zynpagua. Was he returning? They crowded around the soldiers to get more details of the threat. 'Drudan is the threat!' yelled one, announcing it to the others. 'Drudan?' repeated some others in a state of shock. Then everyone decided to head for the palace to help Vivian build the houses.

Back in the palace, Queen Sussaina was sitting with Vivian and Anika. She had a diagram in front of her which revealed the proposed underground structure of the palace.

Sussaina was explaining the design to Anika and Vivian 'Children, this will be the entrance to the underground corridors. One door will be situated on the floor beneath the throne in the main hall and the other beneath the jail cellar'

'Mother, I understand that the intention to keep the entrance hidden is for keeping our people safe and secure from Drudan, but what is the idea of having them in the jail cellar and beneath the throne' asked Vivian

'Son, God forbid if we are taken into captivity, and somehow Drudan forces us to reveal where the people are, I will tell him the route to underground houses from beneath his throne. Even if he captures them, we will be able to reach them through this secret passage from the jail cell and help them' said Sussaina

'Mother, why are we assuming that Drudan will capture us? Anika asked.

'Anika, Venus has indicated that there would be a situation when the stars will be helpless. This indicates that we have to use our good sense. As the queen of Zynpagua, my duty is to protect our people. Wisdom says be hopeful but also be prepared to face the worst' said Sussaina.

'Mother, but Venus also said that the result for any situation would depend on our determination and decision. I will never decide to stand defeated in front of Drudan' said Anika empathically.

'She is right mother. None of us will let Drudan rule Zynpagua again' assured Vivian.

'Son, I know, under no circumstance would we be ready to let Drudan win, but remember ten years back, I was more powerful than Anika in terms of predicting the stars and winning their favours. Despite that Drudan tricked us' Sussaina said sadly.

'Yes mother, you are right. We have to be prepared for the worst' said Anika

'But always hope for the best' beamed Vivian, hugging Anika.

'Children, we don't have time. The underground construction will have to start today itself. I do not know how many people would volunteer to build the houses. Our houses have to be ready as soon as possible.'

Suddenly, they heard some commotion outside the palace.

'Queen Queen
We are here
To help Prince Vivian
Build houses
In palace premises'

They went out and saw that all the people of Zynpagua, both men and women, had gathered outside the palace and were willing to build the houses. Sussaina smiled and addressed them

'Dear Citizens, we might face an attack from Drudan. To keep you safe, we will have to build houses within the palace. How many of you know how to construct?'

Some fifty men and women stepped forward. 'Great' said the queen. 'Then you will lead the team to build five houses each.'

One of them asked Sussaina 'My queen, when Prince Vivian can do magic, why can we not make houses with the help of magic'

Sussaina smiled and said 'Because Vivian's magic is equal and opposite to that of Drudan. What Vivian builds with magic, Drudan can destroy with magic.'

Everyone nodded in agreement.

Vivian stepped in front and said 'Friends, we have made the arrangements. There are spades for digging the soil, bricks and cement to build houses and water for construction work. The leaders, please come forward!'

The leaders who knew construction stepped forward. Vivian showed them the diagram and took their suggestion to commence work. The leaders then addressed the people and selected their teams to build houses. The Sun was high up in the sky as they commenced work. Building two hundred and fifty houses in underground tunnels was not a joke. But none revolted. After all, even Vivian was with them and his enthusiasm kept them going.

Anika was quietly watching them. The onus of saving her people actually lay on her shoulders. She was the one who had the power to influence the stars and protect her people but no one was putting pressure on her to save them. She felt her people loved her so much that if there was ever a threat to her life, they would give their life to save her.

As she was thinking about them, her eyes fell on a single ray of Sun falling on Vivian. It was giving a reddish glow to his forehead.

A sinking feeling engulfed her. She turned around to look at the people and saw the same reddish glow on the forehead of every worker. She knew the colour red signified danger. Was the danger approaching Zynpagua faster than she had thought? Venus had told Anika that the shadow of demon planets would turn Moon reddish. Was this evil planet also casting a shadow on the Sun? A sudden realization unnerved her. She muttered

'Red rays of the Sun
Indicates a shadow on the Sun
Who can challenge the Sun?
The demon planets- the evil ones
The red rays of the Sun
Indicates that evil planets
Have commenced casting their red shadow
On the Sun
Danger is coming faster towards Zynpagua
Faster than expected by anyone'

This realization made Anika tremble. If Drudan was planning to attack Zynpagua then, it will happen in a matter of only few days, not even weeks.

Anika rushed towards Sussaina and told her about the premonition. Sussaina looked worried but continued to portray a calm demeanor. They instantly headed towards the construction site, to urge the workers to hasten the process. But when they reached there, the scenario silenced Sussaina and Anika.

The people had only been able to dig the ground. Everyone looked exhausted and out of energy. While the head cook was continuously providing food, juices and energy drinks to the people, it wasn't enough to give them strength to finish the task with rapid speed.

Sussaina thought for a while and asked Anika to come to a side. She said 'Anika, pray to Mars to give our people super strength and stamina. We have to finish building the houses. The sooner we do it, the safer we are'

Anika nodded and sat down to pray.

Sussaina stopped her and said 'Wait; first let me inform them that we are seeking help from Mars.'

'Mother, why do we need to inform them?' asked Anika

'Mars is a harsh teacher. When it will cast its rays on the people, they will get an acute burning sensation. If our people do not know the reason for this sudden pain, they might think this is being inflicted by Drudan. I do not want to frighten them. Let us keep them informed' said Sussaina.

Anika nodded. Sussaina called Vivian first and briefed him on Anika's premonition.

Then Sussaina stepped forward and addressed the crowd 'My dear people. You are very precious for us. As you already know, we feel we will be attacked by Drudan. So far we had no idea when this was happening. But unfortunately, Anika senses it is going to happen very soon. We have to build the houses by tomorrow.'

'What? That is impossible Queen' said the people, in unison.

'It is possible my children, if we seek blessings from Mars' said Sussaina.

'Thank you Queen' said the people in unison.

'My people, while Anika will pray to Mars, I must warn you that the rays of Mars are harsh and generate acute burning sensation when they fall on anyone. While the result will be magical strength in your limbs, but the initial pain is quite intolerable. Those willing to back out, can move inside the palace' said Sussaina.

'Queen, we are ready to face anything' voiced the people together

Sussaina smiled and said 'Then let us get ready to be showered by the valiant rays of Mars!'

Anika sat on her knees and joining her hands, prayed

'Where are you Mars?
The most courageous of all Stars
We need your powers
To build under-ground towers'

Everyone was looking at the sky but there was no sign of Mars. Anika repeated her prayer and yet there was no response. The Queen and the people were waiting expectantly.

Anika closed her eyes and remembered Venus's advice on using her wisdom in every situation. She calmly thought how she had asked Mars to help her the previous time. The memory brightened her face. Yes, Mars always expects a commitment and a sacrifice. She had to commit something to Mars.

She joined her hands once again and
looking up at the sky, she voiced aloud
'Dear Mars
My people need your powers
I have a commitment to make

I will sacrifice my life
For my peoples' sake
When any threat will come on them
I will give my life but save them
Please ensure, if death knocks at our door
I should be the one taken away
Alive the rest should stay'

'No, Anika, what are you saying?' screamed Sussaina.

'Yes mother, what is the point in living if my supernatural abilities cannot save my people. If there is any threat on Zynpagua, my life should stand as a safeguard for everyone else's' said Anika.

'What have you promised my dear sister? You think we will be able to live without you?' asked Vivian.

'Brother, you and I will ensure that no death like situation arises in Zynpagua. We will strengthen our spirits and strengthen our skills. We will fight Drudan with all our grit. If I have promised my life for Zynpagua I promise my family that I will live for them' said Anika.

The people began to clap and Sussaina hugged Anika, with tears rolling from her eyes. No one had ever seen such a brave eleven year old child. Mars was happy with Anika and showered its valourous rays on the people of Zynpagua. Vivian, Anika and Sussaina also faced the rays with the people. Initially they yelled with pain and burning sensation but within minutes the sensation was replaced by energy flowing in their veins. They had never felt so strong before.

With renewed ardor and vigour, they commenced the construction of houses. Their efficiency was matchless and by the coming morning, the underground tunnels, the secret roads and the houses were ready. People patted themselves and clapped in amazement. They painted each house with beautiful colours. These houses were constructed in such a way that the Sunrays and oxygen could come in through secret windows.

Chapter 15

Spell of hundred rounds

Queen Sussaina proudly announced 'My children, this is spectacular. Your efforts have paid off. We have built our secret houses in such a short time. This is commendable.'

Someone from the crowd said 'Mars gave us the strength'

Sussaina smiled and said 'People, stars support those who are ready to help themselves. Without your personal effort, even Mars strength would be a waste. Thank you my dear countrymen '

Everyone clapped. The Head cook came out hurriedly from the kitchen, followed by a coterie of helpers, with smiles on their faces, balancing huge trays loaded with delicious muffins on their palms.

The people feasted on them and celebrated this achievement.

'Now hurry and get your belongings to the palace. Leave nothing behind. Move your entire family in' said Sussaina.

The people rushed out.

She turned to Vivian and said 'Son, with the help of magic, provide a name plate for each house. This way the people will find it easy to move in'

'Sure mother', said Vivian and blew air towards the houses and instructed

'Emboss names of our countrymen starting from z and reverse!'

'Well thought and well done brother' said Anika

'Yes Son, well done. Anika try finishing your swimming classes today itself. Staying outside the palace is not safe' said Sussaina.

'Yes mother' Anika affirmed and left the palace in haste.

Sussaina called Vivian and said 'Son, I want you to use magic and hide these houses'

'But mother, even if I use magic, Drudan will be able to discover these houses by doing magic himself' Vivian responded skeptically.

'My son, today I am going to teach you a trick. It is called the spell of hundred rounds'

'Spell of hundred rounds? 'Asked Vivian

'Yes. I am sure Drudan will not be able to break this spell easily. Let us try it on that tree. Use the disappearance spell to make it invisible'

Vivian raised his hand and said

'Tree with green pear

Disappear from here'

The tree instantly disappeared.

Then Sussaina instructed him 'Now send the tree to a different location'

Vivian pointed his hand towards the tree and said 'Go from here'

There was a loud noise as if something was uprooting itself and then the movement of wind signified the invisible tree was moving away from there.

Sussaina continued 'Now get the tree back with a different spell'

Vivian again pointed his hand and said 'Appear once again'

'No don't use the same spell. Use a different spell to get the tree here' said Sussaina.

'How mother?' asked Vivian

Sussaina smiled and said, 'say something like take birth here again and be the same'

Vivian exclaimed 'Wow mother, you are superb!'

He nodded and said 'Take birth here again and be the same'

The tree first transformed into a seed and became the same size.

Sussaina clapped and said 'That's fantastic'

Now make the tree invisible through another spell.

'How mother?' asked Vivian

'Say something so that others around cannot see the tree' said Sussaina

'This is so much fun mother!' said Vivian and pointing his hands up, he said 'People in this region, don't see this tree for one long season'

Sussaina and her guards could not see the tree.

Vivian was very excited learning this new trick and said 'Mother, I have understood what you mean. Basically I have to hide the houses using hundred different spells so that Drudan is not able to locate the houses and he will have to use same hundred spells to discover them'

'Good Son. Just make a mental note of the sequence of the spell so that you are able to remove the spells when there is no threat on the people' said Sussaina

'Do you know how to make a mental note?' asked Sussaina

'Memorize the sequence?' asked Vivian

'Yes but memorizing magically. Verbalize the spell, then tap your head and say first of the spell and don't forget. Then pronounce the second spell and tap your head and say second of the spell, don't forget. Do this for all hundred spells' instructed Sussaina

'Got it mother' said Vivian

'Now my son, tell the guards to make haste and tell the people to shift to the houses as soon as possible' instructed Sussaina.

Chapter 16

Mootu and Anika

Anika ran towards her horse and mounted it. She gently pressed her heels on the horse's sides and holding the reins, instructed the Stallion to gallop fast.

Mootu was waiting for her at the river bank. He had worn a cap and a pair of glares. A jute bag was placed on his hump.

The birds began to chirp merrily on seeing Anika.

The stallion halted in front of Mootu. Anika instantly jumped down. She patted the horse and thanked him.

'Good afternoon Sir, I am ready for the classes' she said.

Mootu blew a whistle and silenced the birds. He then inspected Anika's clothes. She had worn a tight shirt which covered her hands and body completely and a pair of fitting pants.

'Great! 'Said Mootu, smiling.

He instructed Anika to take off her shoes and listen to him carefully. Anika nodded and Mootu continued 'Ok Anika, we start our classes today. The reason I wanted you to be fully covered in fitting clothing is that unlike a swimming pool, the river has innumerable living species and plants in it. Some are poisonous for humans. The tight fitting clothes covering your body will ensure these poisonous plants do not touch your skin.'

He then took out two leaves from his jute bag and gave it to Anika. 'Rub these two leaves between your palms and apply the juice thoroughly on your hands and legs. The juice of this leaf will protect your limbs from any harm'

Anika did as she was told. On rubbing the leaves, they changed to a rotten green colour and emitted a horrible stench. Anika felt giddy. As she looked down, Mootu had covered his nose and the birds had hidden their faces in their wings.

'Sir, please tell me what I need to do next or else I may vomit' said Anika.

Mootu said 'Anika, breathe deeply and get used to the smell. Once you get used to, it will not be so irksome.'

'What? Sir, I will puke if I smell my hand' said Anika.

'I understand, but remember this is the only plant that can protect you in raw waters. It can cure poison of any aquatic species be it snakes, fishes...' said Mootu.

'Ugh, it's ugly!' said Anika

'Anika, never treat anyone or anything like that. Listen to me, this is the rule of nature- all ugly things can bestow precious gifts. Learn to respect them' said Mootu

'I am sorry' said Anika

'Now take deep breaths!' said Mootu

Anika did as she was told. Initially she felt giddy but as she continued, she felt better and better. After sometime, she sensed fragrance everywhere. On looking around she saw innumerable plants with the same leaves had grown on the river banks.

'Fantastic!' said Mootu 'Now, Mana will protect you everywhere!'

'Mana? Who is Mana?' asked Anika

'These magical plants are called Mana. They have the power to cure all wounds and bites underwater. They have magical healing properties. In fact, when eaten, these leaves help humans breathe underwater'

'That's wonderful' said Anika

'Yes, and these plants teach us a lesson. Ugly things can be the most wonderful once you know them' smiled Mootu.

'I Apologize for being so mean' said Anika

'Mana seems to like you. See they have grown on the banks to protect you' said Mootu.

'Let us start now. Listen to my instruction. First we will strengthen your leg movement. Follow me' said Mootu and dipped his legs in the river while sitting on the bank. Anika too sat on the banks and dipped her legs inside the river.

'Good' said Mootu 'Now slowly move inside the River, while holding the edge of the banks with your hand.' Anika followed the instructions and Mootu continued

'Now turn towards the bank of river, hold the edge with both hands and move your body inside the river' said Mootu

Anika saw the expanse of the river and got frightened. It appeared very broad and deep with gushing currents. Seeing Anika hesitate, Mootu asked her 'What happened?'

'This is such a huge river. Even if I hold the sides, the undercurrents will pull me away' said Anika.

'Yes, they might and that is the challenge. Holding the banks will strengthen your arms and flapping your legs while they are suspended in water, will strengthen your legs. Now, don't waste time. Step in and while holding the sides, suspend your legs in water and flap them. The more you practice this, the faster you will learn to swim.'

Anika was scared stiff and continued watching the wild torrent.

Seeing her state, the birds began to sing

Anika, this is no big deal
You have Nerves of steel,
Daughter of lovely Queen
On your face we see her gleam
Sister of brave brother
You can do it no other
Hold the banks and flap your legs
Fear you should suppress
Step in, Step in
And flap your legs.
One two three and race in
We will sing throughout this training session.'

While the birds were singing, Mootu held Anika's hand and gently pushed her in the river, still holding her hands. At first Anika screamed but then slowly braced courage and holding the banks, commenced flapping her legs.

Mootu made Anika practice the flapping of legs and hands only for the next two hours. The beneficial rays of Mars had given Anika enough strength to learn fast. When Mootu was confident that her lower limbs had been strengthened, he began instructing

Anika on strengthening the hand movement for swimming. Anika was holding onto the banks when Mootu instructed

'Alright Anika, now focus on the river. Can you see how strong these currents are?'

Anika nodded, still holding the banks.

'Your hands and legs movement should be synchronized with the speed of the current'

'What?' exclaimed Anika.

Chapter 17

Lady Carol

Lady Carol was sitting in her room, studying an old book that had deep secrets of the kingdom of the clouds. This book had been gifted to her by her father and he had instructed her to read it only in privacy.

Before reading, she had closed all the doors and the windows of her room, to ensure no one eavesdrops. She had been worried about Anika and Leo's safety since the time Drudan had escaped from Zynpagua. Reading this book had made her fears grow deeper. When she had saved Anika's soul by borrowing it from Leo's soul, she had no idea about the repercussions. Never in the history of kingdom of clouds had this been tried on children.

In fact while the technique of borrowing souls existed, no one had managed to do the same in the last hundred years. She was surprised that she had succeeded in borrowing the soul of Leo and saving Anika without being trained to do it. Somewhere she knew that the heavens wanted this to happen and therefore such an impossible task could be achieved. The book clearly stated that when a soul is split and shared between two bodies, it indicates that the two have to work together to clean the evil from the world. The only evil she knew was Drudan who had escaped.

She knew that Drudan would not keep quiet for long.

'Drudan has an unusual scientific mind and can bring out a solution to almost everything. After all, even the violet light was Drudan's spectacular achievement, unimagined by any.' Thought Lady Carol

She restlessly turned the pages of the book to find a solution to all possible threats to people who live on a borrowed soul. As she flipped the pages, one line attracted her attention ***As far as an individual is chanting in a language that sends vibrations to every part of the body, the soul cannot part with the body, under any circumstance.***

'Which language can send vibrations to every part of the body?' she thought.

The crackling sound of the lightening got her back from her reverie. She stood up and rushed towards the windows. The scene outside shocked her. The sky of kingdom of clouds which was inundated with blooming roses had begun to have a rust shade. The roses were not looking fresh anymore.

What was happening? Her heart paced fast. She clapped and beckoned a white pigeon that was flying in the sky, close to the roses.

The pigeon obediently flapped his wings and came and sat on her palm. 'Lady Carol, what can I do for you?' he chirped.

'Thank you for coming Birdie. Tell me, don't you find something strange in the sky?' asked Lady Carol

The bird chirped 'Yes lady, there is something strange. The old bird said when the stars move differently, this shade comes'

This information sent triggers in her veins. She asked 'Which bird told you?'

The Pigeon chirped 'the old eagle was saying that she has seen this weather only once in her lifetime and she was very worried and scared'

'Why is the old eagle worried?' asked Lady Carol, her voice shivering.

'Let us immediately meet her. Birdie, please come with me' said Lady Carol.

Saying this Lady Carol raised her hand and flew up in the sky towards the Northern direction.

The pigeon chirped and flew behind her, flapping his wings energetically to catch up with Lady Carol's speed.

The old eagle was a 200 year old bird and had migrated from the Earth. She stayed in the depths of the jungle, perched on the highest tree.

Lady Carol flew in the jungle, avoiding the thick bushes and trunks. The other birds had also joined her as she flew deeper in the woods. She reached the redwood tree and called out.

With swoosh of wings, the eagle flew down, sat on Lady Carol's hand and began to peck it.

Lady Carol said 'I pay my reverence to the oldest and wisest member of the kingdom of clouds. Dear Birdie, please give me guidance from your years of experience. Why does the weather look so strange and why is there a reddish glow in the sky. My heart warns me against a danger, unheard of'

The eagle shook its head and said 'Lady, even I am perplexed seeing the sky. The flowers seem to shrink and the air warns of threat. I have seen this type of weather only once in my lifetime. I was in my twenties then and used to live on the coconut trees on the bank of Indian Ocean. It was a very dangerous site. The Moon had turned red and seemed to be under the influence of some shadows. That night the tides rose high and destroyed everything around. It seemed the skies had turned evil and malicious'

Lady Carol panicked at the revelation 'The Moon turned red?? The sky was under the influence of shadows? Oh my God!' exclaimed Lady Carol.

She thanked the eagle and rushed back. Yes, her father had once mentioned the spell of shadow planets. It was a universal phenomenon that happened only once in 200 years. She knew that there were two evil shadow planets that rotated and revolved around the Sun. Once every 200 years these two shadow planets gained the ability to cast their shadow on every planet. This was the time of natural disasters and birth of evil. The influence of the shadows did not last for more than a week, but that one week gave birth to evil in the universe.

All the negative people in the world who knew about this phenomenon waited for this period to gain victory and rule the world.

She held her head and sat down on the chair. Yes, Drudan must be planning to take advantage of this period.

Chapter 18

Mootu and Anika

'Did I hear a what? Manners lady, mind your manners!' Said Mootu sternly

'Sorry Sir, but these currents will swallow me' Anika replied

'No, they won't. Your legs are now trained to handle these currents. Even if you do not move your hands, simply flap your legs the way I trained you and you will manage to float in the river.' Mootu asserted.

He then slipped in the river and holding his head above the water level, said.

'Now watch my hand movement. Your palms should work like blades and hands should rotate full length'

He demonstrated the movement to Anika and instructed her to practice with one hand, while the other could continue holding the banks. Once he was satisfied that Anika could commence swimming, he instructed. 'Anika, I am swimming from here till the point where there is a coconut tree. Once I reach there, I will blow the whistle. As soon as I do that, leave the banks and start swimming straight towards me'

'Sir, I will drown' said Anika, trembling.

'Stop looking at the flow of the water. Focus on me and your target the tree' saying this Mootu elegantly swam towards the tree and in a matter of some minutes, reached his destination. Turning towards Anika, he raised his head above the water and blew the whistle.

Anika slowly released her grip on the banks and slid back in the river. Some birds were flying above the river and others were sitting on the trees. They cheered and chirped to encourage her. Anika looked at them, took a deep breath and thrust her head in water, slicing the currents with her hands and moving her legs steadily. Despite vigorously moving her limbs, she felt she was sinking down, deep in water. She looked ahead and saw Mootu gesturing to continue moving her limbs. Anika was gasping for breath and yet she pushed herself ahead, slicing the waters strongly and moving her legs speedily.

When she had gained some control on her swimming, she looked up, trying to locate Mootu. To her dismay, she could neither see Mootu nor the birds. Terrified and tired, she yelled 'Mootu sir!' but there was no response. On looking around she realized that the banks of the river were far away. Where had she come?

A sense of panic began to engulf her. What had happened to them? Had Drudan attacked? How was she going to get out of these deep waters? She tried flapping her legs and turning towards the direction of the banks on right. After a lot of effort, she managed to do so, but her hands felt heavy and fatigued. The river currents were very strong and she had to strike the waters with more energy to swim ahead. Anika thrust her head out of water, took a deep breath and with all her might, pushed ahead. She covered some distance, but her strength gave way. She could not even lift her hands and legs.

In a state of panic, she tried flapping her hands, but could not even lift them and soon she began to sink in water. She gasped for breath, but water entered her mouth making her dizzy.

She closed her eyes and began to think. 'When things go wrong, simply use your wisdom!' her inner voice told her. What could she do? What? What? What? She closed her eyes and clearly recalled Mootu sir's instructions 'even if you are unable to use your hands, simply flap your legs and you will be able to float in water'. A sense of relief transpired within

Thus Anika began flapping her legs slowly. She stopped sinking in water and began to float. Some water currents pushed her and she gradually drifted towards the banks. She continued floating for some time and when she regained some strength, she pushed herself forward and reached the banks. She stretched her hands and held the bank but could not pull herself out of water.

Just then she saw several birds appearing from nowhere. They caught Anika's dress with their legs and pulled her out from the river. Mootu came out from the hiding and clapped aggressively 'Fantastic! You have passed the test!'

Anika feebly smiled and said 'Sir, was it a test? It almost took my life'.

'I had complete confidence in you. You would have managed it' smiled Mootu. The birds flew down holding fruits in their claws. One by one they dropped the fruits beside Anika. Mootu instructed 'Have the fruits Anika. You will feel better!'

Once Anika ate the fruits and gained some strength, Mootu solemnly instructed 'Anika, I do not know why the stars want you to know swimming. But if you are stranded in deep waters, remember to seek the help of tortoises. There is a method to call the tortoise in water. Vibrate your lips and blow air through them. These vibrations will reach the tortoise in no time. And once they come close, tell them you are my student. They will help you. While we are feeble creatures in the water, we are great communicators. We can connect with anyone.'

'Thank you Sir, I will remember this'. As Anika spoke, she noticed that the Sun had suddenly disappeared behind very dark clouds. It wasn't the rainy season and the shape of the clouds looked weird. After a while the entire milieu got covered with a reddish tint.

Mootu blurted out 'What the hell is this? It seems there is a celestial war going on'

Anika felt an eerie sensation. She immediately mounted her horse and bidding farewell to Mootu, galloped speedily to the palace.

Chapter 19

Lady Carol

The thought of Drudan made Lady Carol uncomfortable.

She tried using magic to see what was happening in Zynpagua, but the thick clouds and the reddish glow in the sky, obstructed her vision. This disturbed her even more.

Immediately, she clapped her hands and called the helpers. As they came in, she ordered 'Fetch me the messengers of the kingdom of clouds.'

Two Peregrine falcons flew in and bowed before Lady Carol. They were huge birds in shades of brown and white. Lady Carol acknowledged their greetings and instructed them 'My fastest birds make haste and fly. Go to Zynpagua and find out how is everyone there. Don't go inside the palace, just observe from a distance and let me know. I haven't heard from Sussaina for long and it worries me immensely. Ensure you do not descend. If you see threat, one of you should stay there while the other should return to seek my help.'

The birds pecked twice, spread their huge wings and flew away. Lady Carol immediately went back to her books. She was desperately searching for a language that was scientific, ancient and whose pronunciation could make the entire body vibrate. **'The soul cannot part with the body till the person is reciting this language'**, she kept murmuring, while searching for the information.

Chapter 20

Drudan and the Mermaid

'Whose soul do you want to unite with the magical water?'The mermaid asked Drudan

'Ah, it's a long story. I married a lady called Pajaro who was the princess of the clouds. She is the one who taught me magic. She was a pious woman, too good for my taste. I kind of tolerated her goodness until she gave birth to our son Leo. Whenever I faced Leo, my powers depleted and I felt like a cripple.

I created the violet light that could annihilate anything. The same violet light-separated Zynpagua from the Earth. The day I thought I could rule, I betrayed the king and captured Queen Sussaina. Since Pajaro tried stopping me, I killed her and sealed my son in ice. Little did I know that destiny planned differently! I was ruling Zynpagua peacefully when Sussaina's daughter came back from the Earth. With her powers, she began influencing the stars and receiving their favours. I sent violet to kill her. Violet entered her heart and killed her soul.

My wife's mother, Lady Carol, borrowed a part of my son's soul and lent it to Anika. She was saved. Not only that, Anika rescued Leo from ice, impressed the stars and ousted me from Zynpagua. I despise her and want to take back my son's soul from her body. Once the soul is gone, she will die!'

'How could Lady Carol borrow your son's soul? Can anyone do that?' asked the Mermaid.

'Yes, she could do that because my son is Anika's soul mate' replied Drudan

'Hmm', said the mermaid, thinking deeply. 'What is a soul mate? Just the person you marry?'

'It isn't such a casual term as used these days. There are certain couples who have a special purpose in life, for the benefit of mankind. These people have the same thinking process, same missions, and same intuitions. Their souls are like twins, only bodies are different. Nature gets active in getting these people together. That is a soul mate. Actually it was the Moon which united Leo and Anika's soul.'

'You mean to say we are going to put up a fight against the heavenly bodies and even the will of God?' asked the mermaid, dilating her pupils and staring at Drudan.

'Yes, we are evil people and we are meant to disobey nature' chuckled Drudan.

The mermaid let out a loud laughter and clapped happily 'That's why I love you...my evil Hero! I think even we are soul mates, evil soul mates!'

Drudan laughed and hugged the mermaid who continued to snigger for a while.

A sudden recollection of Romeo made Drudan turn 'Why has Romeo not come till now?'

'He is still on his way. I sent rapid waves and pulled you towards me' the mermaid smiled.

'Wow!' exclaimed Drudan.

'We need Romeo to carry the magical water till Zynpagua. It can be carried only on poison. In the meanwhile, let us make the plan. For uniting the souls, both Anika and Leo should face each other or be in close proximity to each. other. Leo should be made to drink the magical waters. Once inside the body, the magical waters would automatically coax Leo's soul to call Anika's soul to unite. Once the soul unites, Anika will be dead. ' said the mermaid.

'And what about Leo?' asked Drudan

'The human who drinks magical water will die. This water creates so much heat and pain in the body that the person will not be able to stand it for more than a day' the mermaid replied.

'Good girl' said Drudan, smiling at the mermaid 'After that I will kill everyone' he continued.

'No, don't kill anyone' said the Mermaid 'We have to focus on impressing the demon planets'

'We have to be good to impress them?' asked Drudan

'No! We are negative evil people. We are born to challenge the goodness. Why do you think there are two evil planets in the universe? 'The mermaid said, looking intently at Drudan.

She laughed and continued 'we are doing justice with the role nature has assigned to us. Being evil is such a burdensome and difficult task!'

Drudan too began to laugh. He was absolutely smitten by the mermaids charm and wisdom. For a moment he wanted to forget the revenge bit and spend his life happily with the mermaid. All he desired was to lead a happy life with the mermaid, but then the evil instinct overpowered these tender feelings and he began plotting again.

'You are very sure that the two evil planets will support us throughout? What if the Sun and Mars send their benefic rays to Zynpagua and I get overpowered?'

The mermaid smiled and said 'That is why I am insisting on conquering Zynpagua during the week the demon planets cast their shadow on other planets. Any conquest done then will get the favour of these two demon planets and the other planets will not be able to do any good.' The mermaid replied.

'Great! In that case, I am game. I will get Leo close to Anika, kill her and use my magic to win Zynpagua back. But wait; there is another hurdle –Vivian. He can defeat me with his magical abilities.'

'So can Leo. If he faces you, then you will lose your powers!' said the mermaid.

'Yes, that's right. Very intelligently thought' said Drudan

'This is so obvious. When Leo will drink the magical water, it will create immense heat in his body and he will wreathe in pain. You can capture him then'

'Are you listening to me?' Asked the mermaid, when she saw Drudan lost in his thoughts.

'Of course', said Drudan

She continued 'As I have heard from you, Vivian is an emotional boy. When he will see Anika die, his focus would be on saving her rather than combating you. That would be the right time to capture him.'

'You are superb!' said Drudan, admiring her.

'Besides, the demon planets will be powerful and all evil beings would have more power 'she continued

'Oh yes, I forgot about the great demon planets' said Drudan, nodding his head.

The mermaid smiled and said 'And listen, I wish I could accompany you, but Romeo will be with you. Besides a mermaid cannot leave the sea when she is going to give birth to a baby'

'Going to give birth to a baby? Asked Drudan totally surprised.

'Yes, I am carrying your child' she smiled merrily.

Drudan was elated. He instantly declared 'No, I don't want to seek revenge from anyone. I want to live happily with my wife and child'

The mermaid smiled and asked him 'Sure?'

But Drudan was a vicious man. How could he live without ruling, without inflicting pain, without shedding blood? He smiled and said 'First let me conquer Zynpagua and then we can live happily ever after.'

'This is exactly what I like about you -the will to seek revenge' said the mermaid. Then she silenced Drudan and concentrated on the movement of water. 'Romeo is very close; I will quickly take you to your house.' Saying this, the mermaid held Drudan's hand and swam with him till his house. 'Romeo is coming, I will hide somewhere' she said.

Chapter 21

Romeo and Drudan

'Hello brother, you made a quick dash' said Romeo entering the house. He looked tired and fatigued carrying Juliet with him.

Drudan smiled and asked Romeo 'How is your Juliet?'

'Unconscious. I will have to take her to Mother. She will cure her. Just came to inform you that I have saved magical waters in my gland. Once Juliet feels better, I will come back to discuss our plan. Till then strain your dumb head to make a plan. I want to get rid of the burden of helping an evil man, as soon as possible'

Drudan got a fit of rage but he bit his lips and controlled his temper 'I have a plan. You better return by evening to discuss it.' he said

'Sayonara!' said Romeo, swaying his head

'What?' asked Drudan?

'Well, this is the Japanese way of saying goodbye' smiled Romeo

'Now, how do you know Japanese?' asked Drudan irritated

'I had entered a Japanese tourist's bag once....so you know' winked Romeo

'See you in the evening' Drudan said bluntly, trying to get rid of Romeo soon.

Romeo caught his expression, smiled and waving his tail said 'Sayonara, Sayonara. I will come back to sit on your head. Till then Sayonara!'

'Idiot!' said Drudan when Romeo had left.

The mermaid came out from the hiding and chuckled seeing Drudan's reactions.

'Why can you not lock him inside the pebble again?' asked Drudan, exasperated by Romeo's teasing.

'Because I know he is required to help you right now. Besides, I intend to kill the entire snake clan once you conquer Zynpagua.'

'Wonderful. That sounds exciting!'

'What do you intend doing with Soto?' asked Drudan

'I had captured him to get married to him. Now I have met you and can get rid of him' the mermaid replied.

'No, don't do that. He has to live and be in chains. Till he is alive, I can threaten Sussaina and rule in peace.'

'Can I not see him?' asked Drudan

'Of course, come with me' said the mermaid, leaving the house.

Chapter 22

King Soto

The mermaid took Drudan in the depths of the sea where ugly fossils grew amidst swamp. A wet stench was poisoning the place. As they swam further, Drudan saw tiny sea caves gaping at them. The mermaid held Drudan's hand and entered one such cave.

It was pitch dark inside. For a moment Drudan could not see anything. Then the mermaid raised her fins which began to shine like silver, giving the area a silvery shimmer. In that silver light Drudan saw King Soto, Sussaina's husband and Anika's father.

He was tied with a sea creeper and looked worn-out and famished. His body below the torso was immersed in marshy water. His head was drooping down and his hair had turned grey and green. His hands hung loosely and lifelessly to his sides while his legs were haphazardly stretched, touching the walls of the caves.

'Oh my God, what a piteous site' said Drudan, with his face glimmering with excitement.

'He is responsible for his state. Anyone who refuses to marry me, suffers like this' said the mermaid.

'How can anyone refuse to marry a beauty like you?' smiled Drudan.

The mermaid blushed.

Suddenly they heard Soto murmur 'I know God will be kind to me and send someone to free me'

'Oh hello Soto' said Drudan walking towards him.

Soto lifted his head gradually and strained his eyes to focus on Drudan. He slowly moved his lips to say 'Oh Drudan the traitor is here. I just hope you die soon!'

Drudan laughed aloud viciously 'Nope, I wouldn't die. In fact we are currently planning to kill your daughter and put wretched Sussaina and Vivian back in jail.'

'I don't have a daughter. Why will you capture them again? That means they are free now' saying this Soto smiled unconsciously and continued 'I knew Sussaina would defeat you'

'Poor Soto is not aware of the existence of his own daughter' laughed Drudan.

'My daughter?' repeated Soto in a state of trance 'Am I dreaming or this is happening for real?'

'Dream on... loser! I have better things to do than to explain stuff to you' said Drudan.

The mermaid smiled and said 'Drudan let us leave now. Romeo must be coming. You can settle scores with this fellow later'

She held Drudan's hand and swam out of the caves.

Chapter 23

The Vicious Plan

On reaching the house, the mermaid transformed back to a complete human. She sat on the sofa with Drudan and made the plan. After discussing for a while, the mermaid said 'Now here is the plan- Get Leo to Zynpagua, make him drink the magical waters. Anika will die instantly. Her death will throw Vivian and Sussaina in sorrow and pain. Capture them then. You can ask the people of Zynpagua and others to surrender once Sussaina and Vivian are captured'

'Awesome' said Drudan, admiring the mermaid. 'I don't even have to tax my brain'

'I am glad to be of help, my hero' the mermaid said.

'Let us find out where your son Leo is. We need to ensure he is in Zynpagua when you attack' the mermaid continued.

'Sure' said Drudan and closing his eyes began to visualize Leo's location.

'East West North and South find Leo and spell his location out'

'How do you that?' asked the mermaid

'Magic' smiled Drudan

'Yes, I can locate him. What place is this? It isn't Zynpagua' said Drudan, trying to find Leo with his eyes closed.

'The place isn't Zynpagua?' asked the mermaid, looking intently at Drudan's face.

'No!' Said Drudan

'Where is Leo?' asked the mermaid

'In an exquisite hotel that faces the sea' Drudan said.

'This is not even the kingdom of clouds. This place is different.' He continued.

'Then how are we supposed to find out where Leo is?' asked the mermaid.

'I can go there magically but then I have to meet Romeo and plan for the attack' said Drudan.

'Let us see what is written at the name plate of the hotel' said the mermaid.

Drudan smiled at the suggestion and said 'That is a great idea. I am proud of you'

'Thank you and now concentrate on finding the entrance of the hotel' said the mermaid.

'Yes, here you are. On the entrance gate is embossed, the Taj hotel, Mumbai, India' said Drudan

'Why should Leo be in India?' the mermaid asked, surprised at the revelation.

'Let us hear what Leo is talking. We will come to know why he is there' said Drudan.

'He is sitting with Frederick, another wretched fellow. Why are they wasting time with three tiny girls?' Drudan murmured.

'Indian girls?' the mermaid asked skeptically.

'Why is there uncertainty in your voice' asked Drudan

'Indian girls are one of the very few girls in the world who know how to swim against the tide and win' said the mermaid.

'My God, what are Frederick and Leo trying to accomplish in India?' thought Drudan and then voiced aloud 'Let me try and hear their conversation'

Chapter 24

Leo and Frederick

'Do you know how to solve formulas and numbers?' asked Frederick, trying to simplify the question for Aarna.

Saanvi laughed and said 'She is too young to understand formulas!'

'Then how is she going to solve the formula that binds Femina?' whispered Frederick in Leo's ears.

'I hope we have found the right Aarna' said Leo

'Just focus on what these three girls are engaged in doing!' suggested the angel birds

The three girls had commenced playing yet again. Frederick and Leo sat watching their activities. After sometime they noticed that Aarna was particularly attracted to people holding Laptops. Leo asked Frederick 'What is this gadget?'

Frederick looked at it and said 'I am not sure'

'It's a Laptop and is used for typing words and finding information on the internet.' Said the angel bird

'I see. This is like a handy computer, the one Radhika used for finding Aarna's address' said Frederick.

'Wait a minute....it is used for typing words' said Leo, thinking of a solution.

'Let us get a laptop, maybe Aarna types something which would lead us to the solution' said Leo

'Awesome idea, now from where do we get a laptop?' asked Leo

'The seven of us will secretly pick it from a gadget shop. Once our work is done, we will leave it back' the angel birds replied.

'Thumbs up' said Frederick. 'By the way it is an electronic shop and not a gadget shop' he smiled, teasing the angel birds.

'That's nice. You know a great deal about gadget err.. electronic things' Leo complimented.

'Radhika told me' said Frederick. Leo smiled and said 'Great'.

The angel birds had flown by then to fetch a Laptop.

They entered a big store through the main entrance as they could not find a window. The people in the store were surprised to see colourful birds flying in unison. The birds panicked for a moment because every eye in the store was on them. The green bird began chirping distinctly trying to ask the red bird how were they going to lift such a heavy laptop amidst full attention of the shop. The red bird chirped merrily trying to say 'If I can send Frederick from Siepra Nevada to Shillong, this is just a Laptop. Yellow bird, fetch me a twig'.

The yellow bird chirped, flew out of the door and in no time returned with a twig in its beak'

The red bird chirped again 'Now place the twig beneath the pink Laptop'. The yellow bird did as she was told. Then the red bird inhaled ample air and blew it on the twig. The twig shifted a little beneath the laptop and then commenced rising with the Laptop perfectly balanced on it. The people were awestruck while the shop keeper yelled 'these birds are thieves, catch them'

Just then the red bird perched itself on the shopkeeper's nose and said 'We need the Laptop for a day. Once our work is done, we will leave it back'

Shopkeeper was in a state of shock to hear the bird speak. He opened his mouth to say something but the red bird yelled 'Do not move or the droppings will fall in your mouth' saying this, the red bird shat while sitting on the shopkeeper's nose.

The crowd in the shop was repulsed at the site. The bird's droppings fell on the shopkeeper's hand with which he had closed his mouth. In no time the droppings changed to pieces of gold. None could believe what they saw. The red bird flew high up and before leaving the shop chirped aloud 'Keep the gold in exchange of the Laptop'

Someone from the crowd shouted 'Catch the gold giving birds!' but by then the birds had flown away.

They reached the hotel and located Frederick and Leo sitting in a remote lounge. They chirped to make their presence felt and then flew towards them. The Laptop was tagging along, perfectly balanced on the twig.

The birds announced 'someone please take the Laptop off the twig'

Leo stood up and held the Laptop while Frederick kept the twig in his pocket, to avoid littering the place.

'Let us now locate Aarna' said Frederick

They didn't have to search long and found the sisters playing near the staircase. Aarna was instantly attracted to the Laptop and raced towards Leo.

Leo asked Aarna, while handling over the Laptop 'How do you use it'

Aarna smiled and took it in her hand. She opened the cover and pressed on the start button. Just then Leo sensed someone around. He said 'Shh...I feel someone is observing us'.

'Who can it be?' asked Frederick.

The angel birds volunteered to check if someone was eavesdropping.

They looked around but could not find anyone. Leo and Frederick also tried locating the presence of someone, but failed. 'I don't know why I sense danger' Leo repeated. Frederick instantly suggested they talk to Sussaina.

The red bird sent message to Sussaina through the wind. Sussaina got the message and called Leo and Frederick aloud. She had the power to make her voice reach anywhere. Listening to her voice, Frederick asked 'Mother, Is there a threat on Zynpagua?' Sussaina was surprised at the question. She asked 'What happened children?'

This time Leo spoke 'Aunt Sussaina, we have found Aarna, the little girl, and she may be able to save Femina. However I sensed someone was listening to our conversation when we were with these little girls'

Sussaina guessed Drudan could be spying. She immediately alerted them 'Children it could be our only enemy trying to plan something wicked. I do not want to discuss anything further, just try finishing your work, and return to Zynpagua soon!'

Chapter 25

Drudan and the mermaid

Drudan had indeed located Frederick and Leo through his magical abilities and was observing them, from the depths of the ocean.

The mermaid asked Drudan 'How could your son sense that we were observing him?'

'Leo's mother was from kingdom of clouds. They are gifted humans with great ability to sense their surroundings. Not only that, they can fly like birds' said Drudan

'Oh that is wonderful. Even you can fly like birds?' The Mermaid asked

'No, I fly because I know magic. He is like a human bird. His body is equipped to fly' said Drudan

'What are they trying to do?' asked the Mermaid

'Stupid fellows are wasting their time. I turned a girl to stone in Zynpagua. They are trying to bring her back to human form' said Drudan

'What if they succeed?' asked the mermaid.

'They have no sense of science to find a solution. Moreover, as I see it, they think a little girl will be able to help them. That is the height of being foolish' said Drudan, smirking.

The mermaid also smiled and said 'We have to send Leo back to Zynpagua. How are we going to do that?'

'Simple, I will imitate Sussaina's voice and tell him to hasten to Zynpagua. I will instruct angel birds and Frederick to stay in India and continue finding the solution to save Femina'

'What if Leo checks with Sussaina?' asked the mermaid.

'Good question' said Drudan thoughtfully.

After thinking of a plan, Drudan told the mermaid 'I will leave for Zynpagua with Romeo tomorrow morning. When we are half way, I will call Leo in Sussaina's voice and ask him to hasten to Zynpagua. At the same time, I will block all signals travelling to and from Zynpagua. Sussaina will not be able to communicate with anyone' said Drudan

'That sounds to be an excellent plan!' said the mermaid excitedly.

'Do let me know what I need to do with Soto?' asked the mermaid.

'Keep him, he is valuable. Incase our plan fails, I will use Soto to make Sussaina surrender!' Saying this Drudan laughed aloud.

'That's wonderful. Drudan how will I meet you? Till the time I am carrying this child, I will not be able to leave the sea, or else the child will die' the mermaid voiced.

'I will bind Zynpagua by my magical spells and come and meet you. Though I wish I had soldiers and guards to take care of Zynpagua in my absence. Alas, I have none' said Drudan.

'I can give you my soldiers' said the mermaid

'Your soldiers?' he asked

'Yes, my soldiers' said the mermaid 'They are with me all the time'

'I can't see any. Where are they?' asked Drudan

'Watch closely' the mermaid smiled

Drudan looked around and saw small creepy worms surrounding the mermaid. They were not touching her but very close to where she stood.

'Oh my God' exclaimed Drudan 'These worms are your soldiers?'

'These are not ordinary worms. These are sea worms and can live both on land and in water. When they are on land, they can inhale air and be fifty times their size. Moreover their poison can put anyone to sleep for days'

'That is astounding. How do I take them with me when I will be accompanied by Romeo?' asked Drudan

The mermaid took out a small gunny sack and handling it to Drudan, said 'This little bag has thousands of worms. Once you reach open the sack and let the worms out' the mermaid said.

'You are fantastic 'Drudan praised the mermaid.

Just then they heard some commotion outside the house. The mermaid hid herself immediately.

Chapter 26

Drudan and Romeo

Romeo wriggled in with great speed and pounced on Drudan's lap.

Drudan yelled in a state of shock and spat out 'What is wrong with you?'

Romeo sniffed Drudan's face and said 'Why do I always suspect mischief from you?'

'Mischief? What mischief? I plan to attack Zynpagua tomorrow. The timing is perfect. I have traced Leo and will cajole him to reach Zynpagua by tomorrow. Once he drinks the magical water, Anika will die and I will conquer Zynpagua' said Drudan

'This sounds to be a perfect plan. Has someone been helping you?' asked Romeo

'Will anyone have such sharp brain like me? 'smirked Drudan.

Romeo continued to look intently at Drudan. He felt there was something fishy about his behaviour.

He told Drudan 'You plan for tomorrow. I forgot to inform mother about my wife's medicine'

Drudan was preoccupied in planning for the next day and did not pay heed to Romeo's actions.

The mermaid stepped in as soon as Romeo left. She had a sharp knife in her hand. Pointing it towards Drudan, she said 'Take this with you. This is a lethal weapon and paralyses the part of the body it is pierced. But remember, it can be used only once. Use it when you are left with no other option'

'You really understand me. I was actually thinking of carrying a weapon' said Drudan.

'I will leave now. Victory will be yours for sure. Love you' saying this, the mermaid hugged Drudan, triggering a pang of pain in Drudan's heart. He hugged her back. The mermaid transformed into half fish and swam out.

Chapter 27

Romeo and Drudan

Romeo rushed back and instructed the snake clan to change their residence and hide in secret places. He told them that he was going with Drudan to Zynpagua for some days but wanted his clan to be safe in his absence. He had been finding Drudan mysterious and suspected mischief from him.

After ensuring that his family was safe, Romeo returned.

He could have spitted out the magical waters and deceived Drudan. But he was a snake of integrity. Drudan had saved him and his wife. Romeo was indebted to him for that. He had to repay the favour.

But the thought of conquering a land and capturing the people pricked him. Somewhere his conscience, his inner voice told him that he was doing wrong. Before starting for the trip he mentally told Lord Shiva, his favourite deity, 'God I know I am doing wrong, please show me a path to undo my sins'

'I have never seen a snake think so much' said Drudan, who was seated on Romeo as they were cruising in water and heading towards the sky. Romeo had decided to carry Drudan on his back to reach Zynpagua fast.

'I don't speak to useless people' said Romeo.

'You will know how useless I am once I conquer Zynpagua' retorted Drudan

'Useless people remain useless even if they become kings' smirked Romeo

Drudan hated these spiteful remarks. He had planned that once Leo drinks the magical waters, he would kill Romeo. On the other hand Romeo was sick of Drudan and wanted to pay off his debt soon.

Thus Romeo flew at a lightning speed, with Drudan screaming intermittently, too shocked by the velocity of the movement.

When they were nearing Zynpagua, Drudan asked Romeo to descend and land at the outskirts. He wanted to stop all communication going out from Zynpagua.

Drudan then magically imitated Sussaina's voice and called Leo. He had rehearsed it several times.

Chapter 28

The Scheming Plan

'Leo my child, can you hear me?'

'Did you hear that voice?' asked Leo, sitting beside Frederick.

'No' replied Frederick, straining his ears to hear.

'Leo my child, can you hear me?' came the voice once again.

'Who is it?' asked Leo attentively.

'Your aunt Sussaina' said the voice.

'Aunt Sussaina?' asked Leo skeptically.

'Yes my child, this is Sussaina' said the voice

This time Frederick spoke 'This is not the way mother Sussaina calls us. Who are you?'

Drudan panicked. He had modified his voice quite a bit to make it sound like that of Sussaina but had failed in his attempt.

'Who are you?' called out Frederick once again

Drudan remained silent. He thought for a while and then decided to confront Leo directly.

'Son, I am surprised you are unable to identify your father's voice. What's up?'

'Drudan is that you?' asked Frederick.

'I am talking to my son, do you mind keeping your mouth shut' said Drudan.

'An evil man like you cannot be my father. You thought you could trick me by aping aunt Sussaina's voice?' asked Leo

'Yes, Now think it would be better if you face reality' said Drudan

'What reality?' asked Leo

'Reality is that I have captured Zynpagua once again and that I am heading to kill Anika, Sussaina and Vivian. In case you want to save them, come fast. I need a favour from you and for that I will spare them' said Drudan.

'I don't believe you' said Leo 'You are a coward!'

'No, I am a very brave scientist who believes in spreading evil' chuckled Drudan. If you have any doubt, ask your mother. Oh my God, how will you ask her? She is dead and Drudan the great killed her'

Leo got a fit of rage hearing that. Though he was very young then, he remembered how Drudan had hit his mother Pajaro and killed her.

'Drudan, I promise, I will be the one to bring your death to you' said Leo.

Drudan laughed aloud and said 'First be heroic and save Zynpagua'

'I am coming' said Leo outraged by the memory of his mother's death.

'Don't 'said Frederick, trying to calm him.

'Don't stop him stupid Frederick or else you will find everyone dead in Zynpagua' said Drudan

Frederick yelled back 'I don't trust you and will not believe you'

'I will give you half an hour. Decide whether you want to save Sussaina and others, or let them die' warned Drudan.

Frederick silenced Leo who was about to retort.

He told Leo 'Let us first try talking to mother Sussaina. Let me call the angel birds'. Saying this he clapped his hands and said '*Chin chunaki chin chin*'

The angel birds had been secretly tracing Aarna who now had the laptop and was sitting in the hotel balcony.

The birds instantly flew back towards Frederick. After listening to what had transpired the angel birds tried sending messages to Sussaina through their aerial communication, but could not. They waited for a while to hear Sussaina's voice but did not get a response. They tried contacting Anika with the help of crystal ball, but failed. This worried Leo and Frederick. The angel birds decided to fly to Zynpagua and check what was going on.

In the meanwhile, Drudan's voice called Leo and said 'My foolish son, I am sure you have made up your mind. Come to Zynpagua now!'

'I don't believe you and I am not coming' replied Leo.

Drudan fumed and said 'Then bare the consequence' and his voice faded.

'What if he has actually captured everyone in Zynpagua?' asked Leo

Frederick replied 'Don't think negatively. It could be his trick. Let us wait for the angel birds to return'

Chapter 29

Drudan reaches Zynpagua

Drudan decided to inspect Zynpagua. If his trick with Leo failed, he would need another plan. As Drudan entered Zynpagua, the bright virtuous rays of the Sun began to burn his face. He covered his face with a black cloth, sparing only his eyes.

While flying, Romeo had stretched his huge body longitudinally to gain pace and enter Zynpagua. Sitting on Romeo, Drudan peeped down to see what was happening, but everything looked like ants from such a distance.

'How will I see anything from here? Fly little lower' said Drudan

'This is being very rude. Romeo only works on requests. I am worried that being with you will spoil my pleasant disposition' retorted Romeo

Drudan fumed inside but feigned a polite request 'Romeo I can't see anything from this height. Can you please fly a little lower?'

'That's like a good scoundrel' said Romeo smiling.

Drudan thought 'Romeo, you are so naïve. You don't even know your death awaits you. Laugh as much as you want to because after today your Juliet will cry all her life'

'Why are you not saying anything? Planning evil for me? Are you?' asked Romeo.

'No I am trying to concentrate. There are only the two of us against entire Zynpagua. One mistake and we both can be killed'

'Yes, I like it when you use your brains sometimes' smirked Romeo.

Drudan chose to remain silent. He was focusing on the ground. As Romeo lowered himself gradually, Drudan could see clearly. The people of Zynpagua seemed to be in a great hurry. Some were busy packing their belongings and placing them on the bullock carts while the others had already done the same and were heading towards the eastern direction, with their family

'Where are they going?' thought Drudan and then answering his own query, he said aloud.

'The palace lies in the eastern direction. They are heading towards the Palace!'

'Go further down' Drudan told Romeo.

'Oh hello uncle, if I do that, the people will notice my handsome physique with a cockroach mounted on it. Do you have a plan to handle the attention? Romeo asked

'Good point Romeo' saying this Drudan lifted his hand and pronounced the invisible spell.

'One, two and three, let the imperceptible spell work for Romeo and me' said Drudan

'You are sure we cannot be seen?' asked Romeo

'Yes. Now we can walk with the people towards the palace' assured Drudan.

Romeo flew down and landed near a tree, little away from the people. None took note of their arrival and the people continued to walk with their normal pace.

Drudan marched ahead while Romeo wriggled behind him. Suddenly a voice made Drudan turn. A young girl was standing and watching the ground with great astonishment. 'What marks are these?' she was asking her friends pointing towards the mud. Drudan looked down and saw that Romeo had been wriggling on the floor and had displaced the mud in such a way that clear marks of the snake's movement were visible.

Before others could get excited about it, Drudan lifted his hand and blowing air said 'Disappear!' The marks faded instantly.

'Oh my God, I can't see them anymore' said the girl.

'Must be made by the movement of the wind' said a man standing beside her.

'Whatever it is, we will let the queen know' said the girl.

'Idiot' Drudan mentally snapped the girl and told Romeo to fly instead of wriggle.

'Sure I would do that but I must admit, girls of Zynpagua are genuinely sharp and beautiful' said Romeo smiling.

'If you don't mind, may I please take a round and see the people of Zynpagua. They seem to be very interesting' asked Romeo

'Ok..' said Drudan' He desperately wanted to move away from Romeo for a while to communicate with the mermaid.

Once Romeo had flown away, he whispered 'My mermaid, my senorita, can you hear me?'

'Yes, my hero, I am with you' the mermaid giggled and responded.

'Could you find when the shadow planets would commence casting their shadow?' asked Drudan

'They have started casting their Shadow. Look at the sky. The twilight of today will see a complete change in the milieu. You can attack right then, and victory would be yours.' The mermaid assured.

Drudan looked up and was shocked to see that a dark red tint had enveloped the sky.

'Oh my God, this is due to the demon planets?' asked Drudan excitedly.

'Yes...don't you feel a strange strength coming in your body?' asked the mermaid.

That is when Drudan realized he had begun to feel stronger and invincible. He felt bouts of confidence entering his veins. A feeling similar to the one when he had violet light with him.

'You are absolutely correct. I feel as powerful as I used to feel when I had violet light with me' affirmed Drudan

'Wait till tonight and you will witness miracles' giggled the mermaid.

Her giggling sounded like music to Drudan's ears.

'I miss you Senorita' he whispered.

'Don't miss me, I am with you. Remember we have only a week to conquer the world. Let us make hay till the demon planets are casting their effects' said the mermaid

Drudan smiled and said 'I love you and I am sure we will rule the world because you are with me'

'Take care and focus on your mission' said the mermaid.

Drudan saw Romeo return and hushed the mermaid.

Chapter 30

The warning

'The people look so innocent. I feel guilty of being your accomplice'. Romeo said pensively.

'Before you allow that nonsense to enter your head, always remember that you had become stone and I rescued you' said Drudan.

'Nothing is worse than being indebted to an evil man' sighed Romeo.

'Alright... concentrate, we are entering the palace'

Sussaina was standing near the entrance trying to hasten the process of people shifting in. The guards were blowing whistles and announcing

'People whose names start with A B C D E,
Take the corridor that is set near the tree,
F, G, H, I, J, K
Turn left your houses are near the hay,

LMNOPQR
Your houses are beneath the North Star
STUVWXYZ
You stay right at the start
Now everyone hurry up and part
Stock your houses with food and water
You may not get a chance day after'

Vivian was standing near the houses, binding them with the spell of hundred rounds. Drudan and Romeo being invisible entered the palace. They had taken only a few steps when Vivian cried 'Mother, I sense an Intrusion. There are some unknown figures around us'.

He looked around and pronounced 'Appear whoever is hiding here'

Drudan immediately murmured 'Don't obey and reverse the say'

Nothing happened. Vivian stared at the place where Drudan was standing. He told Sussaina 'Mother, someone is here'

Sussaina replied 'Son, why should we fear enemies who are chicken-hearted. Those who are hiding from us will have no courage to withstand our strength'

Vivian looked puzzled but Sussaina winked at him and said 'No man in this universe has the courage to face Zynpagua's army'

Drudan heard that and fumed but chose to remain silent. 'First let me kill Anika and then I will see your reaction', he thought.

Vivian tried another spell 'Hiding devil come out and show your face so very evil!'

Drudan instantly reversed the spell by saying 'Devils don't show their face. Spell of hell shower water from the well!'

The water in the nearby well swelled up and with great speed began to shower itself on everyone standing there. As soon as Vivian got distracted, Drudan raised his one hand and holding Romeo's tale from the other, yelled 'Disappear and reach the river bank'.

Vivian stopped the flow of water from the well with another spell and turned to face the invisible Villain but could not sense anything.

Frustrated he said 'Mother, I knew there was someone here. Someone powerful, who had the power to reverse my magical spells. This knowledge of magic always proves useless for me. Look at this, I could not even figure out who had intruded.'

Sussaina had also sensed an infiltration.

She was tense but said 'Vivian knowledge of magic is not enough but one needs to have the wisdom to use it correctly and aptly. I am very sure Drudan had intruded just now and he was reversing your spells. But what I am most surprised is that he remained silent and did not speak a word when I was instigating him. I have an eerie feeling; he has planned something much more dangerous than what we can imagine!'

Anika had come out of the palace listening to the commotion caused by the water shower. She heard the conversation between Vivian and Sussaina and got even more puzzled. When she looked at the sky, she saw the red shadow enveloping it and knew the demon planets had begun to cast their shadow on other planets.

'How are we going to face Drudan and the demon planets when the stars will not be able to help us?' she thought.

She rushed towards Sussaina, and pointing towards the sky, she said 'Mother, look, the sky has a red tint. The demon planets have started casting their shadow'.

Sussaina looked up and became stressed.

'Mother, we have no plans in place. We don't even know what happens when the demon planets rule the universe. How are we going to handle the situation' asked Vivian.

'Son, when we don't have a solution, we have only one weapon and that is to bc bravc' said Sussaina.

'Mother, Venus had said our willpower will decide whether we will win or lose' assured Anika.

'Yes Anika, we will be alert and we will be valiant.' Sussaina said, smiling faintly.

She immediately called the soldiers and instructed them.

The bugle of threat was blown in the palace and all the people were moved in and the gates of the palace closed.

In the meanwhile Drudan landed on the banks of the river with Romeo. He did not know how to get Leo to Zynpagua. He looked up at the sky and was delighted to see the demon planets enveloping the sky with their reddish tint. The night was approaching and he knew it was a full moon night.

'The demon planets shadow on the Moon will make it red and evil', he smirked.

No point hiding from these people now. Saying this he raised his hand and said 'Romeo and I want to be visible for everyone'

'How do you know people can see us?' asked Romeo

'They can, I have used the appearance spell' replied Drudan.

Romeo shook his head. He was thinking fast.

'Let me see where Anika is' saying this, Drudan closed his eyes and located Anika. She was looking at the sky and praying in the palace garden.

Wonderful! This is the best location to get Leo and make him drink the magical water, thought Drudan

He then closed his eyes again and attempted to locate Vivian. After a while, he found Vivian sitting in his room. Drudan's attention instantly went to Femina and seeing her as a stone statue, made him laugh. 'Alas! this trick could work only on common people like Femina and not on supernatural beings like Sussaina and her family, not even on Leo' he murmured.

In fact Drudan had tried to convert Frederick into a statue as well when he was eight, but the trick did not work on him. *Perhaps Soto's parents were also special in some way. Who knows*, he thought again.

Just then, someone gave a hard blow on Drudan's back. He turned instantly and found Romeo sitting half curled up, attempting to attack again. 'What is the matter with you?' asked Drudan

'I am soooo hungry' replied Romeo.

'Then jump in the river and find fishes for yourself' said Drudan

'Listen, I will swim deep in as I need big fishes. The ones floating atop will be like having a snack. I need a proper meal' said Romeo

'I don't think there is any danger in the river. Go wherever you feel like going. But yes, come back before the Moon rises in the dark tinted sky'.

'Of course' said Romeo and happily jumped in the river.

Once Romeo had left, Drudan took out the sack of worms and thought 'I will wait for the Full Moon to appear with the red tint of demon planets. Then I would release these worms that the mermaid has sent with me. First I will capture Sussaina and then ask Vivian and Anika to surrender.'

In the meanwhile, Romeo swam deep in the river but did not eat any fish. The only reason he wanted to swim in waters was to warn his river inmates of Drudan. He was hoping someone could carry his message till Queen Sussaina and warn her. The inhabitants of river were shocked to see such a huge snake in their waters. But when Romeo did not harm them, they relaxed. Romeo asked them 'Is there someone here who knows the Queen? I wish good for her and want to warn her?'

A tiny frog jumped forward and said 'There is an old tortoise Mootu here. He is Princess Anika's teacher. I can take you to him'

'Please take me fast' requested Romeo.

The frog took him to Mootu who was scared stiff seeing him.

Romeo said 'Please don't be frightened. I have come with this evil man called Drudan. He intends to harm the princess of this place. Please go and warn the queen!'

'When you know Drudan is evil, why are you supporting him? Asked Mootu

'Because he saved my life and I owe a favour to him. When I came here, I saw the simple people of Zynpagua and the Godly face of the queen. They are innocent people and I want to save this land. I have carried magical waters in my mouth. This water will take Anika's soul out under the Moonlight and kill her' said Romeo

'Oh my God!' said Mootu. 'Why don't you puke it out?' he asked.

'I can't do that as Drudan has saved my life and rescued my wife. I cannot ditch him. But I can warn the people to save themselves'

'Ok. I will go and warn the queen immediately' said Mootu.

'You will walk slowly and we have very little time. May I please fly you till the palace?' asked Romeo

Mootu climbed on Romeo's back and flew high till they reached the gates of the Palace. Romeo descended silently in a nearby bush and let Mootu dismount. He then steadily wriggled back to where Drudan was.

The guards stopped Mootu but one of them recognized him. He had seen Mootu teach Anika swimming. He accompanied Mootu till the garden where Anika was praying. Queen Sussaina was also sitting with her. Mootu greeted everyone and then told them about Romeo and how Drudan had come to Zynpagua to take Anika's life. Queen Sussaina held Anika tight and asked the guards to call Vivian immediately.

As Vivian came in, Sussaina said 'Son, as Mootu tells us, Drudan has only two powers, the water to kill Anika and his magic. You can tackle his magic. Anika, going forward, do not drink any unknown water or drink. Little precautions are needed and I am confident we can defeat Drudan and ensure our land is safe.'

She then thanked Mootu and asked him to leave and be safe in the river, but Mootu insisted on staying back.

Romeo reached the banks and found Drudan observing the Moon with a wicked smile on his face. Drudan saw Romeo and greeted him 'Come along and watch the Moon. Doesn't it have a nice reddish tint? That is the shadow of the demon planet on the Moon. This Moon gave Anika life and this very Moon will take away her life tonight.'

Romeo knew that the magical water grew stronger under the rays of the Moon. Since the Moon was under the influence of demon planets, it had become evil too. *What would be the effect of evil Moon on magical water? More devastating and more painful!* Thought Romeo. A pang of guilt hit him.

He was carrying the magical water in his mouth and this same water would take Anika's life. He decided to ditch Drudan and escape. He flew up in the air and said 'Drudan I cannot be responsible for so many killings. I am going back with the magical water. While you saved my life, I cannot repay my gratitude by taking an innocent life'

Drudan waved at him and said 'Good Bye Romeo, but before you go, I have to show you something' and saying this Drudan waved his hand in the air and said 'Vision of the Indian Ocean, show Romeo the condition of his wife and kins'.

Instantly a halo appeared. Romeo was shocked to see the site. His parents, Juliet and his friends were in the mermaid's captivity. The sea worms had tied them with poisonous creepers. Romeo yelled 'you scoundrel! You cheated me! You partnered the treacherous mermaid!'

'Stop calling her treacherous! She is my wife'

'What?' said Romeo in a state of shock.

'Don't be so shocked. Didn't you suspect something and hid your family. It is a different matter that we followed you and located the place where you had hidden them. If you do anything with the magical waters, the mermaid will kill your family. Don't even attempt betraying me.'

Romeo could not believe what he was listening. He said 'You are making me a fool. This scene is not real. You have created it magically'

'Senorita, can you hear me' asked Drudan

'Yes, I can my Drudie' said the mermaid.

'Can you update this snake on what has transpired behind the scene' said Drudan

The mermaid laughed and said 'Philip or Romeo, whatever you want to call yourself. Your dear family is in my captivity. Follow Drudan's instructions or else I will kill your wife and make your parents my slaves for life. Speak to your father'

The mermaid's voice was followed by a feeble coughing voice. Romeo immediately recognized it and yelled 'father!'

'Yes Sonny, it is me' said Romeo's father. 'Come back son, this mermaid has captured us'

'Enough of father and son talk. Thank you Senorita' said Drudan.

'Bye and all the best' said the mermaid.

'Romeo, finish my work and your father will be fine' said Drudan. He looked up towards the Moon and his pupils dilated in excitement. 'The Moon is full now. How big and evil it looks with that reddish tint. The sky will favour us and now is the perfect time to attack!'

He excitedly rushed ahead and looking at the sky, said 'Oh demon planets, you have finally conquered the Moon. How will I know that you will favour my rule?'

There was no response.

Chapter 31

The shadow of the demon planets

Drudan looked up again and continued to gape at the Moon and the stars. By now they had gained a deep blood red tint which was spreading in the whole sky.

'How do I know whether the rule of demon planets will favour the evil?' Drudan continued to think when he heard the mermaid whisper 'A huge storm is rushing towards Zynpagua. Go and face the storm and you will know the Demon planets are active now'

'What?' said Drudan but before he knew, huge cyclone erupted, swirling in circular movement and rushing towards Drudan.

'Face it' The Mermaid whispered yet again.

'It will tear me apart' Drudan said looking frightened.

'Just face it. Go and stand in front of it' insisted the mermaid.

Drudan walked forward and stood at the face of storm. It whirled around Drudan and took him in its confines. Drudan rotated first and then held the ground to stop moving with the wind. It was then he realized that every swirl of wind around him was making him stronger and stronger. He felt he was walking in air, crushing all the people who disobeyed him.

After sometime the wind receded almost as suddenly as it had appeared. Drudan looked at his sinews. They had turned a shade of red but his muscle looked more defined and strengthened.

He excitedly looked around and saw Romeo wriggling towards him.

'What happened to you? Why have you turned red?' asked Romeo

'Notice the sky...can't you see the demon planets have started influencing the universe...' before Drudan could complete

'...and making evil powerful 'Romeo blurted out, looking despondent.

'So you knew that the demon planets were casting their shadow?' asked Drudan.

'Yes and hoped you would never come to know about it' said Romeo

'Oh my God, all your hopes are shattered. My wife, the mermaid has kept me abreast with every secret of the universe.'

Saying this, Drudan released the bag full of worms and said 'Go and tie everyone in your fold'

Romeo was shocked to see Drudan's deceit. For a moment he felt like killing Drudan but his mind was now connected to the mermaid's. Any harm to Drudan meant harm to his family. He swallowed the bitter pill and wriggled behind Drudan who was marching towards the palace.

The creepy crawly and tiny worms escaped the soldiers' eyes and entered the palace. Each one of them then became fifty times of their size and wound themselves around soldiers and

Sussaina, Vivian and Anika. It happened so fast that Vivian got no time to use his magic. The worms circled around his hand and mouth stopping him from doing magic.

Then two worms opened the palace gate and let Drudan in. Drudan instructed the worms 'Get everyone out to the garden.'

Sussaina was furious and fumed 'Drudan you cheat. I wish you had the courage to defeat us in war instead of playing such vile tricks'

Drudan laughed and said 'All's fair in love and war'

He looked around and asked 'Where are all the people of Zynpagua?'

'If you want to harm us, do so, but spare the people of Zynpagua' urged Sussaina.

While Drudan was preoccupied, Vivian moved is lips somehow and pronounced a spell to kill the worms. But none of the spells were working on the worms. Drudan laughed aloud 'These are creatures of the sea and no human can influence them.'

'Where is my dear Anika?' he asked, trying to locate her.

One of the worms had tied Anika on the bench where she was sitting.

Drudan saw her and said 'Great, so what do you prefer? Would you like to die while sitting or standing? Wormies, please get her closer to her mother'. The worms pulled Anika and dragged her till Sussaina.

Sussaina was standing quietly in one corner with her eyes on the Moon which had turned blood red. She remembered Anika's prediction and murmured

'When Red Evil Moon will shine behind the tree
And its light will fall on water of stormy sea

A drop will rise from a hole
To unite our soul
Taking away my power
I will become a shrunken flower'

She looked at Anika and gestured her to run.

Anika nodded and tried dragging herself but the grip of the worm was so tight that she could not even move. Vivian had somehow managed to drag himself near Anika. His hands and mouth were tied but his legs were somewhat free. Vivian somehow lifted his legs and hit the worm which was wound around Anika.

Nothing happened and it tightened its grip on Anika. In fact it was going to bite Anika, when Vivian hit him on the face. The worm instantly loosened its grip. Vivian continued hitting on the worm's face till it fell off.

As soon as Anika was free, she hit the worms holding Vivian, by attacking on their faces. They fell off.

Vivian whispered in Anika's ears 'Run my sister, run and hide in a place where you can influence the stars and save Zynpagua'

'There is no point running brother. The stars are under the shadow of demon planets and cannot help us' saying this, she kicked the worm trying to circle around Vivian. The worm let loose and fell off.

Vivian raised his hand and said 'Capture Drudan and let him not flee'

By this time Drudan noticed what Vivian had done and he instantly raised his hand and said 'don't capture me arrest him please'

Vivian raised his hand and said 'Make him fly high and dump him on the ground'

Drudan flew high but instantly commanded 'Fall safely and make Vivian stand still'

'Wormies attack Vivian and Anika, why have you set them free?' He called out.

Drudan fell safely on the ground and with full force gave Vivian such a hard blow that Vivian flew up in the sky and fell far away.

Drudan laughed aloud and looking at the sky, he said 'I bow before you, my demon planets. Thank you for giving me supernatural strength'

Just then a lightning flashed in the sky, as if the demon planets were acknowledging Drudan's greetings.

Drudan's gaze feel on Sussaina and he yelled 'Wormies, double your strength on this wicked lady'

The worms tightened their grip on Sussaina.

Once the worms had taken Vivian and Anika in their grip, Drudan chanted a spell 'My voice has to reach Leo. May the spell of communication erase the obstruction'

He then called aloud 'Leo, you wretched fellow, can you hear me?

Leo and Frederick were sitting in the Indian hotel, trying to interpret the meaning of letters which Aarna was typing.

When Leo heard Drudan's voice, he thought he was hallucinating but when Drudan repeated his call, Leo yelled back 'Drudan, I am not scared of you. Stop playing tricks on me.'

'Stupid boy always pay respect to your father. I don't have time to waste on you. Just thought of letting you know that I am in Zynpagua and Sussaina, Vivian and that wretched Anika are in my captivity. I will kill them, if you do not reach here soon. Before wasting time, see the images of your dear friends' and saying this Drudan sent an Image to Leo.

Frederick and Leo were shocked to see everyone in the confinement of some ugly looking worms. Leo instantly decided to leave for Zynpagua, but Frederick stopped him and suggested 'Wait for the angel birds to return'.

Leo was apprehensive that waiting might bring disaster for Zynpagua and people there.

He suggested 'Frederick, Please wait here for the angel birds and try finding a solution to rescue Femina as soon as possible. I have to be in Zynpagua!'

Frederick nodded and told Leo 'My brave friend I am sure you will defeat Drudan. I will hasten the process of finding the solution to save Femina. Once that is done, I will come to Zynpagua with the angel birds. Good luck my friend and always remember- I can stake my life for you. Don't hesitate to call me when you need me'

Leo hugged Frederick and bid adieu! He flew high in the sky and with the speed of lightening headed towards Zynpagua. When he was on his way, he also noticed the change in the sky. The universe was lit up by the reddish tint and he felt that this reddish tint was sapping his energy. He must have gone a little ahead when he found the angel birds trapped in a cyclonic wind.

Leo inhaled air and with full energy blew on the wind. The cyclonic pressure got diluted with the force of the wind and dissolved. The angel birds flew towards him and sat on his shoulders. Then the red bird said 'Leo, this red tint in the universe symbolizes the advent of demon planets. They are casting their shadow. What are you doing here? Please return to the Earth'

Leo informed the birds that Drudan had attacked Zynpagua and has called him there. The angel birds insisted 'Leo, go back.

He wants you there to kill everyone in one go'. The red bird wanted to tell Leo about his soul connection with Anika but as per rule of nature he had to discover that himself. Red bird told the other six birds to fly with Leo while she decided to go back and help Frederick decode what Aarna had been typing.

Chapter 32

Frederick

Aarna was fascinated seeing the pink Laptop and could not keep her eyes of it.

In fact she and her sister Saanvi spent the day typing stories and strange syllables. Before they left for the wedding, they handed the laptop back to Frederick.

Frederick opened the laptop but the letters typed by Aarna made no sense. 'Ah Anika, are you sure you dreamt of Aarna and not someone else' Frederick murmured in a state of exasperation.

Just then the red bird returned and told Frederick about Drudan's attack on Zynpagua. Frederick panicked. He had to find a solution to save Femina fast.

'Oh God, show me a way' he murmured again and looked helplessly at what Aarna had typed.

ψ Nacl+H2O+ ⇧

'What could this mean?' he thought.

The red bird peered towards the symbols and said

ψ This symbol... I have seen it somewhere nearby.

Frederick instantly requested the red bird 'Angel bird, let us not waste time. Let us fly to Radhika's house. She may know the meaning of these symbols.'

The angel bird chirped and said 'Chin chunaki chin chin'

Frederick diminished in size and sat on the red bird. But the laptop became much bigger than him. The red bird then repeated 'Chin chunaki chin chin' and tapped on the Laptop. It instantly became puny. Then they flew towards Radhika's house. She was standing in her balcony when Frederick and the red bird dashed in. Frederick showed Radhika the symbols.

Radhika looked carefully and said 'Frederick, Nacl and H_2O are formulas of chemistry'.

'Great! Go on. Drudan is a scientist and may have mixed spells and formulas to turn Femina into a statue.' said Frederick.

'What is chemistry?' the red bird asked.

'A branch of science concerned with the substances of which an object or thing is composed' said Radhika

'Ok, if I am right then the solution to saving Femina lies with something concerned with salt and water' said Frederick

ψ 'This is the sign of the Trishul of Lord Shiva' said Radhika

"Trishul?' repeated Frederick

'Yes. Lord Shiva is a powerful Hindu Deity and he keeps a Trishul as his weapon'

'Then these symbols could mean that we need to collect salt water near Lord Shiva's temple' said Frederick, straining his mind.

'There are many Shiva temples in this world. Salt water of which temple?' asked the red bird.

'I don't think any temple uses salt water for worshipping Lord Shiva. Most of the people use water from the river Ganges' said Radhika

'River Ganges? A river? Wait a minute, I get this clue. I think salt water symbol is for a water body, like river. Only sea has salt water. This means that we have to collect the water of sea which is near this Shiva temple' said Frederick

'Yes Frederick, you are right. Sea water could be the solution as there is no sea in Zynpagua. Drudan would definitely use a formula whose solution is not in Zynpagua' said the red bird.

'There are many Shiva temples near the sea. Which temple would this be?' asked Radhika.

⇧'I think this symbol can give us a clue' said the red Bird, pointing towards the upward looking arrow.

'Aarna has typed this symbol way above the other letter. See....' said Radhika pointing towards the Laptop

ψ +Nacl+H2O+ ⇧

'Could this mean the highest Shiva temple near the Sea?' asked Radhika

'Yes, yes, this sounds perfect. Which is the tallest Shiva temple near the sea?' asked Frederick.

'Frederick I don't know but we can search on the Internet' saying this, Radhika switched on her computer and searched for the tallest Shiva temple near the sea. The first came out to be Kailashnath Mahadev in Nepal, but it was not near the sea. What about the second tallest? She thought.

In no time she discovered and read aloud 'Murudeshwar temple dedicated to Lord Shiva, lies in the holy beach town in Bhatkal Taluk in the state of Karnataka. It lies on the coast of Arabian sea.'

'Excellent! Let us leave for this place and collect the water of the Arabian sea there' said Frederick.

'But how do you know that we have guessed the symbols correctly?' asked Radhika.

'We don't have an option Radhika. I have to find the solution fast and reach Zynpagua. Please pray that this solution is the correct one' said Frederick.

'I will pray to Lord Shiva. He can cure anything' smiled Radhika.

Bidding adieu to Radhika, Frederick sat on the red bird and left for Murudeshwar temple located in Karnataka. On reaching the temple, the red bird and Frederick bowed before Lord Shiva and prayed to him for saving Femina and for defeating Drudan. They collected the water of the Arabian Sea in a bottle and left for Zynpagua.

Chapter 33

Lady Carol

The two Peregrine falcons sent by Lady Carol, reached Zynpagua and were shocked to witness the scenario. They immediately recognized the sea worms. Once upon a time these used to be their favourite meal. They used to fly from kingdom of clouds to the Earth to feast on them. But this was a dangerous sport. The falcon had to attack the worms on their face and kill it instantly, attacking anywhere else would give these worms more powers and they would increase their size and swallow the falcon.

Seeing these worms, the peregrine falcons immediately took a decision. The older one decided to stay back while the younger one returned with speed to let Lady Carol know about Zynpagua.

The younger Peregrine falcon reached the kingdom of clouds in no time. She informed Lady Carol, who immediately left for Zynpagua. Lady Carol knew that Drudan's return signified threat to lives of both Leo and Anika. She had to stop Drudan from playing mischief.

She did not know why but this one line was echoing in her mind 'an ancient language that sends vibrations to the entire body can stop a split soul from uniting'

'Which language is this? Oh God, please help and give me a clue 'she murmured. Throughout her journey till Zynpagua, she continued to rack her brain to remember a language that sent vibrations to the body.

But when she reached Zynpagua, the scene was appalling. Huge and dirty worms were crawling everywhere and they had fastened Sussaina, Vivian and Anika in their grip.

Drudan was asking Sussaina 'Tell me where the people have vanished? I had seen underground houses here. Where are they?'

Sussaina smirked and said 'Even if you try finding them, you will not be able to locate them Drudan. I am glad my people are safe'

Drudan fumed, raised his hand and said 'Give this woman some pain'

Sussaina winced in pain as Drudan's magic hit her. Vivian struggled as he had become speechless by Drudan's spell.

Anika was watching the scene, holding her nerves and praying to God to show her a way. She asked Drudan 'Why are you torturing us? You want to kill me?'

'What a naive question! You want to die? I am planning to do so. Just let my son come. Once your souls unite, I will kill you immediately.'

'Uniting Leo and Anika's soul? What will you gain from it?' asked Sussaina.

'The sweet taste of Revenge by inflicting a painful and unnatural death. Anyways, what you borrow, you should return. She borrowed my son's soul to live. She must return it' laughed Drudan.

Something struck Drudan and he immediately raised his hand and said 'Demon planets, please bless me. No magic should affect me.'

The skies roared as a red coloured lightening came and struck Drudan's hand.

Drudan looked at the sky and bowing his head, he said 'Thank you my demon planets!'

Lady Carol regretted having missed the chance to use magic on Drudan. 'I am dumb and stupid' she cursed herself under the breath.

While Drudan was talking to the demon planets, Romeo silently wriggled towards the soldiers and killed the worms that were holding the soldiers. Then he indicated to soldiers to attack Drudan from behind.

Lady Carol was seeing this and immediately instructed the falcons to secretly attack the worms that were holding Sussaina, Anika and Vivian. The falcons flew with a speed of lightening and hit the worms on their faces. They instantly fell off. Lady Carol rushed ahead and freed Sussaina and others.

She quickly reversed Drudan's spell and cured Vivian.

The soldiers were going to capture Drudan, when he paced ahead and captured Sussaina.

'I will slay your Queen and this time there aren't any good stars to protect her' screamed Drudan.

The guards backed out. Drudan raised his hand to kill the guards, when he heard 'Drudan, don't harm the guards. I have come. Seek your revenge on me'

On turning around he saw Leo. Drudan deliberately stood at a distance from him. He knew anyone facing Leo ends up feeling powerless.

'Oh my God, what a handsome boy' said Drudan, melodramatically.

'My darling son has finally come. Romeo, please do what you have come here for' he continued.

Romeo hesitated and stood wordlessly watching Anika and Leo. How could he be instrumental in taking their lives? Tears rolled out from his eyes.

Drudan looked at his expression and said 'You can spare them and let your family die. Up to you'

He heard the voice of the mermaid as well 'Romeo hurry or your mother will be the first to die'

Romeo nodded and pounced on Leo from behind. Leo was stunned to see such a huge snake and staggered under his weight. He could only exclaim 'Ah!'

As soon as Leo opened his mouth, Romeo poured the confluence water in his mouth. Leo began to shiver and scream with pain, as the water entered his veins.

People around were not even aware what was happening to Leo. Lady Carol and Sussaina screamed in unison 'What have you made him drink?'

'Fruit juice 'laughed Drudan and turned to Romeo.

Chapter 34

Drudan's Victory

'That was fast Serpie and now you useless fellow, it is time for you to die' saying this Drudan magically got a huge sword and struck him. Romeo jumped fast, but the blade slit his skin. Blood began to ooze out from it.

Anika was dumbfounded, like the others. It took her a while to fathom what had happened. Her gaze moved from Romeo to Leo and back to Romeo. 'They will die!' she mumbled.

Vivian had come close to her by then. Things had happened at such a fast pace, that even he was numb, the only thing that came to his mind was to reach close to Anika. He held Anika tight and shook her. 'Anika!' he called out.

Anika was still in a trance and cried out 'God, show me a way to save them'

While Leo had fallen on the ground and rolling with pain, Drudan raised the sword again and hit Romeo. He escaped and fell on Drudan and began to tighten his grip on him. Drudan pulled out his hand somehow and put the sword straight inside Romeo's body. He tried pulling out the sword but it got stuck. Romeo began to bleed profusely and fell off Drudan.

Lady Carol and Sussaina had reached where Leo was lying. Lady Carol held Leo who had become as cold as ice.

She asked aloud 'Drudan, what have you made him drink. You coward, tell me, what have you done?'

'Welcome mother in-law! I have made him drink the magical water, which will unite his split soul. In other words, this water will pull Anika's soul out of her body. Since this water is extremely powerful, I am not sure if Leo can withstand the pain and continue living' laughed Drudan.

'You felon, what have you done!' Sussaina cried out.

'Just devised a new and permanent way to kill these two rotten people, so called soul-mates'

Sussaina began to cry while Lady Carol rushed towards Romeo and patted him. Romeo feebly opened his eyes and looked at Lady Carol 'I am sorry' he mumbled.

'Is there a way to save them?' asked Lady Carol

Romeo was almost unconscious now; he garnered strength and managed to say 'I don't know!'

The magical water began to show its effect. While Leo was shivering with pain, Anika too had begun to feel giddy and weak. But she did not realize that, as her mind was desperately searching for a way to save Romeo and Leo's life.

She suddenly remembered her Indian mother's words 'Lord Shiva can grant life to anyone'. In fact she had taught Anika a powerful chant of Lord Shiva which could save lives.

Anika strained her memory to remember it and began to murmur

'Om Tryambakam yajamahe
Sugandhim pushti-vardhanam
Urvarukam-iva bandhanan
Mrityormukshiya mamritaat'

Leo was miserable with pain when Anika started chanting the mantra. She looked at Leo and then at Romeo and called out 'Lord Shiva please save them.'

She continued to pray as her limbs were losing strength. Vivian held Anika tightly and shook her hard 'Anika, what is the matter?' He asked.

She did not answer and fell on the floor with her eyes fixed on Romeo and Leo. She yelled out with all her might

'Om Tryambakam yajamahe
Sugandhim pushti-vardhanam
Urvarukam-iva bandhanan
Mrityormukshiya mamritaat'

Romeo heard the mantra and a new stream of energy entered his body. He worshipped Lord Shiva and knew that this mantra was coming as a message from him. Garnering all his strength, he jumped on Drudan and choked him, till he fainted.

Sussaina rushed towards Romeo and caressed him. Weeping she said 'May I please pull out the sword from your body? You will feel better'

Romeo vaguely nodded and said 'save Anika' and fainted.

Sussaina could not understand what Romeo was saying and pulled out the sword from his body. Romeo winced in pain and collapsed. Anika saw Romeo dying and screamed even louder.

'Om Tryambakam yajamahe
Sugandhim pushti-vardhanam
Urvarukam-iva bandhanan
Mrityormukshiya mamritaat'

She softly repeated 'The three eyed Lord Shiva, please liberate us from the fear of death'

In the meanwhile Lady Carol cried aloud 'Don't let Leo faint, once he faints, Anika's soul may leave her body. Don't let him faint'

Vivian dashed towards Leo and holding him said 'Brother, don't close your eyes stay awake'

'What is the connection between me and Anika's soul?' asked Leo, shivering.

Vivian continued rubbing his hands and said 'I will let you know but for now just focus on breathing'

'Please tell me. I know my soul is connected to hers. Always felt it. What is the connection between us?' asked Leo.

Vivian said 'Brother, I am not supposed to tell anything. You have to discover it.'

Leo had become very frail as he said 'I had discovered this when Anika had saved me. I knew there is a connection between us. Tell me how'

'Drudan's violet light had killed Anika's soul. She got life back when Lady Carol borrowed your soul to save her. Anika and you share a common soul' said Vivian.

'She had saved my life, please don't let her die. Kill me so that my soul dies and does not unite with hers but don't let her die' saying this Leo fainted.

Lady Carol screamed aloud 'Oh no! Leo has fainted, Sussaina come here....'

Lady Carol ran towards Anika. She called Sussaina and said 'Come fast Sussaina. Leo has fainted and his soul will be pulling Anika's soul. Do something, pray to the Moon'.

Sussaina sat down on her knees and prayed to the Moon 'Save my daughter!' But her prayer gave rise to a big storm, which came roaring in, pulling the trees and flooding the river. Nature looked so wild and frightening.

'This is the time of demon planets which have cast their shadow on everything including the Moon. I don't know what to do?' Sussaina told Lady Carol

'How do we save them?' asked Vivian, running between Anika and Leo.

Lady Carol was flustered and so nervous that her senses failed to work. She turned numb. All she could say was 'Leo has fainted. I don't know how to save Anika'

They could hear Drudan laugh from the background. He had become conscious now and was elated to see the scene of disaster.

Sussaina stood up and said 'Lady Carol, if Leo has drunk the water, how is it that Anika is still alive and reciting the same prayer?'

They looked at Anika whose attention was on Romeo and Leo as she continued chanting. In her heart she praying 'Please God save them. They cannot die'.

Anika took a deep breath as weakness was engulfing her and recited again

'Om Tryambakam yajamahe
Sugandhim pushti-vardhanam
Urvarukam-iva bandhana
Mrityormukshiya mamritaat'

Every line of Anika's prayer, continued to give strength to Romeo and he woke up.

His blood had stopped oozing and his wound looked healed. Slowly he wriggled towards Anika.

Seeing Anika awake, Sussaina asked Lady Carol 'If Leo has drunk the magical water and has fainted, how is it that Anika is still alive?'

Lady Carol looked at Anika. She was beginning to lose consciousness when Romeo joined her in reciting the prayer

'Om Tryambakam yajamahe
Sugandhim pushti-vardhanam
Urvarukam-iva bandhanan
Mrityormukshiya mamritaat'

He told Anika to repeat it. Anika feebly opened her mouth, while unable to fathom anything, continued to say

'Om Tryambakam yajamahe
Sugandhim pushti-vardhanam
Urvarukam-iva bandhanan
Mrityormukshiya mamritaat'

'What is she reciting?' asked Lady Carol

'This is a powerful mantra to defeat death. It is addressed to Lord Shiva' said Romeo

'Which language is this?' asked Lady Carol.

'This is Sanskrit, the most ancient Indian language' said Romeo

Lady Carol began to weep. Anika was trying to save Romeo and Leo by chanting in Sanskrit, the same language which sends vibrations to the body. That is why her soul did not leave her body and unite with Leo's soul.

'Everyone please repeat this prayer with Anika. Till she recites it, her soul will not part. Usage of Sanskrit is vibrating every muscle in her body, stopping the soul. She has got the blessing of God, how else would she start reciting it on her own' said Lady Carol.

Drudan was shocked to see the turn of events.

How could the magical water fail? His mind was running fast and he quickly thought 'Let me arrest Vivian first and then spell bind everyone with magic. He looked around and saw Vivian sitting on the floor holding Leo, who was slowly coming back to consciousness. Vivian was making Leo chant the same prayer. Drudan thought 'This prayer is more powerful than the magical waters? It is the time to conquer the world. The demon planets will support me. I want to learn all the hidden mysteries in India.'

He thought for a while and said 'No wonder Sussaina chose to send her daughter to India'.

Without wasting any further time, Drudan hit Vivian on the head and pointing his finger towards Leo and Vivian, he said 'Deep sleep should capture thee' Vivian was caught unaware. He was bleeding profusely with the blow on his head. While he had no time to counter the spell, he quickly voiced 'This sleep should break with the first call of our name'

Drudan did not know that Vivian had said another spell before dozing off to sleep. He laughed aloud and sent an imprisonment spell for everyone. When everyone was getting captured, Romeo who was unaffected by magic, quickly wriggled and hid himself in the bushes. He was still very weak to fight Drudan at that moment and he had to plan something fast. When everyone was captured, Drudan walked towards Anika and said 'It is simple. I can kill you with this dagger which my lovely wife, the mermaid gifted me. Why did I have to bother for magical water and stuff?'

Sussaina yelled 'Drudan you cannot kill her. She has the blessings of the stars'

Drudan looked at the sky and noticed that all the stars were covered by the red shade. He laughed and said 'let me show you how the planets will protect her. In the meantime, Sussaina quickly tell me where are the people of Zynpagua?'

'Vivian has hidden them through a special spell. You know magic then why can you not discover them?'

This infuriated Drudan and he began to try all possible spells to find the people. He was so preoccupied that he did not realize that thousands of birds had appeared in the night sky and between them Frederick was flying on the red angel bird. Lady Carol and Sussaina's face lit up with hope.

Frederick first flew straight inside the palace where Femina's statue was placed. He joined his hand and said 'Lord Shiva, please cure Femina'. Then he sprinkled water on Femina's hand. As the water touched her hand, a crack appeared in the stone revealing Femina's frail yet beautiful hand. Slowly Frederick sprinkled water everywhere and she came back to life. She coughed and asked for water. Frederick immediately picked the jar placed nearby and made her drink water. She was very weak and could hardly speak.

The red bird handed her the banana they had carried with them and told her to eat it slowly.

Back in the garden, Drudan went very close to Anika 'Now let me see what can protect you', saying this, he pulled out the dagger and aiming it towards Anika yelled 'kill her!'

Just then, thousands of birds hovering in the sky attacked him.

Drudan tried pronouncing a spell to kill everyone but Romeo flew up and wrapped himself around Drudan, covering even his mouth. The birds looked at Vivian and Leo who were lying unconscious. They saw Anika who had become very weak, and was lying on the floor.

Lady Carol used her magical spells and in seconds, Lady Carol rescued herself and Sussaina.

Lady Carol advised 'Sussaina please take Anika inside. She is very weak. Let me see how I can wake Vivian and Leo'

'No mother, Drudan is dangerous. First capture him' said Anika

'Kill him before he does anything evil' said Romeo

Just then they heard a melodious song.

'I am the mermaid of the sea
Have come to set him free
Who is he?
Beloved of the mermaid of the sea
Don't challenge evil in evil times
You will lose and nothing will be fine
And victory shall always be mine.'

'Who is it?' asked Sussaina

'This is the voice of mermaid of the sea. Drudan is my husband and I will set him free' said the mermaid.

'He is an evil man and we have captured him.' said Sussaina

'Let us make a deal. You release my husband and I will set your husband free' said the mermaid

'My husband? How do you know him?' asked Sussaina.

'How do I know him?' the mermaid chuckled 'I have kept him hanging between life and death for the last eleven years' she continued.

'I don't believe you' said Sussaina

'Then see for yourself' said the mermaid

Just then a halo appeared in the sky with the image of King Soto. He was tied in the deep sea with worms crawling all over him. He looked haggard and scrawny. Green scum had accumulated on his legs and his head was stooping down, as he sat unconsciously in water.

Sussaina was aghast seeing his condition 'King Soto, my Lord, you are alive!'

The mermaid chuckled and said 'He can't hear you. Now be quick. Release Drudan and I will release Soto'

Romeo cried aloud 'Don't believe her, she will not keep her promise'

'Dear Snake we have to save King Soto.' Said Sussaina

'Hurry up' said the mermaid.

'Romeo release Drudan' instructed Sussaina

Romeo left his grip on Drudan. As soon as he was let loose, he hit Romeo on the head and captured Sussaina, Lady Carol and the soldiers with his magic. He yelled 'Thank you my mermaid my love'

'You are welcome my Lord' said the mermaid

'Mermaid, I have kept my promise, now you should keep yours' requested Sussaina

Mermaid chuckled and said 'Evil people only cheat. Otherwise how would they keep their names alive? Goodbye Sussaina and King Soto would never come back to you. Drudie, get this girl in sea. Once the demon planets' influence fades, we will use her to influence the stars. Ensure she comes'

'Good idea' saying this Drudan lifted his hand which had the dagger gifted by the Mermaid. Pointing it towards Anika, he said 'Fall in the deep sea where resides the mermaid my wife.'

Romeo yelled aloud 'Anika move from there'

Instead of listening to Romeo, Anika stood up

Romeo dashed ahead and stood in front of Anika. He told her to curl behind him so that the lethal weapon could not touch her. But instead of moving behind, Anika came and stood right in front of Romeo. She said 'My father is lying in the sea Romeo. Let this weapon take me to the same sea. I want to save him and set him free.'

Sussaina continued to yell 'No Anika, don't do that' but by then the weapon came and hit Anika on the leg. She flew up with the strong force and started heading to some destination. Romeo dashed ahead and wrapped himself around Anika. Before they vanished he cried aloud 'Queen Sussaina, I swear on Lord Shiva, I will not let this little girl be harmed. Kanya Kumari...'

But before he could complete, they vanished with the force of the wind.

Sussaina was shocked to see what had transpired.

Drudan laughed and said 'Sussaina, I have made you taste sweet revenge. Now, I am going to conquer the world'

'So long Sussaina. Once Anika leaves Zynpagua, Femina too will die since she is bound by the spell of her life. Pay her my deathly regards!'

Chapter 35

The search Begins..............

Once Drudan had left, Lady Carol and Sussaina were grieved and thunderstruck. Anika had been taken away while Leo and Vivian were unconscious.

Sussaina and Lady Carol rushed towards Vivian. He had lost lot of blood which made him turn pale. Lady Carol immediately sent the angel birds to fetch a special leaf from the jungle.

In the meanwhile, she went close to Leo and tapping him, she said 'Leo wake up!' Calling out Leo's name broke Drudan's spell and he got up with a terrible pain erupting from his heart.

He cried out in pain 'Ah grandma, it seems someone is trying to pull my life out. I can't bear this pain. My body feels lifeless'

Sussaina and Lady Carol could not fathom what to do. Leo's face was vibrating with pain. Lady Carol touched his forehead and pronounced the spell 'Sleep!' Leo closed his eyes and went off to sleep.

'Drudan has made him drink the magical water which tried pulling Anika's soul. I do not know how to cure this pain caused by this water' Lady Carol told Sussaina.

'We will find a way to cure Leo. I am sure there must be a way' said Sussaina, defeating the tears rolling out from her eyes.

'I have never seen you so shaken' said Lady Carol.

'Be courageous Sussaina, we have faced worse days and have been victorious in the end'

Sussaina held Lady Carol and began to weep. 'My daughter is taken away, Leo is suffering, Vivian is wounded and Femina is lifeless. I feel helpless, so helpless!'

'Sussaina, you cannot lose hope. Let us first cure our children here. Anika took the wound to reach Soto. She is a tough girl and will find a way. Romeo is with her and I am sure he will protect her' said Lady Carol

Sussaina nodded and looking up at the Moon said 'Please save her!'

Just then, Frederick came out with Femina in his hands. She had scales on her skin and looked much emaciated and feeble. While she was no longer a statue, she didn't look human either. The complexion of her skin had become chalklike.

'Frederick my son, you have come!' exclaimed Sussaina on seeing Frederick.

'Mother, I thought it was important to bring Femina to life. I am sorry, I could not come to help you' said Frederick.

'How is Femina? Is she fine? Could you save her?'

'Yes mother, she is fine. I managed to get the seawater which dissolved Drudan's spell on her' assured Frederick.

'I am so glad son. Femina is alive!' said Lady Carol.

Sussaina saw Femina alive and felt a little better. 'Frederick, I am glad you are fine. Drudan wounded Anika and took her with him' she said, wiping tears from her eyes.

Frederick was stunned to hear that. He looked around and saw Leo unconscious and Vivian bleeding. He placed Femina on a bench in the garden and hugged Sussaina 'Mother, everything will be fine. Don't worry about Anika. She will be fine.'

The angel birds returned in no time with the leaves. Lady Carol quickly made a paste of the leaves and applied it on Vivian's forehead. Blood stopped oozing out. Then she slowly called him 'Vivian, son, how are you feeling?'

Vivian gently opened his eyes and nodded.

While Lady Carol dressed Vivian's wounds, Sussaina's mind rattled with pressing questions. What would Drudan do with Anika? Would he torture her to impress the stars? But stars would not be influenced by the mission of spreading evil. What would Drudan do then? Would he kill her? Sussaina knew she had to devise a speedy plan to rescue Anika and King Soto. But the mermaid ruled the sea. How were they going to enter the sea and defeat the mermaid?

Sussaina also feared that their inability to capture Drudan would bring disaster for people on the Earth. Drudan had married a vicious mermaid. How could nature allow victory for such vicious and evil people? It seemed the rule of the demon planets would bring disaster for the world. How could the Moon, the Sun and other stars get so helpless?

By this time the people of Zynpagua came out from their hiding. They were grateful that Sussaina had saved them from Drudan but were aggrieved to hear about Anika. Everyone decided to support Sussaina in finding Anika and King Soto.

They voiced in unison

'To find our Princess,
We will enter the sea.
And set our King Soto and Anika Free'

'Ladies and gentleman, it is not going to be easy. You have no idea what it is to swim in a sea. It could risk your life' said Sussaina.

'We owe our life to Anika and will do whatever to save her' said the people in unison.

'Thank you my dear people. We have to make a plan. As of now, we know nothing about the sea. Moreover, we have to find a way to defeat Drudan. The demon planets are ruling the sky and we can get no support from the Moon and the stars. Be patient and use your wisdom to find a way. Let your mind race to find a solution. Together we will tide off any obstacle.'

The people nodded in agreement.

Lady Carol came close to Sussaina and whispered in her ears 'Sussaina, Leo is moaning even in his sleep. I am flying back to Kingdom of clouds to get the ancient book of solutions. I am sure I can find a way to cure him. Even Femina needs special cure. I can only start the treatment once I gather the information. Frederick has left Femina in your room. I did not want Vivian to see her. He is in a state of shock. While blood has stopped flowing from his forehead, he is feeling frail. Frederick has gone to leave Leo in his room. He will then help Vivian reach his room. Sussaina, you too take rest. I will be back in a day. Remember, we have to be healthy and fine to cure others. I have asked Frederick to be alert in my absence.'

Sussaina concurred and said 'Yes Lady, we have to be fine. I have a suggestion. We can send the angel birds to the earth. Maybe they will be able to find some clue on the whereabouts of Anika'

'That is a wonderful suggestion. Let me call the angel birds' said Lady Carol and clapped her hands. The angel birds came and sat on Lady Carol and Sussaina. The red bird sat on Lady Carol's palm and asked 'Yes Lady, please tell us how can we be of help'

'Angels, please fly to the Earth and try finding where Anika is' said Lady Carol

'Where should we start from?' asked the Red bird.

'Before Romeo disappeared he had shouted a name- I think he said Kanya Kumari'

'Kanya Kumari! Is it a place?' asked Lady Carol.

'I don't know Lady but will surely find out 'saying this, red birds bid adieu and flew towards the Earth.

Chapter 36

Anika and Romeo

Anika had become unconscious by the assault of Drudan's weapon. Romeo used all his powers and pulled out the weapon from her leg when she was falling. While the weapon was out, Anika's leg was bleeding profusely. He knew that as soon as they reach the Earth, the mermaid's magic would start pulling Anika towards the sea. Romeo tried his level best to stop Anika from falling in the Indian Ocean but he could not defeat the mermaid's magical pull and landed straight in deep sea, in front of the mermaid. She laughed mercilessly seeing Anika injured and unresponsive.

Romeo tried to escape, but the mermaid captured him. He was immediately locked behind the bars while Anika was made to sleep on a huge leaf. The mermaid kissed Anika's hand so that her skin could function like gills and she could breathe freely in the sea. She blew air on Anika's leg and stopped the flow of blood.

Anika woke after a day and was totally frightened to see the scene around. She was suspended in water and dirty worms were crawling everywhere. On one side, in a prison kind of structure, she saw huge snakes locked behind the bars. Romeo was one of them and he was bleeding from various places. A very beautiful girl was sitting on a huge stone right in front of her. On looking closer, she saw that half of her body was that of a girl and half of a fish. 'Mermaid!' she exclaimed. Anika tried moving, but was frail and could not do so. She was given a plate full of swampy leaves to eat. Anika felt giddy seeing the site of the leaves.

A melodious voice said 'Eat this or pick one of these fishes and have them'

Anika looked down and saw few fishes floating in the water. 'Live fishes?' she asked.

The mermaid chuckled and said 'Of course, once you bite them, they will be dead'

Anika feebly said 'I can't eat this. I am a vegetarian'

'Then there is nothing else we can offer you. You are free to die' the mermaid chuckled.

Just then they saw Drudan descend. He came down and hugged the mermaid

'My love, thank you for saving me!' he said.

The mermaid blushed and smiled happily. By then Anika was feeling so weak that she fainted again.

'Let her collapse and die. I don't need her' said Drudan

'But I do. You don't know how much power this girl has. Can you imagine if she impresses the Moon, we can control the tides, if she impresses the Sun, we can control the day and night'

'The celestial bodies support for doing good and not evil' said Drudan

'Even then, she has the power! We will use it somehow' the mermaid chuckled.

Drudan was exhausted and in an urgency to conquer the world. 'Do whatever you feel like. I need to have a word with you' saying this he swam out and the mermaid followed behind.

Once they had gone, Romeo called out 'Anika, wake up. Can you hear me, wake up!'

Anika stirred a little and opened her eyes. She feebly whispered 'Romeo? I am sorry to see you wounded'

Romeo smiled and said 'No problem. Anika you need to gain strength to be able to save yourself. Please eat whatever is being served to you'

'I cannot eat the swamps and I don't eat fishes. I am a vegetarian'

'Anika, listen me. You will have to survive in order to save your father. If you don't eat, you will die' insisted Romeo.

Anika looked around feebly and asked 'Is there anything better I can eat?'

'What about Sea grapes? 'Asked Romeo's mother

'Yes mother, a great option, but how to get it when we are behind the bars?' asked Romeo.

'You have not tried rescuing yourself because of Anika. She is conscious now, let us try and escape'

'You are right mother. I can take help of Mashy. He has not been made captive' said Romeo.

'I will try communicating with him mentally. Let me see if he responds' said Romeo.

Romeo closed his eyes and tried connecting with Mashy. Romeo and his clan were gifted with this unique ability to mentally connect with each other and read anyone's mind.

Thus Romeo called out 'Mashy can you hear me?'

There was no response.

Romeo called out yet again 'Hey Mashy, can you hear me'

After sometime, a faint voice said 'Hey Romeo, are you back?'

'Yes I am. Where are you?' asked Romeo

'Hiding in the sea caves. The mermaid has issued an arrest warrant for all the snakes.'

Romeo got a fit of rage. He felt like strangulating the mermaid then and there.

'Where are you Romeo my friend?' asked Mashy.

'The mermaid has arrested me and my parents' said Romeo

'I told you don't trust that human. He looked untrustworthy. You know there is a man lying in these caves. He is unconscious. I think he is under the mermaid's magical spell. Should I spit on him and kill him?'

'Hey, don't harm him. I think he is Anika's father' said Romeo

'Whose father?' asked Mashy

'I will tell you the details. Just take care of him. Mashy is there any way you can rescue us?' asked Romeo.

'I am coming to save you' said Mashy

Is there a way to break the jail?' he continued.

The sea jails were locked by special cave rocks and sealed by the mermaids spell. No one could break the locks and escape the jail.

Romeo thought for a while and said. 'Mashy, I don't think I can break the mermaid's spell but there is a little girl here who is not locked in the jail. She saved my life. Can you please get some sea grapes for her?'

'Little girl? You mean human? Why are you helping a human? They have never been faithful to snakes' said Mashy.

'She saved my life Mashy and I have to save hers. If she doesn't eat anything, she will die. Is there a way to get sea grapes for her?' asked Romeo

'Romeo, the sea grapes can only be found in the mermaid's garden. I will have to escape the eyes of the worm guards. But don't worry, I will try' said Mashy

Mashy reached the garden which was heavily guarded. Juicy sea grapes could be seen hanging in water. Mashy was a huge snake and did not know how to escape the eye of the guards. He thought for a while but the only solution that came in his mind was a direct combat. He went straight in, hit the guards at the garden gates and wriggled fast towards the grapes. He pulled out few grape plants and holding them in his mouth, he rushed out, hitting the guards with his tail and crusading forward. He rushed towards the prison and on reaching there, hit the prison guards and entered the jail. He found Romeo and his family confined in a small cellar. As soon as Romeo saw Mashy, he was overwhelmed and cried aloud 'Mashy my friend you are here!'

'I have carried the sea grapes. Whom should I give these? Sea guards are following me' Mashy screamed.

'Oh' said Romeo and pointing towards Anika, said 'Give it to the girl there'

Mashy turned around and saw Anika. He went close to her and kept the grapes behind a huge boulder. He then licked Anika's face and realized she had very high fever.

'Oh my God, her body is burning' said Mashy.

'Catch him' a voice alerted Mashy

As he turned around, he saw fifty sea worms had surrounded him.

Mashy blew in air and stepped forward. With agility he jumped high in the sea and came back full force, falling on twenty worms. They fainted immediately. He wrapped himself around two others and strangulated them. But soon more worms joined in, holding thorns in their mouths, and began piercing Mashy with it. Mashy recoiled in pain, unable to hit the worms. Some fifty thorns had been pierced in his body.

Romeo yelled seeing the site 'So many worms surrounding one single snake. I dare you, release me and we will show you what real combat means!'

The worms laughed and continued piercing Mashy. Anika woke up with the turbulence in water. She saw this wounded snake that looked so much like Romeo and understood he belonged to the Romeo's clan. Garnering all her strength, Anika moved her limbs and swam towards Mashy. She smacked the worms with one swift movement of the hand. They fell far away from Mashy. Before the worms could swim back towards them, Anika quickly pulled out the needles from Mashy's body who nodded in gratitude.

She then told Mashy 'Run from here before the other worms attack'

Romeo yelled as well 'Mashy run as fast as you can'

By then some hundred worms came back and surrounded Anika and Mashy. When one of the worms tried attacking Anika, the other worm said 'No, the mermaid has instructed us not to harm her'

When Anika heard this, she swam towards Mashy and stood like a barrier between Mashy and the worms. 'Run Mashy, they will not harm me. Run' said Anika.

Mashy jerked his body and with great agility, swam out of the prison. The worms tried following him, but Anika picked a huge stone from the water and hit it on the worms. Many got wounded while the others swam behind Mashy.

Anika fell in the seawater, exhausted and sapped. She felt her wounded leg had become lifeless and was merely hanging to her body.

Romeo called her 'Thank you Anika for helping my friend escape. He has got sea grapes for you. Do you have the energy to swim till the rock there?'

Anika looked towards the grapes that were kept on the boulder. She nodded and feebly lifted her hands and moved one leg to drift towards the grapes. She somehow managed to get there. As she popped a few grapes, a current of energy ran in her veins.

'Thank you Romeo, I feel so much better' she said.

Romeo smiled and said 'Yes, I had asked Mashy to steal them from the mermaid's garden. Sea creatures say these are powerhouses of energy'

'Yes, indeed they are. Romeo, how can I break this lock to free you and your fellow snakes?' asked Anika

'Oh this is my family, my parents and my wife' said Romeo, introducing his family to Anika.

Anika looked at the other snakes. They were injured and weak. Anika felt a pang of guilt seeing the snakes 'Have you been imprisoned because of me?' asked Anika.

'No, not because of you but because of me' smiled Romeo as he continued 'The sea is a crazy place Anika. There are millions of creatures in it, the fishes, the snails, the whales, but none of them have the courage to revolt against the vicious rule of this mermaid. Only the snake clan has managed to rebel against her. The first time I revolted, the mermaid locked me in a stone and my wife in magical water. This time, Drudan ditched us and married the mermaid. He used me to carry the magical water. He had planned to slay me. Had you not been there, I would have been dead by now' said Romeo.

'Drudan used you to carry magical water? What is it? Why did he carry it to Zynpagua' asked Anika

'To unite your soul with Leo's and kill you' said Romeo

'But why with Leo's soul?' asked Anika.

Romeo suddenly realized that Anika was not aware of this fact. He thought the discovery that her soul had been killed by Drudan and that she was living on a borrowed soul, would shock her and threaten her.

He thus said 'I really don't know Anika'

He continued. 'Before I forget, Anika, listen carefully. The mermaid has kept you alive to impress the stars. Keep giving her the assurance that you will do it, or else she will kill you'

'I will speak the truth Romeo. The stars will never get impressed for doing anything evil' said Anika.

'Listen, if you don't want to say a lie, simply nod your head sideways. Swaying the head sideways symbolizes a yes among animals and reptiles. In humans it means a no. While you will gesture a no to the mermaid, she will think it is a yes'

Just then they heard someone giggle. It was the mermaid

She walked in and laughed aloud 'Guards, get that rogue to me'

Several worms swam in, carrying Mashy on them. He was severely wounded. The mermaid looked at Mashy once and then at Romeo 'Why are you playing tricks with me Philip oh I am sorry, Romeo?'

She stared straight in Anika's eyes 'You little girl! Why are you instigating the snakes to play thieves for you? Look at Mashy's state, he is almost dead and you are responsible for it.'

'Why is she responsible?' asked Romeo

'Because she made this snake steal sea grapes from my garden' said the mermaid.

'No, she did not. I told Mashy. The food you are giving her is awful' said Romeo.

'She should be thankful that she is alive' she said.

'Guards throw this snake with the others in that jail' she continued.

The worm guards stuffed Mashy in with Romeo and others in the same cell.

Romeo's mother squealed as there was no space for them to move.

Turning to Anika, the mermaid said 'Listen girl, I want you to impress the Moon for me.'

Anika took a deep breath and said 'I will listen to you if you free Romeo and his family and make me meet my father'

'Darling Darling, I am not a fool. Once I make you meet your father and release Romeo and the snake clan, you guys will revolt against me and escape. I cannot let you escape. Your life is mine now' the mermaid said, laughing aloud.

Anika panicked 'Is she trying to keep me captive for life?' she thought.

Then taking another deep breath, Anika said 'Fine, you keep me captive but free Romeo and my father'

'If I free your father, he will come back with an army to save you. By now he knows the sea well. I cannot let him escape' said the Mermaid

Anika struggled to sit, with one leg injured; she was finding it very difficult to float in water.

The mermaid looked at Anika's leg and smiled 'I love Drudan. What a right place to inflict a wound. Girl, your leg is terribly injured and will take days to heal. Don't try playing tricks with me in the sea. You will impress the Moon for me for your life. I will neither free the vicious snakes nor will I let your father escape. If you are good to me, I will make you meet him soon. I don't need you this week. My dear demon planets are ruling and giving me enough strength and support to rule the sea. Post this week, you will get support from the Moon'

The mermaid laughed mischievously and slapped Anika who fainted with the blow. Romeo kept yelling at the mermaid, 'She needs proper food or else she would die' but mermaid waved a goodbye and left the place, laughing merrily.

Chapter 37

Lady Carol

Lady Carol flew to the kingdom of clouds to bring back the ancient book of solutions. On reaching the kingdom of clouds, she felt her body was burning. She noticed that the flowers in the sky had all shrunk and withered and the roads were deserted.

Worried, she rushed towards her palace. There were no soldiers at the entrance. She hurried in and saw people hiding within the palace.

'What happened?' she asked them.

'Lady the weather is wild and there is a red shadow in the sky. Our body feels itchy and burning when we step out. Even the flowers in the sky have dried.'

Lady Carol got worried. While she knew that the rule of the demon planets was causing this sensation, she had no idea why it was affecting the people from Kingdom of clouds more than those in Zynpagua. She had not felt this burning sensation in Zynpagua.

She told the people to calm down while she went to read in the library. On reaching there, she opened her father's cupboard. After browsing through the books, she found a book on the rule of demon planets. She quickly opened the **Chapter-The evil rule when the demons command** and began to read. After reading two pages, she reached the page on warnings. It stated 'The evil planets prepare for ruling the universe for about 200 years. That is when they garner all their strength. The Sun, the Moon and the other planets succumb to their power. While their rule lasts for only a week, incorrigible natural disasters happen now, to destroy nature which is so skillfully created by the universe. Thus volcanoes, earth quakes and storms erupt. Moreover, evil people commence to rule.

The demon planets then bless some of these evil people to rule for about two hundred years. People residing on the Earth and universe should strive towards ousting this evil rule within the week or else these evil people selected by the demon planets may bring disaster for mankind. In fact the first region to be destroyed by these evil planets would start receiving signals like body ache or a constant burning sensation. Such region should be evacuated immediately or the people would get burnt by the power of the demon planets.

As Lady Carol read this, her heart sank. People of the kingdom of clouds were experiencing a burning sensation.

Was it her region, the beautiful kingdom of clouds which would meet disaster soon?

She quickly read ahead to find a solution to save the region.

'There is only one way to fight this influence of the evil planet. Only when Saturn, the planet of justice will cast its aspect on the evil planets, would they mellow down. But winning Saturn's favour is not easy. It is the planet of justice and the planet of good deeds. Only such a person can influence Saturn who has staked his or her life to free mankind of evil. Such a person can pray to Saturn for saving the region or else the region will perish.'

Lady Carol continued to stare at the paper even when she had finished reading. The only solution to this impending disaster was to find Anika, the princess who could impress the planets and the stars. But she had been taken away by Drudan's weapon.

Lady Carol held her head '*What should I do? We have to find Anika soon!*'

The thought of Anika gave her goose bumps. How callously the weapon had hit her leg and taken her away. 'Please God, save Anika' she murmured.

A sudden uproar outside made her standup. Two girls flew in 'Lady, the red sky is affecting us inside the palace as well. We are getting rashes' said the girls pointing to the pink blotches on their skin.

Lady Carol knew she had to act immediately or else all the people of Kingdom of clouds would be killed. She walked out and announced 'People, we have to fly to Zynpagua immediately. Cover your faces and skin with thick clothes. We have to leave now!'

The people were traumatized to hear that. Lady Carol saw their perturbed faces and clarified 'Ladies and Gentleman, this is the first day of the rule of the demon planets and we have started getting rashes. The way this weather is affecting us signals an imminent destruction of our land. Let us evacuate now or else by tomorrow, we will not be able to even fly in such wild skies.'

'Yes Lady' shouted the people and rushed back to prepare for the journey to Zynpagua. Lady Carol hurried towards the Library and picked all the relevant books. She then requested the Falcons to carry them to Zynpagua while she herself carried the ancient book of solutions.

Within minutes, all the people of the kingdom of clouds could be seen flying towards Zynpagua. Their bodies itched and burned but they maintained a steady speed, till they were out of the zone of kingdom of clouds.

Chapter 38

Incurable Pain

Frederick was instructing the palace guards when he saw Lady Carol lead an army of people. He called out 'Mother Sussaina, please come out'.

Sussaina was sitting with Femina when she heard Frederick. She rushed out and saw Lady Carol flying with her people. 'How are these people going to fit in the palace?' asked Frederick.

'Frederick, I fear something disastrous has befallen on the kingdom of clouds. Why else would Lady Carol get everyone here?' said Sussaina

'The people of Zynpagua have occupied palace houses. People of kingdom of clouds can occupy the vacant houses of our people outside the palace. I feel Drudan would not return now. He has achieved his goal and taken Anika' she continued.

Lady Carol descended and told Sussaina everything. Sussaina welcomed the people from the kingdom of clouds and instructed

Frederick and her soldiers to help them settle in the houses vacated by the people of Zynpagua. The head cook was instructed to make meals for all.

Lady Carol went inside the palace library with the falcons and placed her books safely on the racks. She then opened the ancient book on solutions and commenced reading. She hurriedly turned pages and reached the section where there was a mention of the magical water.

It stated 'There are some sections in the ocean, where waters of three or more sea unite. When the ray of the Full Moon falls on such water, it makes it magical. The effect of such magical water differs from situation to situation but mainly such water can unite things that were originally one but had got separated. If a human drinks this water, he will suffer with incurable pain. This excruciating pain is capable of killing the person in a maximum of two days'

Lady Carol was shivering while holding the book. Her eyes were frantically searching for a solution. How was she going to save Leo from the magical waters? She finished reading the book but there was no solution provided in the book. She collapsed in her chair and held her head. 'The magical water inside Leo's body would instill so much pain that he may die' she vaguely muttered.

She was almost in tears when a sudden thought flashed in her mind? When the magical waters are so dangerous, how was Romeo able to carry them in his mouth? What do snakes have that humans don't?

'Poison!' she murmured.

'But how will poison save Leo, it might kill him faster?

Just then a helper of the palace came running inside the library 'Lady Hurry and reach Vivian's room. Leo is not well. Not well at all. Queen Sussaina has asked you to hasten'

Lady Carol's heart skipped a beat. What was she going to do now? She flew towards Vivian's room instead of walking. On reaching there she saw Leo was still asleep but his entire body had turned crimson and he was shuddering. Sussaina was placing wet towels on his face, while Vivian was holding Leo's hand.

Vivian's head was bandaged but patches of blood were visible on the dressing. Sussaina saw Lady Carol and said 'Lady, wake Leo. He is under your sleep spell but is shivering with pain'

Lady Carol went and touched Leo's feet. Instead of being cold, now his body was burning with temperature. Sussaina told Lady Carol that she had given him medicines but none seemed to be working.

Lady Carol said helplessly 'Sussaina, I have read in the ancient book of solutions that if someone whose soul had once split, drinks magical water, his soul tries to unite with the split soul. If that doesn't happen, the magical water inside the body of the person creates intolerable pain and kills the person'

'Oh my God' said Sussaina, placing her hand on her mouth and exclaiming in a state of shock.

'There must be a solution to this Lady' said Vivian.

'None that I could find in the ancient book of solutions' said Lady Carol, panicking.

'What are you saying Lady? I'm sure there is a way out 'said Sussaina.

'Sussaina, I couldn't find a solution in the book. However, the thought that Romeo could carry magical water in his mouth for so long, is building some hope'

'Yes indeed he carried the magical waters all along' said Sussaina and before Lady Carol could reply, she said 'What do snakes have that humans don't? Poison!'

'Yes Sussaina, I thought the same. Maybe poison is the solution. But how will Leo survive if he drinks poison and moreover what kind of poison?' asked Lady Carol.

'Lady we don't have time to think. Let's find a snake like Romeo and request him to sting Leo in such a way that the poison does not enter the heart' said Vivian

'But where do we find such an understanding snake?' Vivian continued.

'Only Romeo can do this and no one else' said Sussaina.

'We have only a day. What do we do?' asked Lady Carol.

'Let us call Anika's teacher Mootu. I am sure Romeo is in water near this place called Kanya Kumari. We will send Mootu to swim in the mermaid's sea'

A guard was sent to call Mootu. Since Mootu walked slowly, two falcons were sent with the guard to carry Mootu on their back.

As Mootu came in, Sussaina asked 'Sir, we have to save Leo's life. Can you please go to the Earth and enter the sea near this place called Kanya Kumari. You have to fetch Romeo from there. I don't know how you will manage to break into the mermaids' kingdom, but can you please try?'

'Sure Queen but I would need help. I have heard in tortoise stories that these mermaids spell bind the sea. How will I break her magic?'

'I will go with him' Vivian said instantly

'But you are wounded son!' Sussaina objected.

'Mother, I have to go else Leo will die' said Vivian.

Sussaina nodded because there was no other option.

'Please take Vivian with you. He can do magic. But how will he breathe in the sea?' asked Sussaina

'You needn't worry about that. Mana leaves can make anyone breathe in water'

'Wonderful!' said Sussaina.

'Vivian, remember, you have to find Romeo and get him here. Even if you see Anika miserable, don't lose focus. Just bring Romeo as soon as possible' she continued.

'Mother, I will get Anika back' said Vivian

'The mermaid wants to use Anika to impress the stars. She will not kill her. Defeating Drudan and the mermaid will not be possible in a day. We have to save Leo first. I am not discouraging you my son. If you can save Anika, nothing like it, if you cannot, ensure you come back with Romeo. We will wage a war against them and save Anika.'

'Mother, should I stay back while I send Romeo here'

'No Vivian, you are injured and not prepared to face the mermaid or Drudan alone, that too in the sea. We will attack together but let us save Leo first'

'Remember, we have less than twenty four hours' said Lady Carol.

'Fine, let us leave immediately. We will pick Mana leaves on our way' said Mootu.

Lady Carol called the two peregrine falcons and instructed them 'Both of you accompany Vivian and Mootu. When they enter the sea, you remain on the sea shore to render any help they need. If they do not return in next twenty hours, ensure you return at great speed to let us know'

Sussaina and Lady Carol bid adieu to Vivian and the falcons. Once they had left, Sussaina said 'Lady, I think we should also have a second plan. In worst case scenario, it is possible that Vivian gets captured and may not return. In that case, what should we do?

'Yes Sussaina, in that case the only option left with us is to infuse poison in Leo's body. However, I am not sure whether it would be of any help. In fact it may prove fatal'

Sussaina looked at the Moon which had turned crimson. 'I wish I could pray to the Moon for help. Alas! It is under the influence of the demon planets'

'When destiny does not favour, it is the man's will that determines victory or failure. Sussaina we have no option but to save Leo and our children' Lady Carol said emphatically.

'Yes Lady, no harm shall fall on our children as long as we are alive' assured Sussaina.

Chapter 39

Drudan commences to rule the Earth

The angel birds reached the city of Kanya Kumari to find Anika and Romeo. The seashore was inundated with people. They checked every face to locate Anika, but could not find her.

They looked at the huge expanse of the sea to find any snake floating on its surface, but failed to get any evidence. Exasperated and tired they sat on the bark of a tree. Some fishermen were on the sea shore, tying nets. They were talking about the shade on the Moon and the turbulent sea, when all of a sudden they began to scream.

Drudan appeared from the sea and flew towards them 'You nasty people. You are the ones who obeyed the snake and insulted me. I will take revenge for every insult. Sea worms capture them!' yelled Drudan.

Just then millions of sea worms came out from the sea and began to grow in size. People at the beach ran seeing them. Some were so petrified that they simply fainted. Drudan captured the people with a magical spell and suspended them in the air.

'Now I need my special army to capture this world' thought Drudan.

He smirked and raised his hands towards the sky 'Demon planets, send your blessings. Make my magic so powerful that I am able to create an evil army of my own' voiced Drudan.

Just then, a red lightening appeared in the sky to support Drudan in this evil act. Drudan laughed aloud and said

'Demon planets,
I seek your blessings,
Let my magic create an army
That will cause only suffering
Mercy will be given to none
I promise you an evil rule
And make you as powerful as the Sun'

Saying this, Drudan pointed his finger towards the beach and said 'My evil and magical army appear now'

Millions of armed men in red uniform appeared on the shores. Drudan laughed aloud 'Yes the demon planets are blessing me. My magic is getting powerful.'

He then pointed his fingers towards the armed men and said 'my magic will make you run, make you fly, make you swim. Just go and capture the world for me. I will rule the Earth!'

The armed men ascended high in the sky and commenced spreading everywhere, to every nook and corner of the Earth. They commenced capturing all the leaders and rulers of various places. Those who agreed to become Drudan's slaves were spared, the rest killed.

Drudan created a palace for himself on the shores of Arabian Sea. He inspected his people with his magical vision and was delighted to see that his red army had captured the Earth in a day. The newspapers, television and the radio screamed against this alien invasion but not a single sole was spared to revolt against Drudan. People around the world were shocked at what had happened.

Drudan entered the newsrooms of various news channels and announced 'People, I am Drudan the evil scientist who is now going to rule you. If you quietly obey my orders, I will spare you or else, you will be killed. If you have to live, live in my fear or die. Please stay in your houses and wait for my next instruction. Any layman found roaming on the road will be killed'

Most of the people locked themselves in their houses.

Drudan then decided to buy a modern vehicle to ride on. He entered an automobile showroom and confiscated a red coloured Ferrari 458 Italia. Unable to decipher how to drive it, he magically instructed the car to move. It roared and dashed ahead. Drudan instructed the Ferrari to fly in the sky. The car raced in the sky.

The journalists and media personnel captured this scene and the news went viral that this powerful alien could make a Ferrari fly!

Radhika and her family were seated in the living room, when they saw Drudan on the television. They were petrified to see him.

This Drudan had tried killing Anika once and was now going to rule the Earth. Radhika rushed inside her room to find the crystal ball which Anika had sent. Radhika's heart was sinking 'If Drudan has conquered this world, what happened to Anika and others in Zynpagua?' Frantically she tried locating the crystal ball.

Chapter 40

Drudan

Radhika found the crystal ball and peering in it softly called out 'Frederick, can you hear me?'

There was no response.

Radhika cleared her throat and emphatically called out yet again 'Frederick, can you hear me?'

Some visions began to appear on the crystal ball and then suddenly Drudan appeared and said 'Hello!'

Radhika panicked seeing him. Drudan laughed aloud and said 'Hello Ma'am, this is Drudan, the evil scientist. I don't like people disobeying me. Why were you trying to connect with Frederick? I can catch all signals moving from the Earth.'

Radhika continued to gape at him. Drudan looked intently in her eyes and screamed 'Don't you dare disobey me. I have sent my soldiers to capture you. Welcome to my jail!'

Drudan laughed viciously. Radhika turned around and saw men in red uniform in her balcony. They broke the door and arrested Radhika and her parents.

The angel birds were sitting on the tree, watching Drudan take over the entire world. They were shocked to see Radhika and her parents being brought by Drudan's soldiers. The red bird secretly followed them. Radhika and her parents were taken to the palace jail on the Arabian Sea.

The red bird hurriedly flew to inform the other angel birds. They had to rush back to Zynpagua to let Sussaina and Lady Carol know about Drudan's rule.

They had noticed the place in the sea from where Drudan had risen. Anika could be in the sea from where Drudan had come out.

Before Drudan cast spells to stop any movement from the Earth, the angel birds had to reach Sussaina.

Using the disappearing spell they became invisible and flew with full force towards Zynpagua.

Chapter 41

Vivian

Vivian and Mootu flew towards the Earth.

Sussaina had instructed Vivian to fly on peregrine birds and not use magic, so that he could meet the angel birds on the way.

When they were about to enter the hemisphere of the Earth, Vivian heard a piercing sound. He tapped the peregrine falcons to stop. On looking around he saw the angel birds fluttering in the air. The red bird flew towards Vivian and said 'Drudan has conquered the Earth. His magical army of men has spread everywhere. Where are you going?'

'Angels, Leo drank the magical water and is suffering in pain. Lady Carol has read in the book of solutions that such water kills the person, if it is unable to unite his soul. We need Romeo to transfer poison in his body. This seems to be the only solution to save Leo. If we fail, Leo might die.'

'Oh!' exclaimed the red bird. 'We have seen the place in the ocean from where Drudan emerged. I am sure Anika is down there in the ocean. We are coming with you 'said the red bird.

'Thank you angels, let us leave immediately' said Vivian

'Hold on, please use the disappearance spell and make all of us invisible. Drudan has created a magical army which is floating everywhere. They might catch us' said the red bird.

'Thank you Angel' saying this Vivian raised his hand and said 'Disappear for others, to be seen only by us. Never show your face till my voice commands'

'How do we know that we cannot be seen by others? As of now I can see everyone' asked Mootu.

'Sir, I have used a magical spell that makes us invisible for others but we can see each other' said Vivian

'How do we test this?' asked Mootu

'We will come to know once we enter the Earth. Instead of flying, I am using magic to reach the city of Kanya Kumari. It will hasten everything' said Vivian

'Surely' said Mootu

Vivian raised his hand and said 'Take us to the beach of Kanya Kumari'

In a few seconds everyone disappeared and reappeared near the palm tree on the beach.

Men armed in red were busy whipping few fishermen. Vivian got a fit of rage seeing the scene, but the red bird stopped him 'Don't do anything now. Let us first reach Romeo and Anika. Any commotion here will alert Drudan and he is much more powerful under the rule of demon planets.'

Then the red bird flew ahead and hovered over the Arabian Sea. She chirped aloud 'Vivian, this is the place from where Drudan had risen'

Suddenly they saw a group of men in red uniform, coming towards them. One of them said 'Where did you hear voices? I can't see anything?'

Vivian and Mootu stopped their breath so that the men could not sense them. They were invisible but their breath could be felt. The red bird was hovering on the sea and could not stop fluttering her wings. Drudan's men followed the movement of the air and reached the place where the red bird was. The red bird flew away from the place, with the men in red uniform chasing her with the movement of the wind.

Vivian yelled 'We have to save the red bird!'

But the other angel birds suggested 'Vivian you enter the sea till the men are chasing the red bird. We will follow these men and flutter in all directions so that they get confused. Do not worry about us but enter the sea before anyone notices'

Saying this, the angel birds flew in the direction of the men and distracted them.

Seeing them safe, Vivian picked Mootu and magically flew towards the sea. He then dived in the place from where Drudan had appeared. Vivian and Mootu were quite surprised that there were no guards in the sea.

As they reached the depth of the ocean, Mootu whispered 'Vivian, if you start feeling giddy, just remember to chew the Mana leaves in your pocket. You will feel better'

'How do we know where we have to go? I am feeling choked' said Vivian

'Don't worry; just place a Mana leaf in your mouth. You will get acclimatized to the sea in sometime.'

Vivian placed Mana leaf in his mouth. Soon he began to feel better. He did not know how to swim but had managed to float in water with magic. The sea was so vast and they did not know where to go.

Moreover they feared that sea worms would capture them.

Mootu asked Vivian 'Can you find where Anika is with the help of magic? You are able to float in the sea, which means your magic is working in water'

'Great idea Sir, I can trace Anika with magic. I feel my brain has stopped working in this moment of crisis.' Vivian reacted.

'Don't panic, just be composed. In threatening times, it is the will of a person that determines victory' said Mootu.

'Thank you Sir' said Vivian. He then closed his eyes and whispered

'Spell of magic working in this sea
I have to set Anika my sister free
Can you tell me where is she?'

Saying this, Vivian blew air in the sea. It instantly started creating a route in the sea. Vivian held Mootu and magically dived ahead to follow the route. They were cruising inside with great speed with gushing seawater splashing on their faces. After sometime, they saw a region in the deep sea, where there were patches of land. Several worms were crawling outside this area. On looking closer, Vivian saw a small cave.

Vivian took a deep breath and said 'My magical abilities be with me. Ensure none can see Mootu Sir and me.'

Saying this, with minimal speed, Vivian moved towards the cave, holding Mootu. The opening to the cave was oval and almost the size of a football. Vivian let Mootu get in first and then he murmured 'Magic dear, reduce my size and let me in here'.

Vivian shrunk in size and entered the cave. It was very dark inside and both Mootu and Vivian kept swimming in darkness. After sometime, they saw some light coming from a corner of the tunnel they were passing through. Mootu held Vivian's hand and said 'Swim this way'

They dashed forward and as they approached the light and swam ahead, they saw rock boxes with thick bar like structures in which strange sea creatures were kept. Many sea worms were freely crawling outside these boxes, as if guarding them. *Is this some kind of a jail?* Vivian thought.

Just then Mootu pulled Vivian's hand and whispered 'These worms are talking about Romeo'

Vivian came closer to Mootu and bent his head to listen to their conversation but it was sounding gibberish. They were murmuring in some unknown language but were taking names of Romeo and Anika. Then, one of the worms hurried in the direction of another cave. Vivian and Mootu followed him.

As they reached the other side of the cave, Vivian gasped 'Anika!'

She was lying unconscious on a huge mushroom, with her leg swollen and blue. She looked frail and famished. Vivian rushed towards her and hugged her. Anika instantly opened her eyes to see who was holding her, but there was no one.

Vivian whispered 'Anika, my sister, I am here. You cannot see me'.

Anika stared in the air. 'Brother Vivian, are you here?' she whispered.

Vivian murmured 'Magic dear, make Mootu Sir and me visible only to my sister'

Instantly Anika could see Vivian. Tears of joy rolled down her eyes.

The giggle of the mermaid alerted her 'She is coming' she warned.

'Who is coming?' asked Vivian

'The mermaid is coming. Don't do any magic now. If she senses it, she will capture you' Anika replied.

Vivian nodded.

The mermaid swam in. She was the most stunning woman Vivian had ever seen. She came close to Anika and said 'I have good news for you'. Anika looked at her feebly.

The mermaid smiled and said 'I have decided to kill the snake clan'

Anika was shocked to hear that. 'I promise I will impress the stars. Please don't kill them' she urged.

The mermaid did not respond. She clapped her hands to call the worms.

Several sea worms came marching in with a huge axe.

Anika yelled 'No!'

But the sea worms pulled out a key and opened the lock of the jail. They dragged Romeo out and held him tightly. Another set of worms straightened the axe.

Vivian, who was invisible to others, instantly whispered 'Magic dear, stop this axe and put everyone to sleep!'

While the spell stopped the axe midair, it could not put anyone to sleep. 'It seems your magic does not work on sea creatures' whispered Mootu.

'Why is the axe not moving?' yelled the Mermaid

The sea worms were shocked as well. Vivian knew that soon mermaid would use her magic to find who is around. He was also worried that she might capture them. If this happens, how would he save Leo! Thinking fast, Vivian stepped forward and tightly held the mermaid. He hit her hard on the neck and she fainted.

The sea worms could not understand what happened to the mermaid. Vivian pronounced 'Magic dear make Mootu and me appear'.

Holding the Mermaid, Vivian said 'Sea worms, back off or I will kill the mermaid!'

Vivian yelled 'Romeo, I need your help to save Leo. If we are unable to reach Zynpagua within twenty four hours, Leo will die'

Romeo smiled and said 'I am coming with you Vivian. Can I take my family along?'

'Of course' said Vivian

By this time the mermaid began to toss and turn. Vivian pointed his hand towards Anika's leg and said 'Heal my sister's wound and give her strength'

But Anika's wound did not heal. Vivian yelled 'Anika I am unable to cure your wound, let us leave immediately, the mermaid will wake up in no time'

'No brother, I cannot go. If I leave the sea, the mermaid will kill father!'

'Where is father? Let us quickly rescue him' said Vivian

'No, the mermaid will wake up any moment. She may then use special sea magic and capture all of us' said Romeo

'Brother, you leave with Romeo, Mashy and their family. I will stay back' said Anika

'I will stay with you Anika. I know where King Soto is' said Mashy

'Even I will stay with you' said Mootu

'No, please don't stake your life' said Anika

By then, Vivian heard the mermaid murmur Drudan's name.

Romeo instantly said 'Vivian hurry, let us leave. Anika is right, if she leaves the sea, the mermaid will turn violent and kill King Soto. Mashy and Mootu, you hide behind the rock. When the mermaid wakes up, she should see Anika. By then we would have crossed the sea. Once the mermaid leaves, Mashy you take Anika to King Soto.'

Chapter 42

The Escape

The mermaid opened her eyes once but fainted again.

Vivian yelled 'Romeo hurry' and saying this he held his hand up

'My magic will carry Romeo, his family and me out from the sea' saying this Vivian swam out of the cave with a lightning speed. Romeo and the snakes followed him with the same speed.

Once Vivian had left, Mootu and Mashy hid behind the boulder. Anika somehow moved her leg and swam towards the mermaid. She tenderly stroked her forehead and said 'Wake up mermaid. Are you hurt?'

The mermaid gently opened her eyes. She had splitting headache and the back of her neck had turned blue. Anika stroked her neck gently. It was swollen and looked sprained.

The mermaid could not move her neck and tears of pain gushed out from her eyes. Before interacting with Anika, the mermaid began to murmur 'Drudan, can you hear me?' She looked in trance attentively and asked 'Drudan, can you hear me?'

Drudan's voice could be heard coming from a distance. 'Yes Senorita, what is the matter. You don't sound well'

'A young boy just attacked me and has taken the snakes with him. My neck is wounded and I cannot move. Don't let him escape, catch him. He may be coming out from the sea.'

Drudan fumed 'How dare someone hurt you? I will give this boy death, whoever he is'

'I think he can do magic and had entered the sea in an invisible state' said the mermaid.

'It means Vivian had entered the sea. Where is Anika?' asked Drudan

'She is here. Who is Vivian?' asked the mermaid

'Anika's brother.' said Drudan

'Then you must catch him fast. It is very strange that he had come to rescue the snakes and not this dame' said the mermaid.

'Drudan you must catch him. My neck hurts terribly. Let me first take care of it' saying this, the mermaid blew air on her palm and rubbed it slowly against her neck. Then she gently turned her head towards left and right.

'Yes, now I feel better' she murmured and looked at Anika.

'You sly girl, I know you stayed back for your father. Don't play tricks with me.'

'Guards, come fast. Lock her in the same cell where the snakes were trapped. Don't give her any food. Once she dies, you can feast on her' ordered the mermaid.

'No!' exclaimed Mootu.

'Shhhh...she will sense you' said Mashy.

The worms circled around Anika and stuffed her in the snake's cell. Then, one of the worms pulled out a big key from his mouth and locking the cell, swallowed the key.

'The worm has swallowed the key. How are we going to rescue Anika? They look just the same, how will we locate which worm has the key?' asked Mootu.

'They look the same to you Sir. For me they are all different. I can recognize them from their mouth. Each worm has a different mouth' whispered Mashy.

'Did I just hear someone' asked the mermaid, looking around.

Anika instantly realized that the mermaid was sensing Mashy and Mootu. She immediately began to pray aloud 'Oh God, save me!'.

The mermaid pepped inside the cellar and saw Anika praying. She giggled hysterically and said 'Your God is sleeping. Our demon planets are ruling. No one can save you.'

Anika did not respond. She closed her eyes and pretended to be weak.

The mermaid looked at her and said 'Oh my poor girl! I wish I could take you out of the cell and make you work. I detest weaklings and that is what you seem to me'.

Anika did not respond. The mermaid stared at her and murmured 'Useless girl'. She turned and swam away, leaving Anika being guarded by the worms.

After the mermaid had left, Mootu sat on Mashy. They came out from the hiding, prepared to attack the worms. Mashy had told Mootu that attacking the worms on the face injures them.

As the worms saw the two, they charged towards them. While Mashy used his tail to attack their heads, Mootu balanced himself on his two hands and raised his body to hit on their heads with his leather back shell.

The blow was so hard that the worms fainted instantly.

Just then Mashy cried 'He is running away...the worm with the Key'

'Catch him fast' cried Mootu

Mashy dashed high up in water and landed on the worm. He squealed as Mashy throttled his neck and forced him to vomit the key. Then Mootu balanced himself on one hand and rotating his body, hit his shell on the worm's face. He fainted. When they turned around, they saw other worms wriggling away.

Mashy dashed towards Anika's cell and opened it. 'Anika, quickly sit on my back. We will leave immediately. The worms would be coming back with weapons' instructed Mashy.

By then Anika's wounded leg had become totally swollen and blue and she was struggling to move it.

She began to weep 'Mashy, I can't move my leg. What should I do? I promised mother, I would save father and would return to Zynpagua'

Mashy and Mootu pulled Anika out from the cell. Then Mashy went close to Anika's leg and inspected it.'

'This looks like you have been wounded by a poisoned weapon' said Mashy

'Yes, Drudan attacked me with a dagger. Romeo pulled out the dagger.....but'

'If this poison is of a sea creature, my saliva will cure it' saying this Mashy spitted on the wound.

Anika screamed with pain as the wound began to burn. Mootu held her hand tightly. Soon a blue liquid seeped out from Anika's leg.

'God, this is the severest form of poison. How are you alive?' asked Mashy, absolutely shocked.

'We have been blessed by rays of Mars which has made our body very strong. That is why the poison could not kill me' said Anika

'Try moving your leg now' said Mashy

Anika moved her leg. It felt lighter and better and she could move it.

'Thank you so much. I can move it' she replied gratefully.

'But don't strain you leg. It will take time to recover. Come and sit on my back' said Mashy.

Anika and Mootu sat on Mashy's back and instantly left the place, hitting the worms that came on their way. Once they were out of the jail, Anika said 'Mashy we have to find father before the mermaid harms him.'

'Yes Anika, we are on our way. The mermaid cannot travel faster than me even if she can sense me.'

They cruised through the foaming sea, rising and falling on the waves. Anika looked at the Moon. The sky still had a reddish tint and the Moon seemed totally shadowed. *I wish the stars could support me,* she thought.

Suddenly Anika saw an army of sea worms darting towards them.

She yelled 'Mashy, watch out. Worms!'

These worms had spades and spears in their mouth. A few were also holding long and thin swords in their mouth.

Mashy instantly slowed down and gasped 'Oh my God! The mermaid has alerted the special sea worm force. They are ravenous and swallow the sea creatures alive. They are armed with poisonous swords and spears!'

'What do we do now?' asked Mootu.

'The only way to escape them is to jump high up in the air' said Mashy.

'But Drudan might catch us there. I have seen his red army of uniformed men, hovering over the sea' said Mootu.

'We can fight these worms? ' Anika suggested

'How? We have no weapons and the swords they are carrying are poisonous. One prick and you will faint immediately' said Mashy.

Anika looked around. The worms were circling them from everywhere. She peeped down but the depth of the sea was unfathomable.

She said 'Mashy, we have just one option. Dive deep inside the sea with great speed. I cannot see any worms down there'

'Anika, I have never gone so deep in the sea. Romeo always said that the snakes are unable to swim in great depths due to the strange water down there. What if I am unable to move a limb?' asked Mashy.

'Anika and I will carry you safely' said Mootu.

By this time the special action sea worms had circled them totally. Mashy yelled 'Let's go!' and dived in the deep sea. As they sank lower, none of them could move their limbs.

The sea worms were circulating above but none dived deeper. Both Mootu and Mashy began to gasp and struggle. Anika too was finding it difficult to navigate the sea. 'What do we do now?' asked Anika. Mootu thought for a minute and said 'Anika, let us lie still. The worms might think we are dead and leave the place'.

The three agreed on the suggestion and began to float in water, without moving a limb. The worms thought that they had died. The mermaid had specially instructed the worms not to kill

Anika. Thus the worms panicked. The mermaid would be furious about Anika's death. In a state of panic, they rushed back to inform the mermaid.

Anika, Mootu and Mashy took advantage of this and quickly swam up and rushed towards the place where King Soto was locked.

Mashy yelled 'Can you see the scum? Just behind the scum are the deserted caves. King Soto is locked there'

Chapter 43

King Soto

Anika moved her limbs aggressively, in an attempt to reach her father soon. Mashy led her inside the dark caves. It was murky and filled with a pungent smell. The place was so foul and slippery that Anika felt she would vomit. The thought that her father had been locked here for almost eleven years, shook her completely.

As she swam ahead, she froze. Her father was tied with dirty weeds and was floating in that pungent water. His skin had become swollen and green and he hung there lifelessly.

Anika continued to gape at her father, without moving, without uttering a word. Mootu and Mashy rushed ahead and pulled away the weeds that were wound around King Soto. But his hands were tied with some rubbery string and Mashy could not pull it out.

He rushed back to Anika and said 'I am unable to untie his hands, can you please help us'. When Anika did not answer, Mashy asked again.

'I think she is in a state of shock. Mashy, fill water in your mouth and sprinkle on her face' Instructed Mootu

Mashy filled water in his mouth and splashed on Anika's face.

She immediately came back from her state of shock and said 'Oh father!'

'Hurry up, the mermaid can come any moment' yelled Mashy

Anika swam ahead and touched king Soto. His body was so swollen that he whispered 'ah!' in pain. Without giving in to her emotions, Anika quickly pulled the weeds, but could not untie his hands and legs.

'Time is running fast, use your teeth to tear this string' instructed Mootu

Thus Mashy and Anika placed the string between their teeth and began to grind them. Mashy was able to break the string first and told Anika

'You pull the string out from the hands while I chew the one which ties the leg'

Anika's jaws were already hurting. She thanked Mashy for the kindness, and quickly pulled out the weed that was tying King Soto's hands. As she did that, blood started oozing out from her palms. The weed was very rough which caused a painful irritation in her hands. 'If by merely touching it, I am feeling the pain, father has been tied with it for years' this thought saddened her even more and weeping, she kissed King Soto on the cheeks.

'Who?' murmured King Soto, trying to open his eyes.

Anika whispered 'Father!'

'Go away vicious mermaid. None of your tricks will work on me' said King Soto, with eyes half open.

'I am not the mermaid, father! I am your daughter Anika and I have come to rescue you' said Anika.

'Do I have a daughter?' murmured King Soto.

Before Anika could reply Mashy exclaimed 'Yes, I have untied the legs now. Anika let us leave'

Anika looked at King Soto. He had fainted again and his hands and legs had become limp, which were droopily floating in the sea.

'How are we going to take father? How will he swim?' voiced Anika.

'Never mind, Mashy just place King Soto on my hump. I will carry him' said Mootu

'Don't worry Sir, I will wound myself around him and pull him with me. You are so tiny, how you will carry his weight?' Mashy asked.

'Don't worry about that Mashy. You just give us the directions to get out from the sea' said Mootu.

'Sir I will do both, carry King Soto and give you directions. Trust me I can do both'

Just then they heard the mermaid giggle. She was standing at the entrance of the cave.

Mashy first looked at the mermaid and then at King Soto. In a split of a second, Mashy dashed towards King Soto, wrapped himself around him and swam towards a small exit that opened from the other end of the cave, yelling

'Anika and Mootu....swim fast and follow me.'

Anika and Mootu followed him immediately.

'Catch them and bring them to me at once 'yelled the mermaid.

Anika could not catch up with Mashy.

Mootu instructed Mashy to swim as fast as he could while he slowed down with Anika. Mashy went ahead with King Soto. The mermaid and her soldiers were very close now. Seeing Anika's inability to swim with speed, Mootu instructed Anika 'Let's swim vertically down and try reaching the depth of the sea. I am sure the mermaid will not be able to catch us.'

This decision was taken just in the nick of time. The mermaid had almost reached the spot when Mootu and Anika dived deep in.

'That snake and that man Soto are not with them. Catch them first, these two will come chasing them' instructed the mermaid

Chapter 44

Vivian

As Vivian came out of the sea, Drudan's army of red men was waiting for him. While Vivian had used the disappearance spell, Drudan yelled 'Coward son of Soto and creatures with him, appear now!' as he sensed someone coming out from the sea.

Vivian and the others were visible instantly.

Seeing Vivian, Drudan yelled 'capture them at once'

Vivian turned around and told Romeo 'I will face him while you escape and reach Zynpagua. Do not wait for me'

Saying this, Vivian came out from the sea and faced Drudan 'Why can we not fight valiantly? I try magic on you and you try on me, is no game. If you have courage, challenge me for a combat, a physical fight, where we face each other and none else'

Drudan roared aloud. Seeing Drudan distracted, Vivian nudged Romeo and said 'please escape.'

By then Drudan noticed Romeo and he ordered his uniformed men to trap him. Romeo and his family spewed venom on the men, which made deep fissures in their skin and caused such pain that the men fell down.

Vivian yelled once again as he stood in front of Drudan for a combat 'Romeo run, fly away. Zynpagua needs you!'

When Drudan saw his red uniformed men fall in the sea, he created more force. But by then Romeo and his family had escaped.

The angel birds were sitting on the coconut trees, waiting for Vivian. They had hidden themselves behind the huge coconuts which were hanging from the trees.

Drudan ordered his men 'Catch this rat Vivian and bring him to me.'

Vivian yelled 'magic dear, please give me a sword right here'

The sword appeared in his hand and with the speed of lightening; he dashed ahead and attacked the men. While they were magically created, none could match Vivian's agility and gallantry. Soon they were lying wounded on the shore.

Vivian bellowed 'Drudan, I challenge you for a combat'.

Drudan pounced on Vivian. He soon realized that Vivian had become much stronger and adept since their last confrontation in Zynpagua. Vivian could have defeated Drudan easily if the demon planets were not ruling. Drudan continued to attack Vivian with his sword but could not overpower him.

Suddenly a thought entered his mind.

When demon planets rule, deceit is a good weapon for victory. Thinking this, Drudan grabbed a fistful of sand from the beach and threw it in Vivian's eyes. Vivian lost control as the sand entered his eyes. Taking advantage of the situation, Drudan hit sword on Vivian who jumped back but the tip of the sword sliced the skin on his chest and he began to bleed.

Drudan instantly used magic and ordered 'Tie his hands and cover his face and stop him from uttering any magical spell.'

Within seconds, Vivian's mouth got gagged and his hands and legs tied with a rope. He helplessly fell on the ground.

Drudan laughed aloud and said 'All is fair in love and war'

Vivian struggled to get up, but could not.

'I will kill you now, before you play any games with me' saying this Drudan pulled out his sword to kill Vivian

'No, don't do that' the melodious voice of the mermaid stopped him.

Drudan halted 'Mermie, is that you?' he asked.

'Yes, it is me. Don't kill Vivian; instead use him to get Sussaina and her family from Zynpagua. Give them a day to come. If they fail, just kill Vivian. Anika has escaped, and I will use Vivian as bait to trap her' she asserted.

Drudan laughed aloud and said 'I am married to the most intelligent and beautiful woman in the world'

The mermaid giggled and said 'Take care and hope to see you soon'

'Very soon, let me capture Sussaina and then we can live happily ever after' said Drudan.

'I will wait for you Drudan' said the mermaid with a pang of pain. She was already missing him.

Chapter 45

The war begins

Romeo reached Zynpagua and informed Sussaina about Vivian's capture. Sussaina was shocked to hear that.

Romeo was immediately taken to Leo's room. Lady Carol was sitting beside Leo, holding his hand. Leo was unconscious and his body shuddering with pain. When Lady Carol saw Romeo, tears of hope and joy rolled down her eyes.

She rushed towards Romeo and said 'Thank you for coming'

Romeo nodded and smiled feebly. A sense of guilt overtook him. He was Drudan's accomplice who had tricked Leo to drink the magical water.

'I know the magical water can be carried on poison. Is there a way to inject poison in Leo's body so that the magical water inside him does not harm him' asked Lady Carol

Romeo was perplexed. How was he going to transmit poison in Leo's body without harming him?

'What is the matter Romeo? Tell me can you do it?' she repeated.

'I do not know Lady. I am a very poisonous snake. What if my venom harms him?'

'He is a strong boy and has faced many atrocities from his father. Please try infusing poison in his blood.' Lady Carol requested.

Romeo bent low and gently stung Leo's hand. He then gradually commenced transmitting poison in Leo's body. As he did that, Leo began to turn bluish but his shuddering stopped.

Lady Carol panicked as Leo stopped moving. She touched his nose to feel his breath. He was breathing. She placed her ears on his heart. It was beating, in fact beating faster. She placed her hand on Leo's forehead and said 'Son, can you hear me?' Leo did not respond.

She looked at Romeo and said 'I think he is fine but why is he not waking?' asked Lady Carol.

'Lady, a snake's poison is heavy and dangerous. I am surprised it did not harm him. It is too early to say anything. Let us wait for some more time' Romeo replied.

Lady Carol and Romeo sat beside Leo for another hour, intermittently checking his pulse and heartbeat. Everything seemed normal to them. But Leo was not responding.

Two hours passed then three and then four but Leo did not wake. Frederick and Sussaina also joined Lady Carol in the room.

'Don't worry Lady, he will be fine' Sussaina comforted Lady Carol.

Lady Carol looked around and asked Sussaina 'Where is Vivian? Is he with Femina?'

Sussaina smiled feebly and said 'Let us first cure Leo'.

'Where is Vivian?' asked Lady Carol, in a state of panic.

'Drudan has captured him' Sussaina replied.

'No!' exclaimed Lady Carol

'What are we going to do now?' she asked.

'Brace courage and attack with all our might' said Sussaina

Someone knocked at the door just then. It was Femina. She was struggling to walk, but her countenance clearly revealed that she was determined to overpower all weakness.

She walked in and said 'I am with you mother Sussaina. Just give me a day to practice and gain strength and I will lead our army'

'I am proud of you my daughter' said Sussaina

Lady Carol came closer and hugging her hard, she said 'My magic will give you strength'

Moving back she asked 'Are you feeling better?'

'No Lady, I think magic is failing to cure me. Please don't worry; I am much better than before. Milk, bananas and good meals are helping me gain strength' said Femina

Lady Carol hugged her and said 'My courageous girl. Yes I know by tomorrow our bravest soldier would be ready'

'Is Leo still sleeping?' asked someone from behind. It was Romeo's father, an old snake who wriggled in slowly.

'Yes father' said Romeo

'Should I try once? I have been living for more than hundred years. My poison can make him conscious'

'Please Sir, please try' requested Lady Carol

The old snake wriggled up and sat beside Leo on his bed and continued to observe him. After sometime, he looked around and told Lady Carol 'I think there is too much concentration of poison in his brain which is keeping him unconscious. See his forehead. Has it not become a shade of dark blue?'

Lady Carol looked perturbed 'What are we going to do now? 'She asked.

'I think we need to ensure that the venom circulates in his body' said the old snake.

'If venom circulates in his body won't he die?' asked Lady Carol

'He is sleeping peacefully and is in a much better state than before. I think the venom is helping him' said Sussaina

Frederick walked in just then and asked 'How is Leo?'

'Still sleeping' said Sussaina

'Frederick, can you please make Leo sit' requested Lady Carol

'Yes of course' saying this Frederick placed his hand behind Leo's back and helped him sit.

Leo stirred a little which built some hopes in everyone. Frederick was still holding him.

'He is moving, I think this suggestion is working' said Lady Carol

'Yes, you are right. Then should we make him walk?' asked Lady Carol

'I think there is no harm in trying' said Romeo's father.

'Frederick can you make him walk?' asked Sussaina

'Sure mother' responded Frederick and tried making Leo stand. He held his shoulders and pulled him up. Leo jerked his head and whispered 'Anika!'

'He is calling Anika! Frederick balance his weight and help him walk' instructed Lady Carol, watching Leo attentively.

Frederick staggered but could not pull Leo forward to walk.

'Let me help you' said Femina.

'My child, you are very weak, don't strain yourself' Sussaina said.

'No mother, I am fine. Please let me help' saying this, Femina held Leo's left hand and sliding her shoulder below his shoulder, gave Leo support. Frederick then supported Leo and together they made him walk.

After two or three round, Leo feebly opened his eyes and said 'Aunt Sussaina!'

'How are you feeling now Leo?' asked Sussaina

But Leo continued 'Aunt Sussaina, Anika is in the deep sea. She is wounded, and is struggling to swim!'

Lady Carol and Sussaina were surprised. How did Leo know where Anika was.

Leo was still in a subconscious state and continued to utter 'She just escaped the worms. She is swimming fast but struggling to breathe' Saying this Leo fainted again.

Tears began to pour from Sussaina's eyes, listening to Leo.

'This too shall pass' she whispered

Chapter 46

Femina

Femina came out from Leo's room and headed straight towards the stables. She had overheard Sussaina tell Lady Carol about Vivian's arrest. The memory of Vivian, her best friend and love, forced her to take charge of her frail body and prepare for the war with Drudan.

She was feeling very weak and exhausted. She pushed herself to reach the stables, mount her horse and gallop to the house where once Vivian stayed. This was the same place where she had trained Anika.

As she reached the place, the recollection of Drudan's violet rays entering Anika's heart and annihilating her soul, became fresh in her mind. That was the last time she was here. She closed her eyes to stop the flow of all the terrible memories that were disturbing her.

She dismounted the horse and walked towards the patch where she had trained Anika previously. She raced her eyes to and fro, trying to find a symbol. A flicker of smile appeared on her parched lips as she located the sign of the star on a nearby tree. She instantly rushed towards the tree and began to claw the mud at its root. Unable to make much progress, she got up and feebly walked towards her horse, only to fall down midway.

'I have to be strong to fight Drudan' she murmured and dragged herself to sit. Overwhelmed with weakness and grief, she began to cry.

Just then, she heard a sound. On turning around she saw Frederick approaching the place. He got off the horse and rushed towards Femina 'Are you alright Femina? Why have you come here? I was worried for you and therefore followed you' he said.

'I came here to fetch my old sword. It will be easier for me to fight with my sword. We have to leave tomorrow and I thought of using this night for practicing. My body feels like stone and I am in dire need of practice' said Femina.

Frederick smiled and nodded 'Alright then, let us practice. Where is your sword?'

'I had hidden it beneath that tree' replied Femina.

Frederick rushed back and pulled out a bottle and an apple from a bag hanging on the horse 'Femina drink some water and have the apple. You need energy. In the meanwhile, I will dig out that precious sword.'

Frederick walked towards the nearby bush and picked a thick branch of tree which had fallen there. He took the branch till the tree and began to dig near its roots. Though the job of digging with the branch was tough, he somehow continued removing the mud. The sound of the branch hitting something hard made him stop. He quickly removed the loose mud with his hands and pulled out a sword sullied with moisture and mud.

Walking back to Femina, he asked 'Is this the one?'

Her face brightened and eyes lit up instantly. 'Yes!' she exclaimed, grabbing the sword.

'Femina can I practice with you?' asked Frederick.

'Yes of course. But you don't have a weapon' said Femina

'Hang on, I have carried it along.' Saying this Frederick rushed back to the horse and pulled out a sword from the bag he was carrying.

Racing back towards Femina, he said 'I quickly borrowed the sword from the palace guard when I saw you mount the horse'

Femina smiled and stood up. As she held the sword, its weight felt like thousand elephants. She could not even lift it. In a state of despair, she sat down.

Frederick got concerned seeing her. She really had no strength to face Drudan.

'Listen, please stay back with Leo. You will put yourself in danger if you come with us' asserted Frederick

Tears were rolling down Femina's eyes but with a look of determination she said 'Don't discourage me! If you want to help me, please practice with me.'

Frederick nodded and picked up his sword. He then voiced aloud 'Alright Femina, I am challenging you. Get up now!'

Femina staggered and got up. Before she could pick her sword, Frederick hit it. The sword fell far away. Femina took a deep breath and rushed towards the sword. She yelled with all her might 'Drudan, I hate you' and lifted her sword and hit on Frederick's. This time she continued the fight for some time and then fell down.

Frederick ran back to his horse and pulled out two bananas. Offering them to Femina, he said 'Femina please have them for gaining strength. Lady Carol instructed me to give them to you'

Femina devoured both hungrily. She thanked Frederick and commenced practicing again. The bananas gave her the much needed strength.

Both Frederick and Femina continued practicing till dawn, when they heard the morning bugle being played. Both mounted their horses and raced towards the palace.

Chapter 47

Flight to the Earth

'Queen Sussaina, please hurry. Drudan is killing Vivian' chirped the red bird as she flew inside the palace fluttering her wings nervously.

Sussaina was taken aback. 'What?' asked Sussaina.

'Please hurry and stop Drudan. He is killing Vivian' said the red bird, in a state of panic.

Sussaina immediately looked towards the Earth and traced Drudan with her special vision. Vivian had been tied to a tree and Drudan was going to shoot him with a gun.

'Wait Drudan' yelled Sussaina.

Clearing her throat she yelled even louder 'Drudan wait, can you hear me, wait you coward!'

Drudan looked up at the sky and said 'Who is calling me?'

'Sussaina...this is Sussaina Drudan and I warn you, don't you dare touch Vivian'

'Oh my God, the mother is yelling from the sky' laughed Drudan hysterically.

'My son is a brave boy and if you kill him, it is the worst death a valiant boy can get by being killed by a coward.'

Drudan laughed even more hysterically and said 'I have captured your son and I am a coward?'

'Yes, you are a coward. I challenge you, face us in war and then dare to kill us. Is there any valour in killing a boy who is tied? Set him free and fight out. I am coming with my army. First defeat us and then you can kill us. I dare you to defeat us' said Sussaina

'You dare me??' Drudan laughed hysterically yet again.

'Yes I dare you!' Sussaina screamed.

'You have only tomorrow. Come with your army by noon, if you delay, then ....' he laughed uncontrollably.

'Do you understand? Come by noon tomorrow!' he bellowed.

'I am coming Drudan. Brace courage you coward' yelled Sussaina, challenging him.

'Come fast and meet the coward. I am dying to meet you' saying this Drudan laughed even louder.

Sussaina had fire in her eyes when she turned to speak to everyone. With firm countenance and a resolute will, she spoke aloud 'We are waging a war against Drudan. Frederick, Femina, Lady Carol, each of you will lead a team. Get your soldiers ready in next one hour.

Then turning to Romeo, she asked 'Romeo, will you be willing to help us?' Romeo raised his head and said 'Of course Queen Sussaina'

'Thank you Romeo' said Sussaina, and then turning to Femina, she asked 'Femina, my child, will you be able to bear a long journey and fight with a strong and magical army of Drudan?'

'Queen Sussaina, I am prepared to fight Drudan'

'My fearless girl' smiled Sussaina, hugging Femina, who looked frail and exhausted.

'Frederick, hurry and call the people of Zynpagua. We need volunteers for the war. See who is willing to come with us'

Men and women from Zynpagua came out from their underground houses and gathered around Sussaina.

Sussaina stood at the podium and declared 'My dear people, your prince Vivian has been captured by Drudan. I am leading a troop tomorrow, to wage a war against him. My people I will not force anyone to join us...'

Before Sussaina could complete, the people began to shout unanimously 'Dear Queen, we will come with you. Let us face Drudan and defeat him!'

They began to sing collectively

'We will win, we will win
And punish him for his sin
Cruel Drudan should die
Collectively we cry
Please queen take us with you
How can we convince you?
We are always with you
We will win, we will win
And punish him for his sin'

'Thank you my people, my children. Whoever wants to join us can put his hands up' Sussaina said aloud.

Everyone, including children raised their hands.

Sussaina declared 'Children will not go with us. I am leaving Leo behind because he is unconscious. Head cook; please take care of the children of Zynpagua and Leo in our absence. All ladies, please join Lady Carol in her team. All girls please join Femina, boys with Frederick and men with me. We will attack Drudan from East, West, North and South!'

Someone from the crowd came forward and said 'I will take care of Leo!' It was Sachinth Goel, the minister's son.

He told Sussaina 'Queen, I will take care of Leo and the children'

Sussaina smiled and patted Sachinth.

Someone asked Sussaina 'But Queen, how are we going to reach the Earth? We cannot fly and we don't know magic!'

Lady Carol was standing beside Sussaina. She looked up at the sky and clapped. Million of birds came flying in.

Sussaina pointed at them and said 'We will fly on the birds!'

Chapter 48

Anika

Anika and Mootu dived deep in the sea. While Mootu could still breathe, Anika began to gasp for breath. There was very little oxygen in such depths of the ocean. They managed to escape the soldiers, but Anika was gasping terribly. She was left with very little strength to swim. Mootu placed her on his hump and tried swimming, but he could not carry Anika's weight.

Anika had begun to get unconscious when Mootu suddenly remembered the Mana leaves which he had carried for Vivian. He quickly searched his pockets and found 5 Mana leaves. It was such a relief. Mootu immediately pulled out one of the five and gently tapped Anika on her cheeks 'Anika, open your eyes!'.

Anika blinked but could not respond. Mootu quickly thrust the Mana leaves in Anika's mouth and said 'Don't worry Anika, I am carrying the Mana leaves, start chewing them'

Anika struggled to grind her teeth, but garnered strength and chewed hard. As the juice of Mana leaves passed through her throat, she felt the pores of her skin widen and air percolate through them. She began to feel better.

'How are you feeling now?' asked Mootu, looking at her intently.

'Much better' said Anika

'Let us quickly find Mashy and King Soto. We have to leave the sea soon!' said Mootu.

'I wish I could save all the sea creatures locked in the cage' Anika voiced

'Yes, even I wish. They are my water mates and I genuinely want to save them. But we are not equipped to wage a war against the mermaid' said Mootu

'Ahhhh!' Anika screamed all of a sudden, placing her hand on her heart.

'What happened?' Mootu asked in a state of panic.

'Sir, sometimes I feel weird and get a strange pain in my heart' said Anika

'Swimming in the sea may have caused it' said Mootu.

Trying to forget the pain, Anika asked 'How are we going to find Mashy?'

'That is exactly what I am thinking. When I was in Zynpagua, I could communicate with the sea creatures by sending vibration through water. Every specie has a different limit to catch vibrations. Let me try sending some. We may be able to spot Mashy'

Saying this, Mootu began to blow air from his mouth and vibrate his lips. This caused ripples in water. Mootu continued vibrating his lips for a very long time, but did not get any response.

'None of the sea animals are able to catch the vibrations' said Mootu sadly.

'Sir, please try sending all types of vibrations. Mashy may be able to catch one of them' suggested Anika.

Mootu nodded and commenced vibrating his lips again, this time sending vibrations gradually. Anika was about to say something, when Mootu exclaimed 'Wait! Someone is receiving these vibrations and sending me signals through the waves.'

'I hope it is not the mermaid 'said Anika.

'No, these vibrations are very low. A mermaid would not be able to catch them!'Replied Mootu

'Then who could it be?' asked Anika

'I'm not sure but someone from the snake family or a mammal' said Mootu

Chapter 49

Flight to the Earth

Sussaina and Lady Carol sat on the Peregrine falcon, while Frederick and Femina on the angel birds. They had worn fitting clothes covering fully their body and hands.

Metal masks covered their faces leaving only the eyes while their hands and legs were covered with metal coverings. The red bird had used *Chin chunaki chin chin* to reduce everyone's size to travel on birds.

Most of the people of Zynpagua were accompanying them. They had mounted the birds and had formed armies as per Sussaina's instructions. Many people from the kingdom of clouds were also flying with them.

Lady Carol used a magical spell on all the birds, to ensure they reach India in a day.

She wanted to see Leo for the last time before she left. So she dismounted the falcon and rushed towards Leo's room to check on him. He was still unconscious but was uttering 'She can't breathe. There is water everywhere. She is searching for the snake, the good snake!'

By this time both Lady Carol and Sussaina had realized that Leo had been talking about Anika. The magical water that he had drunk had connected him with Anika somehow. But the pressing problem was saving Vivian. Thus Lady Carol ignored what Leo was murmuring.

She kissed him on his forehead and left the room.

Dawn was breaking when Sussaina commanded

'My people, I will reach the Earth from the Northern direction, while Lady Carol will enter from the Southern, Femina from the East and Frederick from the West. But before we leave, let me pray to the Moon.

Joining her hands, she sat down on her knees and looking up at the sky, she said 'Oh Moon, I will fight for the sake of righteousness. Let the evil demon planets rule the sky, but never has evil won over good. I bow before you to send me divine blessings!'

She closed her eyes and prayed for some time.

Then, with a thundering voice she commanded 'We will win, come what may, we have to win' saying this she raised her flag and said 'Femina, leads first.' Femina yelled 'Yes Lady' and flew up in the sky on the red angel bird. Romeo and girls mounted on tiny birds, followed her.

'Now Frederick, you leave' continued Sussaina.

'¡sí!' said Frederick and raising his sword, he flew towards the horizon, being followed by an army of boys. (Si is yes in Spanish)

Then Sussaina pointed her flag towards Lady Carol and said 'Lady Carol, good luck to you'

Lady Carol raised her hand and yelled 'In the name of victory, we fly' saying this, she left Zynpagua, being followed by an army of women mounted on Peregrine Falcons.

When everyone had left, Sussaina looked intently at Zynpagua once

'We will come back as winners Zynpagua. That is my promise to you' saying this, she left Zynpagua with great speed.

Sussaina and her army was first to enter the territory of the Earth from the North because of the speed of Peregrine falcons. She crossed several countries and was surprised on not finding anyone from Drudan's army. Drudan had commenced ruling the world, then why did his army not stop her?

She entered India just before noon.

As she was reaching the city of Kanya Kumari, she realized that her army got surrounded with an army of men in red uniform. She began to ascend near the beach, when she heard the notorious laughter of Drudan

'Ah Sussaina, you have come! Why have you become an ant?'

Sussaina understood that Drudan was referring to her small size. She got off the Peregrine falcon and instantly yelled 'People dismount the birds now.'

From the corner of her eyes, she saw the men descend.

'Chin Chunaki Chin Chin!' she roared instantly to come back to her normal size. This was the spell of the angel birds which could reduce and increase size of the people. But only those trusted by the angel birds could use it. The men of Zynpagua too came back to their normal sizes. The birds flew up and formed their own army in the sky.

'I must say these starving people of Zynpagua have gained much flesh and courage. These insects have the cheek to fight me!' roared Drudan.

Sussaina looked around to locate where he was but could not find him. Then all of a sudden, Drudan attacked from the sky and captured Sussaina.

'Cowards have no courage to attack from front!' yelled Sussaina, struggling to escape.

People of Zynpagua tried attacking, but Drudan warned them 'I can kill Sussaina. This is the time of demon planets and none of the stars or the vile Moon would be able to save her. You scoundrels, back off!'

'My men in red capture them' instructed Drudan.

'You are vile Drudan. This is deceit and against the law of war. You attacked from behind!' Sussaina voiced angrily.

'All is fair in love and war. You expect an evil man to abide by rules?' laughed Drudan.

'If you are so sure of yourself, why can you not fight?' asked Sussaina

'I don't want to waste my time. I used Vivian as bait to get you here and now I will use you to get others. Simple strategy' smiled Drudan looking maliciously at Sussaina.

He raised his hands and yelled 'Net appear and capture all birds flying in this sky!'

Sussaina yelled 'No, let them go!'

'Oh no, I will feast on them. How can I let them go?'

'No net can capture my dear birds of kingdom of clouds. Net disappear and let the birds escape from here' yelled Lady Carol, stopping the birds from being captured.

She had entered in the nick of time and saved the birds. She then sent a magical spell on Drudan and said 'Paralyze!'

This happened so suddenly that he did not get time to send counter spell. Drudan's limbs and face got paralyzed and he fell on the beach. Sussaina moved with agility and captured Drudan.

Lady Carol pronounced the *Chin Chunaki Chin Chin* spell to ensure the women who came with her, regain their size.

Just then Drudan's army of red men began slaughtering the people of Zynpagua. Lady Carol used a magical spell to stop them, but to her despair, her magic could not work on the army of red men. They were so aggressive and ruthless that none of the people of Zynpagua could stop them. When Lady Carol saw this, she told Drudan to stop them. Drudan could hardly move his mouth and gestured to free him from the spell

Sussaina yelled 'No Lady, lets tie him and face the red men. We will be able to fight them'

Lady Carol used a spell and tied Drudan with the tree. She told Sussaina 'You fight from the ground while I will fight from the sky!'

Sussaina asked Lady Carol 'Can you get me a horse with magic. How do I fight on my feet?'

Lady Carol raised her hand and said 'Horses for people of Zynpagua appear now' then turning to Sussaina, she said 'Take one'.

Sussaina sprinted and sat on the horse and called out 'People of Zynpagua, mount the horses and fight!'

The people rushed and mounted the horses. They were carrying weapons with them and the presence of horses empowered them.

Lady Carol and Sussaina began to slaughter the men in red uniform but to their horror, a new set of red uniformed men would stand up and commence fighting. The people of Zynpagua were dying by dozens.

'What do we do now Lady? We can't let our people die like this' asked Sussaina, calling out to Lady Carol who was fighting from the sky.

'Sussaina, cowards die many times before their deaths, the valiant never taste of death but once' said Lady Carol, repeating the famous lines of William Shakespeare's, Julius Caesar.

'Lady, we will die foolishly now. We are unable to fight these men in red. We need to plan a way to destroy them' asserted Sussaina.

'We don't have time Sussaina!' said Lady Carol

'Wait!', saying this Sussaina raced towards Drudan on her horse. As she reached there, the men in red had untied Drudan. They came forward, surrounded Sussaina and attacked from all sides.

Sussaina fought valiantly but the men in red continued to reappear and attack.

Just then she heard Chin Chunaki Chin Chin and saw Frederick land. He got off the angel bird and raced towards the men in red.

Chapter 50

Leo

Back in Zynpagua, Leo continued to be unconscious.

Head cook and Sachinth followed Lady Carol's instructions and tried to make him walk. While walking, though in an unconscious state, Leo began to murmur

'Anika and Mootu are following the direction of the vibration. It's a strange sound unheard of. Mootu feels it could be the mermaid's mischief. But they have no choice but to follow the vibrations. Anika is looking very weak but is swimming. Yes, they are trying to swim towards the wave. Yes, Mootu and Anika are now riding on the wave. It is rising higher and higher. They are on the crest of that wave. Oh my God it has risen as high as mountain. Anika and Mootu are yelling now. They are very scared. Its fall...ling. The wave is falling!'

He became very quiet for some time. The head cook laid him on his bed and left the room. Leo began to toss and turn in his bed. After a while, he began to shiver

'the wave has dropped them far away. But the sound of the vibration is clear now. They are swimming fast towards the vibration. Oh my God, Oh my God....' Yelled Leo

Sachinth ran out to call the Head cook who hurriedly left the kitchen. Leo was shivering terribly. The head cook held him tightly and tried waking him but he did not.

Then he gently asked Leo 'Son, is there a problem with Anika?'

Leo aggressively shook his head and said 'Yes, huge fishes have surrounded them. Sorry, they are not fishes, they are whales. One whale has opened her mouth and is heading to swallow Anika and Mootu!'

The head cook was shocked to learn this. He asked Leo 'Where is Anika now?'

'I cannot see her' said Leo panicking while sleeping.

'Son, try locating her. I am sure you will be able to find her' said the Head cook.

'I can't see her. There are too many whales around' said Leo

Head cook got deeply concerned. *Have the whales eaten her?* He thought.

A deep pain of agony stung him.

He joined his hands and prayed aloud 'Please God save Anika and Mootu!'

Chapter 51

Dangerous whales

Anika and Mootu were indeed surrounded by dangerous whales. They had a brawl on who would eat Anika. They were not interested in Mootu as they had been feasting on turtles. One belligerent whale pushed others to a side, opened her mouth and pounced on Anika.

Anika and Mootu yelled and closed their eyes as the axe like sharp teeth of the whale came as close as the breath.

After this there was silence. Anika felt she was floating in space. She opened her eyes and saw Mootu gasping for breath 'Are we dead?' she asked Mootu.

'I think so, can't feel anything!'

Just then someone hit them on their face. Both got up and screamed 'Mashy!'

'Yes, it is me. Managed to pull both of you in the nick of time or you would have been sitting in the whale's stomach'

'How did you know where we were' asked Anika and Mootu

'I will tell you everything, but I am unable to breathe. We have been floating here for days and there is no air to breathe' said Mashy.

'We had Mana leaves and did not realize that. Wait' saying this Mootu pulled out two leaves from his pouch 'Please swallow one and make King Soto have the other'

Mashy quickly swallowed it while Anika thrust the other leaf in King Soto's mouth. He was unconscious.

'Wow, this is magical. I feel so much better!' said Mashy, feeling relieved. 'Sir, do you have enough of these leaves?'

'Just three more left' said Mootu.

'Oh, then we have to cross the sea fast. The mermaid's magic cannot sense us in these depths but then we will not be able to breathe here. We have to get out fast!' said Mashy

'Yes, but you didn't tell us how you managed to locate us' said Mootu.

'Sir, I could sense the vibrations you were sending but had no strength to return the same. I could hardly breathe. When I saw the whales, I told them that a delicious human was with the tortoise who was sending the signals and if they sent their signal, the human would come and they could feast on it' laughed Mashy.

'Let us hurry now' said Mashy.

'Where do we go from here?' asked Anika.

'We are in deepest area of the sea and will have to swim upwards. We will meet the whales and other dangerous species. Mootu and Anika you sit on my back and hold King Soto. I will cruise fast and escape being caught.'

Just then Anika held her head and said 'there is poison in my head. It is so heavy. I cannot sway it.'

'What is the matter Anika?' asked Mootu, surprised at her reaction.

'I don't know Sir, I feel I am connected to someone. He is sleeping and his head has become heavy with poison.'

'It must be Leo' said Mootu. 'Vivian had come to fetch Romeo to save him. Romeo was supposed to infuse poison in him to make him walk'

'That's right. Why am I able to feel what he is experiencing?' asked Anika.

'We don't know that, but try talking to him. Call him' said Mashy

Anika hesitated for a moment but then focusing on her feelings, she said 'Leo!'

There was no response.

Anika repeated again 'Leo, are you listening to me?'

This time a voice said 'Yes Anika, I am. I know you are in the deep sea'

'You can see where I am?' asked Anika, totally surprised.

'Yes Anika I can but I am unable to get up and help you' said Leo

'Why can you not get up?' asked Anika

'Anika, Drudan made me drink some strange water. My father tried uniting my soul with yours. It did not happen but....'

'But what?' asked Anika.

'Anika hurry and save yourself. I am being treated' said Leo

Anika got very concerned, she called out 'Leo, try waking. Wake up Leo'

A strange connection had formed between Anika and Leo due to the magical water. As Anika called out his name, Leo began to feel better and his pain eased. He woke up instantly and sat up. 'I am fine now! The pain is no longer there' said Leo

The head cook and Sachinth were also surprised. 'This is a miracle' the head cook exclaimed.

'How did this happen?' asked Sachinth.

'Anika called out my name and spoke to me. As she did that, my pain seized. This is so strange' said Leo

'Son, before Lady Carol had left she informed me that Drudan made you drink magical water to unite your split soul and kill Anika. You did drink the magical water but Anika chanted a prayer of Lord Shiva which stopped her soul from leaving her body' the Head cook said.

'But isn't it a miracle that when Anika called out my name, I felt better and could get up' Leo said.

'Son, I think the magical water was trying to connect you with her. Once that connection was established, you could wake up' the head cook affirmed.

'How is Anika?' asked the head cook

'A snake saved her from the whales. She is with King Soto, Mootu and the snake' said Leo

'King Soto!!!' exclaimed the Head cook. She has managed to find King Soto?'

'Yes, he is with her, though he looks famished and is unconscious' said Leo

'I want to help Anika and Queen Sussaina' said Leo

'Son, eat well and recoup first. By then we will get some news on Queen Sussaina'

Sachinth was patiently listening to their conversation. Once they were quiet, Sachinth stepped forward and said 'Hello, I am Sachinth Goel, the minister's son. I promised Queen I would take care of you'

Leo patted Sachinth and said 'Thank you friend'

Chapter 52

Captured

Mashy carried Anika, Mootu and King Soto on his back and cruised through the torrent sea, escaping the whales. He was heading in the direction of the city of Kanya Kumari when a group of worm guards surrounded them. Anika and Mootu had no weapons and simply punched the guards on their faces. They wriggled and swam away with great speed.

'Mashy, swim fast and reach the coast before the worms return' advised Mootu

'Yes Sir, I know, trying my best to reach the coast' said Mashy.

Seawater was splashing on their faces. Anika closed her eyes to avoid the water. As she did that, she saw a blurred Image. It was Sussaina's despondent face. Blood was trickling down her forehead.

Shocked by the vision, Anika opened her eyes. She saw droplets splitting like tears. Her head began to throb. *Was she getting a premonition for the future?*

She closed her eyes again and tried focusing, but this time nothing happened. *Where is mother Sussaina?* She thought.

As they swam ahead, she was surprised to see two tiny swords used by the worm guards. These were stuck to each other in the form of a cross and were simply floating in the sea. Anika's head began to throb even more. *What were these symbols indicating?*

Mootu yelled 'Hey Anika, stretch your hands and pick the swords!'

Anika nodded and grabbed the swords. 'Be careful, they could be poisonous' warned Mashy.

She carefully held the sword upright. As she did that, her head throbbed even more. She began to murmur

'A pair of cross swords,
Are symbols of war,
Splashing water looked like tears
Igniting a strange fear
I saw mother's bleeding face
Not sure, it was all a haze'

Anika was shivering when Mootu touched her 'You are not feeling well?' he asked

'Sir, I am seeing symbols of war. We have to find out what is happening in Zynpagua' Anika said

'Why don't you speak to Leo?' advised Mootu

'Good idea' said Mashy

'Leo, are you listening to me?' Anika called out. There was no answer

Anika called out again 'Leo, are you there?'

'Yes Anika' replied Leo, in a stressed voice.

'Why are you sounding disturbed?' asked Anika

'No I am fine, please tell me why did you call?' asked Leo

'I had a premonition in which I saw mother Sussaina bleeding from the forehead' said Anika

Leo gasped but did not reply

'What happened, where is she?' asked Anika

'Everyone has left for the Earth to wage war against Drudan. He has captured Vivian' said Leo

'Oh!' panicked Anika

'Anika, please save yourself first. Where are you?' asked Leo

'Sir, where are we?' asked Anika, turning to Mootu

'We are in the Indian ocean, near the beach city of Kanya Kumari' Mootu whispered in Anika's ears.

'Leo, we are in the Indian Ocean near the beach of Kanya Kumari city. We are finding our way to the beach' repeated Anika.

'Anika, best of luck!' said Leo.

As Anika's voice faded, Leo turned towards the peregrine falcon that had flown with great speed to tell Leo about Drudan's treachery in war.

Leo decided to help Sussaina and others in the war.

Chapter 53

The Great War

Sussaina, Lady Carol, Frederick and the people of Zynpagua, fought furiously and courageously.

It was the fourth day of the rule of the demon planets. Drudan began to worry.

He had pretended to be paralyzed to gauge their strength.

Drudan secretly got up and sneaked behind the tree. From there he used a magical spell to paralyze Lady Carol and put her to sleep.

Pointing his hand towards Lady Carol, he said 'Magic dear, paralyze Lady Carol. Tie her in chains and get her here'

As soon as he said that, Lady Carol fell on the beach, crippled by the spell. Frederick and Sussaina did not realize that she had fallen.

Drudan then pronounced the second spell 'Magic dear, capture Sussaina and Frederick. Tie them in metal chains and bring them here!'

He used a third spell 'Magic dear, capture all human and creatures from Zynpagua and put them in Palace jail!'

The spell captured Sussaina and others in chains. They rose up in air and headed towards Drudan.

Seeing them, Drudan laughed and said 'this is called cheating, an effective weapon of evil'

'Why did you pretend to be paralyzed?' asked Sussaina

'Obviously, I wanted to see how many insects were coming to face us. You are a fool. I had safeguarded myself against all magic, even before you arrived' he laughed hysterically.

While Drudan was interacting with Sussaina, Frederick wondered where Femina was.

'Hey Sussaina, you look dumb...struck!' laughed Drudan.

'Time to kill!' he continued.

'Sussaina and Lady Carol first, then Vivian then Frederick.... then Anika' said Drudan.

'Sussaina, come forward. How do you want to die?' asked Drudan.

He picked his sword and said 'No planet will protect you today. The Moon will support me!' he laughed hysterically.

'Drudie wait!' warned a voice

'Mermie is that you?' asked Drudan

'Yes' Said the mermaid

'What happened, why I should wait?' asked Drudan.

'Don't kill them now. We will slay them on the last day of the rule of demon planets. It will make you even more powerful. By then I would have captured Anika and Soto. Let us finish the entire clan in one go!' advised the mermaid

'Where is Anika?' asked Drudan

'She managed to find Soto and escape with him' said the mermaid

'How can you let that happen?' Drudan asked furiously

'Don't worry! I have almost trapped her!' the mermaid giggled.

'I trust you completely mermie' laughed Drudan.

'I will spend these two precious days torturing the Zynpagua clan' said Drudan, laughing hysterically.

Chapter 54

Femina

Femina had requested the angel birds to halt somewhere for rest. Romeo was also with her. They flew down and rested on a mountain top.

While they were resting, a flock of birds from the Kingdom of clouds came to warn them. They chirped frantically 'Drudan cheated us. He used magic and captured everyone!'

'Oh God!' exclaimed Femina

'Yes. He plans to kill everyone after two days' continued the birds.

'We cannot let this happen. Let us fly immediately' said Romeo

'Romeo, we need a better plan. If Drudan has captured everyone, he will capture us as well. Let us disguise ourselves and secretly save everyone' suggested Femina

'Good idea' said Romeo

'I have a suggestion. Let us become small ants and enter the prison. No one will notice us. I am passing the power to use the spell *Chin chunaki chin chin* to everyone here' said the angel birds.

'This is a wonderful suggestion. Girls, tap on your heads only twice.' Instructed Femina

'But the spell will not work on me' said Romeo

'This is a special self inflicting spell. Only we angel birds have the authority to use it and pass it on. We have given permission to everyone here to use it'

Femina and her team tapped their heads twice while saying the spell. They became as small as tiny ants.

'It works on me as well' exclaimed Romeo as he diminished to the size of a worm.

The team then set off for Kanya Kumari immediately.

Chapter 55

Captured

'Catch them now' yelled the worm guard as his sword pierced through Mashy's body. They had been secretly chasing Mashy for a very long time. Mashy lost balance with the wound and everyone sitting on him fell in the sea.

The worm guards arrested King Soto who was unconscious and warned everyone else to surrender. Anika gave in and offered to be arrested. The worm cards handcuffed everyone with special weeds and pulled them along till they reached the mermaid's palace.

One of the guards announced their arrival and took them to the mermaid.

The mermaid looked at them with vicious eyes and said 'I don't want to save them anymore. Worm guards take them to the prison deep in the sea where they cannot breathe. Lock them there and let them die!'

'Get out of my sight!' she yelled.

The worm guards pulled them towards the underground prisons. It was a horrible smelling cave. Anika and others felt suffocated inside, as if their body refused to breathe.

The worm guards left them there and hurriedly closed the entrance of the cave with a huge boulder.

'We will die here!' exclaimed Mashy

'Try having the Mana leaves. We have three' said Mootu

He quickly searched inside his pockets to find more leaves.

'Thank God, found one more' he heaved a sigh of relief.

'Let's chew one each and plan to escape this cave' suggested Mootu

But even after chewing the Mana leaves, they were feeling breathless.

'Let me see if I can reach Leo' said Anika, infusing hope in others.

'Leo can you hear me' asked Anika

'Leo!' she yelled with all her might 'Can you hear me?'

'Anika! Anika! Is that you?' said a faint voice

'Yes, yes!' Anika nodded with hope

'I cannot understand what you are saying' said Leo

Anika remembered something and stopped speaking aloud but told her mind. Leo I hope you can read my mind. We are locked in the deep sea and might die in few seconds. Can you save us?'

'I will not let you die Anika, I will save you. I can read your mind. Keep the hope!' said Leo's voice.

Chapter 56

Leo

Leo heard Anika's voice and instantly decided to fly to the Earth and dive in the Indian Ocean.

'How will you enter the sea? You have qualities of a bird' asked the Head cook

'Sir, I remember a song my mother used to sing when I was a child. That is the only memory I have of her. But I don't know why I feel she sang these lines to highlight my strength' he said, trying to remember the song.

'My son is the special one
Who can fly like birds
And make animals flock in herds
He cannot be harmed by ordinary hand
Even if buried in ice or sand
He can call penguins
To fight sea dragons'

'There was more to this song, can't
remember' said Leo trying to recall.
'What was it...' he tried straining his memory
'A true heart can call anyone
He may be in the sea or on the Sun
Call from the depth of your heart
With your loved ones you will never part'
Something struck Leo as he repeated the lines
'Call from the depth of your heart
With your loved ones you will never part?'

'What is the meaning of these lines?' He thought.

Just then he heard Anika again 'Leo, I can't breathe anymore!'

'Anika breathe slowly, I am coming. Be awake so that I can read your mind' said Leo as he rushed towards the roof.

'I want to come with you' insisted Sachinth

'And me too' said the Head cook.

'I cannot stake your life. Please stay here' insisted Leo

'We want to come. Please take us' said the Head cook

Leo did not have much time. He held Sachinth and the Head cook's hand.

'Rise high and let us fly to India!' he voiced.

On the way he told the head cook 'I will leave you in a safe place. Please take care of Sachinth. You will not descend the sea with me'

Leo flew with great speed and entered the Earth and headed straight towards India, but instead of reaching Kanya Kumari, he landed on a beach opposite to the beach of Kanya Kumari.

'Anika!' he whispered

'Leo, I am waiting' he could hear Anika. He felt relieved.

I will try calling the Penguins. I am the Prince of clouds and all the birds in the world should be able to hear me he thought.

Leo closed his eyes and said 'Penguins living in the southern hemisphere, I need your help!'

Nothing happened. Leo gaped at the sea. It looked wild and he did not know how to swim.

'Call from your heart. Ask for help' whispered the Head cook

'Leo, I cannot breathe anyone' he heard Anika's voice.

'I am coming Anika, you will have to wait' Leo spoke aloud

He then looked at the sea and yelled

'Penguins of Antarctica, can you hear me?
Your Prince of clouds is going to dive in this sea
I have to save a special girl and set her free
I don't know how to swim
Please help me'

Leo turned to the head cook and said. 'I am diving in. I can hear Anika and will try locating where she is. She really doesn't have time and if she faints, I will not be able to reach her. If I do not return, please take the help of birds and return to Zynpagua'

The mention of birds brought an idea in Leo's mind.

He called 'Are there any birds sitting on these trees?'

Two crows cawed and came forward 'Prince of clouds!' they exclaimed.

'Friends, I am diving in the sea. If I do not return, please find the birds of the Kingdom of clouds and ensure this gentleman and the boy return safely' said Leo

Before the crows could even shake their head, Leo dived in the sea.

Sachinth yelled 'Leo!' but he was gone.

'Son let us pray for our victory' suggested the Head cook.

Chapter 57

Femina

Femina and her team of girls had become the size of ants after pronouncing the '*Chin Chunaki Chin Chin* 'spell.

It was evening when they landed outside Drudan's palace near the beach. As instructed by Femina, the birds flew away after leaving them.

Drudan's roaring laughter could be heard from outside.

Femina, Romeo and the girls silently tip toed inside the palace and followed the direction of Drudan's voice. The scene ahead was traumatic. Sussaina, Lady Carol, Frederick were tied in ropes and bundled in one corner while Vivian was handcuffed and standing in the centre of the hall.

Drudan was looking at Vivian spitefully 'I want to finish Sussaina and Soto's clan today itself'

Saying this Drudan flew towards Vivian and pounced on him. He slapped him hard and punched him on his face. 'I detest you!' he said.

Vivian looked at him with angry eyes, but did not say anything

Drudan kissed his ring and called aloud 'Mermie!'

'Yes Drudan' a melodious voice said.

'Could you catch Anika and Soto?' he asked

'Yes. I have locked them in an airless underwater jail. They can choke and die there' said the mermaid mercilessly.

'Did you not tell me to wait for another two days?' asked Drudan.

'Yes I did but I do not trust this girl anymore. Better to get rid of her' said the mermaid nastily.

'No!' exclaimed Vivian

'Did I not tell you to keep your mouth shut' yelled Drudan.

'Mermie let us kill everyone and keep only Sussaina alive for the last day' suggested Drudan.

'Perfect plan' said the mermaid gleefully.

Femina and Romeo got alert 'Girls it is time for action, do as I have told you!'

Saying this they raced forward. Femina got on Vivian's feet and quickly moved up till his hands. She took out a tiny sword and began cutting the ropes that tied his hands.

Vivian felt some itching around his palms but did not know what was happening.

In the meanwhile Drudan pulled out his sword to kill Vivian when Romeo entered his pants and began to tickle and scratch him.

'What the hell is this?' exclaimed Drudan as he began to scratch his feet.

By then Romeo had climbed above his abdomen and began to pull Drudan's hair on the chest, one by one.

Drudan yelled in pain and opened his shirt to check. Romeo became alert instantly and stung his chest and transferred poison in his body. Drudan fainted immediately.

Romeo jumped back and ran towards Sussaina and others.

Femina reached Vivian's ears and whispered 'Vivian it is me, Femina!'

'Femina?' Vivian asked excitedly and began to look around

'I am on your ear' she said.

Vivian touched his ear and felt someone on it. He picked her up and placed her on his palm. 'Femina!' he exclaimed once more.

Romeo had untied Sussaina and others. He said 'Please hurry. Under the rule of demon planets my poison will not be effective on him. He will wake up anytime.'

Everyone agreed and using the spell 'Chin chunaki chin chin', diminished to the size of ants.

'Femina, I am so glad you are fine' said Queen Sussaina.

'Hurry and leave!' repeated Romeo.

'How do we escape the men in red uniform?' asked Lady Carol

'Lady, I suggest let us hide from Drudan for the next two days. We will not be able to defeat him. Let the rule of demon planets get over' suggested Romeo.

'What about Anika?' asked Sussaina.

'The mermaid said she would kill her' she continued.

'Queen I will enter the sea to save Anika' said Romeo

'We want to enter the sea with you' responded Vivian

'By now the mermaid's guards would be very attentive. They will catch you instantly' said Romeo as he steadily moved ahead.

The others followed behind. Romeo wriggled towards a huge tree at the far end of the beach.

On reaching there, he knocked at the tree and hissed. Nothing happened. He wriggled on the tree and entered a hole located on one of the branches.

Then he wriggled back to queen Sussaina and said 'Queen, please climb the tree and sit in that hole. It was made by a snake once but is deserted now. Everyone will be safe here.'

Sussaina did not want to obey Romeo and hide from Drudan but agreed because it was prudent to do so. Defeating Drudan during the reign of demon planets seemed next to impossible. He was deceitful and would not follow any rule of the law.

After Romeo ensured that everyone was safe, he flew towards the Indian Ocean and dived in.

As he did that he felt a huge needle pass through his body. He fainted instantly.

Chapter 58

Leo

Leo dived in the sea. Instead of drowning, his body began to float. He had quality of a bird. That is why his body was light and he could float.

He whispered 'Anika' trying to locate where she was.

A Feeble voice responded 'L..e..o!'

Leo panicked but holding his nerves, said 'Anika, don't waste energy in responding. Take deeps breaths. I will follow the sound of your breath.'

'Leo...' came a voice but after that it was all blank.

Leo strained his ears and managed to hear a faint breathing sound.

He pushed his body in the direction of the sound, trying to float on the wave. Suddenly, a group of special sea force worms noticed him and dashed towards him. But as they came closer to Leo, they became powerless and fell in the sea. No one with ill intentions could ever face Leo.

Unable to face Leo, the worms threw pointed swords at him from behind but before the swords could touch him, an army of penguins came before Leo and stopped the swords.

'Don't you dare touch our Prince' said one of them.

These Penguins had guns in their hand. They aimed the guns towards the worm guards and shot them. Some worms fell off while the others backed out and ran away.

'You killed them?' asked Leo

'No, they are just injured and unconscious. We are not allowed to kill any sea creature' said the Penguins.

Then they bowed before Leo and unanimously asked 'We are blessed to meet the Prince of clouds. How can we help you?'

'Thank you so much for coming. The mermaid of the sea has locked my friend in some undersea jail where there is no air to breathe. If I do not reach her, she will die. I cannot swim and do not know how to reach her' said Leo

'Prince, we can hold your hands and make you swim with us' said the Penguins.

'We are from Antarctica and do not know where this sea jail is?'

Leo nodded and said 'I will try locating Anika'

He tried connecting with her through the mind, but could not. He strained his ears trying to locate the sound of her breath. To his dismay, he could not even hear her breath.

He concentrated hard and waited for some time, desperately trying to locate her breath. After a while he was able to trace it.

'We have to head towards the Northwest direction. Please hurry, I think she is sinking!' exclaimed Leo

'The Penguins held his hands and darted towards the specified direction. They injured the worm guards that came on the way.'

Soon they reached a cave like structure from where Leo could hear Anika breathe. 'Please hurry. There is no air here and we are feeling suffocated' said the Penguins.

'Please do not risk your life. Leave me here and you can swim in the higher sea 'urged Leo.

'No Prince, we will be with you but please hurry' the Penguins replied.

The Penguins came close to each other forming a boat.

'Prince, please sit on us' the Penguins requested.

'I won't, you will get crushed' responded Leo

'You cannot swim and this is the only way we can enter the cave'the Penguins said.

Leo hesitated and sat on them. The Penguins swam together and reached a boulder that was blocking the cave.

'Remove it fast' instructed a Penguin

Leo nodded and with full force removed the enormous boulder which was placed at the entrance. As the boulder creaked and shifted, a pool of water fell on Leo, entering his eyes and blocking his vision.

'Welcome' said someone

Leo rubbed his eyes to get a clearer view and saw a beautiful woman standing in a corner.

'Hello, I am the mermaid of the sea and have come to catch thee' she giggled.

Leo looked around and saw Anika, a tortoise, a snake and a haggard looking man lying unconscious, struggling to breathe.

He was feeling choked himself. 'Penguins swim ahead and make me face the mermaid' he instructed. With great agility the Penguins swam ahead, making Leo face the Mermaid.

She yelled as she felt all her energy sap away and she fell.

As she fell, Leo told the Penguins to capture her.

He stooped down and one by one lifted Anika, the snake, tortoise, and King Soto. Once they were balanced on the platform created by the Penguins, Leo told them 'I am holding the Mermaid, please swim fast and leave this place'

Soon they were out of the caves.

The first to wake was the snake 'Hi Leo, you saved us? You actually saved us?' he exclaimed.

Leo smiled and said 'Yes, I am glad you are fine!'

'We must reach the city of Kanya Kumari. Drudan is planning to kill queen Sussaina' said Mashy.

'Yes I know, the birds told me. Who told you dear snake?' asked Leo.

'I heard the mermaid talk to Drudan' replied Mashy.

The mention of Drudan triggered a feeling of disgust in Leo. His father was such an evil man.

Leo looked at Anika. She had lost much weight. Anika's state saddened him deeply. She was only eleven and was forced to fight such a wicked man who unfortunately was his own father.

'Leave me!' yelled the mermaid, struggling to move away from Leo's grip.

'I will not harm you but please let us go' requested Leo.

'I will let you go, please leave me' the mermaid replied.

'I am sorry but I can't trust you. If you want to be free, leave us till the shore' said Leo

Chapter 59

The last Day

Drudan had attacked Romeo with a poisonous needle before he could dive in the sea. It inflicted such a deep wound that Romeo became unconscious and got trapped. The men in red carried him to Drudan's palace.

Drudan tried waking him but Romeo lay lifelessly on the palace floor.

'Is he dead' asked Drudan

'No, but will die soon' said an Indian veterinary doctor who had been captured and brought to inspect Romeo.

'Wake him once, I want to know where are those rogues of Zynpagua' screamed Drudan

'Why can you not use magic and get them here' suggested one of the men in red uniform

'Good idea. Why is my brain not working?' said Drudan.

He raised his hand and pronounced 'Magic dear, get all the people from Zynpagua here!'

Vivian and Lady Carol sensed Drudan's spell and immediately protected everyone through magic. They cast a protective cover around the tree and hid it.

Drudan got frustrated when his magic failed.

He thought *if I cannot get them here, I can reach them there*, saying this Drudan plucked a flower from an indoor plant, and kissing it, he said 'I want you to take me to the location where these goons of Zynpagua are hiding. Magic dear, help the flower reach the scoundrels hiding somewhere near'

The flower commenced flying. Drudan and his army followed it. The flower reached the tree and began rotating near the snake hole. However Drudan could not see the tree as it was hidden by the spell.

Drudan narrowed his eyes and focused on the location. He stretched his hand and swayed it. His hand hit something hard. He instantly pronounced the 'Appear 'spell. The tree was visible now.

The flower was rotating near the snake hole.

Drudan got perplexed. *Why is the flower rotating near the hole?* he thought. He walked closer to the hole and thrust his hand inside it. He felt movement inside the hole. Grabbing a fistful of people, he pulled them out.

They yelled in his grip. **'**Lovely**'** Drudan exclaimed as he saw the people of Zynpagua locked in his fist. Lady Carol was also with them.

'Mother In law, you have become an ant?**'** Drudan roared with laughter

Lady Carol whispered 'Please say Chin chunaki chin chin and tap on your head twice'

The people followed her instruction and regained their size.

Drudan was surprised to see that. ‘Wonderful! This is some new sort of magic. Let me continue pulling out the people. Soldiers arrest them’ said Drudan.

Lady Carol tried saving herself magically but Drudan passed the ‘Still!’ curse on her.

Vivian tried a spell on Drudan, but he was protected by the demon planets against any magic. Drudan scooped everyone out from the hole and handed them to the men in red.

He looked around and said ‘Sussaina and Vivian have not come out’, saying this he put his hand inside and pulled out the remaining lot. ‘Here comes little ant Sussaina and her nonsense son Vivian!’

While everyone from Zynpagua quickly pronounced the spell and regained their height, none could escape the men in red. Vivian tried combating but Drudan punched him on the face and pronounced the ‘Still’ curse on him.

Drudan then peeped through the hole to check if anyone was left. Femina had hidden behind the inner layer of the bark of the tree. Drudan could not see her. In fact Drudan did not know Femina was alive.

He took everyone to the palace.

Chapter 60

Leo

Leo was the first to come out from the sea. He carried King Soto on his shoulders. The Penguins followed him to the shores. Mashy had volunteered to keep the mermaid in his confines till everyone got out.

When Leo was coming out, the mermaid bit Mashy and pulled Anika down in the sea. Mootu sprinted behind Anika.

A mermaid's bite is fatal and Mashy fell in the sea.

Leo waited for Mootu and Anika to come out but when they did not, a sense of panic engulfed him.

He instantly dived back in the sea with the Penguins, leaving King Soto on the shores.

The head cook and Sachinth were waiting for Leo at the beach. As soon as they saw Leo, they ran towards the shore. While Leo jumped back in the sea, they carried King Soto towards a clear patch on the beach.

When Leo jumped inside the sea, he could not find Anika or the mermaid. Mashy was lifelessly floating in the sea. Leo was shocked to see that. One of the Penguins held Mashy 'He is alive!' the Penguin said 'but needs to be cured. I think the mermaid has bitten him' he continued.

Leo caressed Mashy and said 'How do we save him?'

'Please don't worry Prince, let us find Anika first. Two of us will carry Mashy till the shore' said the Penguin.

Leo nodded in agreement, and holding the Penguins, dived deeper in the sea.

The Penguins ferociously fought with the worm guards and swam fast to catch the mermaid.

Once the mermaid was in sight, Leo dashed forward holding the Penguins. The mermaid did not want to become powerless in Leo's Presence. She left Anika and Mootu and swam fast towards the depths of the sea. She was feeling very weak as biting Mashy had sapped her energy.

'Please hurry and get out of the sea, before she returns with more force' pleaded the Penguins.

By this time Anika had become very weak and could not swim. Leo held her hand and requested the Penguins to carry her till the shore. Mootu followed them.

Once they reached the shore, the Penguins lay Anika on the sand. Two Penguins hurriedly came forward and said 'Mermaid's bite is fatal. Mashy can only be saved by our doctor who stays in Antarctica. The two of us will carry Mashy there. Please allow us to leave immediately'

'Thank you for coming my dear Penguins' Leo replied gratefully.

'It is our duty, my Prince' said the Penguin.

'Prince, we will accompany the two Penguins for some distance in the sea. The mermaid may attack them. We will return once they have crossed the mermaid's territory' said another Penguin.

'I agree with you. Please leave immediately' said Leo

The Penguins waved goodbye to Leo and returned to the sea.

Chapter 61

The last day of Rule of demon planets

The mermaid swam fast in the depths of the sea. Once she felt safe, she called Drudan

'Drudie, are you there?' she whispered

Drudan had trapped everyone from Zynpagua and was returning to his palace. He was so engrossed in ensuring that Sussaina and her clan do not play mischief, that he did not hear the mermaid.

In the meanwhile, Femina quickly came out of her hiding. She was thinking fast. *How to save others?* **S**he knew Drudan would capture her, if he saw her.

She remained small in size and wriggled in search of a horse. As she entered Drudan's palace, she heard him instruct the men in red 'Today is the last day of the rule of the demon planets. Start killing them one by one. I don't want you to stop'

Femina's heart sank. She had no time. While she could not find a horse, she saw a man offloading grains from a bullock cart. She immediately said 'Chin chunaki chin chin

'and regained her height. Her sword also became bigger and longer. She rushed towards the cart and patted the bullocks. The man did not notice her. She instantly climbed the cart and yelled 'Run fast inside the palace'

She entered the palace with great speed, slicing all the men in red that tried stopping her. Drudan was so shocked to see a speeding cart, that he could not react. Femina raced fast and hit him on the head. Drudan fell off. The men in red uniform surrounded her from all sides and attacked her. Femina fought bravely, slicing them. But she was alone and they were reappearing in hundreds. She could not find Sussaina and others.

Drudan had asked the men in red uniform to kill them. What happened to everyone?

She called out 'Vivian, Where are you?'

She received no response.

Vivian, Sussaina, Lady Carol and others had been dragged to the shore, to kill them in the presence of Demon planets. The preparation had been done and Drudan had to shoot them under the sky.

When Drudan did not come, the men in red uniform rushed to the palace to call him. They were shocked to see that Femina had injured everyone.

Femina heard one of them tell his colleague, that they were waiting for Drudan on the shore. Thus Femina rode out of the palace with great speed, being followed by men in red uniform. They raced behind her, trying to shoot her.

The men in red uniform woke Drudan. He was furious and ordered 'Kill them now!'

Just then he heard the Mermaid 'Drudie can you hear me? I am trying to contact you for the last one hour'

'Mermie, what happened?' asked Drudan

'The girl has escaped. The inmates of the sea have revolted against me. I am leaving the Indian Ocean and swimming towards Pacific. Don't worry about me. Just remember, today is the last day of the rule of demon planets. Ensure you kill everyone and ask the planets to bless you. I am always with you Drudan. Please remember to seek the blessings of the demon planets' saying this, the mermaid's voice faded.

Drudan was shocked to know about Anika's escape and the revolt in the sea. He kept screaming 'Mermie, talk to me, where are you going?' but he did not get a response. Exasperated, he rushed towards the shore.

Chapter 62

Missing

Leo left Anika and others at the shore and flew towards the city of Kanya Kumari.

He crossed the sea and headed towards the beach. He was flying high in the sky when he saw a young woman being surrounded by red uniformed men. He strained his eyes and realized that the girl was Femina. A feeling of delight and worry passed through him. She was single handedly facing them.

Leo flew towards the shore. Drudan was standing there, pointing his hand towards Femina and announcing 'You will be the first to leave this world'. Before he could pronounce the spell, Leo descended and held him. Drudan began to scream as he felt lifelessly in Leo's arms.

Femina was delighted to see Leo and yelled 'Leo don't leave him. I am unable to find Mother Sussaina and others. Keep holding Drudan as I search for them'

The men in red tried pulling Leo away from Drudan but as they touched him, they also fell off. One of them aimed a gun to shoot him but Femina knocked him off with her sword.

She climbed the bullock cart and rode it with great speed, trying to locate others. 'Mother Sussaina, Vivian, Frederick!' she called aloud but there was no response.

While Leo was holding Drudan, he felt some invisible rays were burning his hands. He looked around and felt the milieu was getting covered by a shade of red. It was getting harder to hold Drudan, who was lifelessly hanging in his arms.

Femina continued to fight with the men. When Femina turned to escape a blow from one of them, she noticed a hand waving desperately from the sea. She raced towards the sea and was horror struck seeing the scene.

Lady Carol, Sussaina, Vivian and Frederick had been tied in chains and suspended in the sea. Their faces were covered with cloth to stop them from calling. Femina got off the horse and tried reaching them, but was stopped by the men in red. Turning towards Leo, she yelled 'Leo, take them out from the sea!!'

Leo hit Drudan hard, threw him to one side and raced towards Femina.

Drudan escaped Leo's grip and staggered to sit.
Seeing the Milieu, he fathomed that the demon planets
were exercising greatest influence before leaving.
He looked towards the sky and called aloud
'My demon planets, I have kept my promise with thee,
Soak these good people in the sea
And let evil reign and malice set free'

A huge storm erupted while Drudan was praying. Femina screamed as the air began to circulate around her and choke her. Leo rushed ahead to save her but the storm lifted him high up in the air and with great speed, threw him down on the shore. He fell on his face.

The storm continued to choke Femina till she fainted and fell.

Chapter 63

The Moon

Anika woke with a searing pain in the head. So acute was the pain that she felt her head would split.

Sachinth rushed towards a coconut tree and carried back a tender coconut that had fallen. The head cook somehow managed to break the coconut shell and instructed Anika to drink the coconut water. As Anika sipped the water, flashes of future began to appear before her eyes. Tears trickled down as she witnessed the scene. She murmured

'The demon planets are ready to set the universe free
Evil on Earth is cheering with a wicked glee
We will lose this battle of good
And let cruel Drudan rule
His son will be worse than him
Don't ever let him sing'

Anika paused midway and yelled 'No, evil can never win, I will not spell out what I can see in future. Evil has to be defeated, Drudan has to lose!'

She turned to the head cook and asked 'What is the time now?'

The head cook said 'Anika, I do not have a watch. It seems twilight is approaching'

Anika panicked 'It is the last day of the rule of the demon planets. If Drudan does not get defeated, this world will fold under an evil rule'

She closed her eyes. Suddenly the words of Venus came to her mind 'It is your determination which will decide everything!'

Anika began to walk helplessly 'We will not obey the command of destiny. We will write our future!'

'Where is Leo?' she asked the head cook

'He has flown to rescue Queen Sussaina and others' said the head cook

Why has he not returned? Has he got captured? Thought Anika

She helplessly looked up at the sky and suddenly noticed that the Moon was visible in the sky. It was still daytime and yet she could see the Moon. While the sky had a deep red tint, the Moon seemed to have moved away from the red tint.

'Is the Moon free from the influence of demon planets?' Anika thought expectantly. She joined her palms and prayed aloud

'My dear Moon,
thank you for coming out soon,
our future is in doom
Who can save us except you
Our Moon
Don't let evil survive

Be with my family in their strife
Please listen to me
I am praying to thee
To destroy the evil
And establish good in people’

Chapter 64

The killer wave

Femina and Leo were lying on the shore, injured and wounded while Lady Carol, Sussaina, Frederick and Vivian were suspended in the sea.

Drudan laughed aloud and said 'My demon planets, please accept my greetings. I have injured the good people. Please swallow them and accept my humble gift. Grant me a very long life so that I can rule this world, under your evil will!'

The clouds cracked and emitted a red lightening, as if the demon planets were acknowledging Drudan's gift.

Drudan clapped happily and said 'Please accept my humble gift. Let this sea swallow them all'

The waves began to rise. These waves had a red crest, as if they were being sent by the demon planets.

As the waves rose higher, Drudan began to sense even more strength entering his body. Drudan laughed aloud and said 'These people should see how their life is ending' saying this Drudan raised his hand and pronounced the wake up spell.

Sussaina, Vivian, Lady Carol, Femina, Leo and Frederick woke up all of a sudden and saw a red coloured wave rising in the sea. Horror struck, they continued to look at it, waiting to be swallowed by the wave.

Drudan laughed aloud and said 'See how death is approaching you!'

The wave rose high and began to tilt

Sussaina closed her eyes and prayed 'God, we are obeying your will and coming to meet you. Please be kind to the people on this Earth and do send someone to save them from this evil Drudan.'

Suddenly she realized Anika was not around. She prayed aloud 'God save Anika so that she can grow up to rescue this world from Drudan'

Drudan heard Sussaina's words. The mention of Anika disturbed him. Yes, he was killing everyone except Anika.

The red wave rose very high and began to fall towards the shore. Drudan flew up magically to save himself from the waves. Leo also tried flying but could not. He had injured his back.

Drudan yelled 'Goodbye everyone, Glad to never meet you again' He closed his eyes to escape the wild scene. Twilight had approached.

Chapter 65

Unpredictable!

Anika felt everything was ending. She looked at the sea and saw a very huge wave with red crest rise unusually high.

Appalled seeing this site, she yelled aloud 'Moon our savior, please come to our rescue'

With a crashing sound the waves began to fall.

Anika prayed even harder

'Oh Moon, please come soon
Please change the command of destiny
We have fought hard
With our loved ones
Don't let us part
You rule the tides
Then why are you not on our side
Please show us your divine light'

Just then, a beam emitted from the Moon and began to spread over the red crest waves. The beam began to turn the direction of the waves. With a huge splashing noise, the waves fell in the sea, sparing everyone on the shore.

Sussaina looked at the Moon and saw the same milky white glow on it. There was no trace of red hue. A flicker of hope crossed her heart. She whispered gratefully 'Oh Moon, you have escaped the demon planets. Thank you for turning the tide and saving us. Thank you our saviour!'

Chapter 66

Anika called out even louder

'Oh Moon!
You have come
To save us from the evil one'

Anika continued to look up as the redness in the sky began to disappear will a crackling sound. She knew the rule of demon planets was ending. She asked Mootu 'Sir, can we not reach the seashore where my family is?'

'Yes we can. I can see some birds flying high in the sky' said Mootu happily.

Saying this Mootu waved at the birds. As he did that, the birds began to descend.

When they were close, they chirped in unison 'Mootu, you are alive?'

Mootu looked up and waved at them 'How are you?'

'We are fine but are very worried for Queen Sussaina and others. They forced us to fly and save ourselves' said the birds

'Please take us there' urged Anika.

'What about King Soto? He is still unconscious' asked the Head cook

'I will go with Anika' volunteered Sachinth.

Anika nodded and said 'Sir, Please let me go with Sachinth while you stay here with father'

'It is not safe for you to go now' replied Mootu.

'Sir, the rule of demon planets is ending. The Moon has risen. I can seek favour from the Moon. I really do not know what Drudan is up to. I should be there to save my family' urged Anika

Mootu agreed.

One of the birds pronounced 'Chin Chunaki Chin Chin!' and pecked on the head of other birds. They grew ten times in size.

Anika and Sachinth sat on the birds and flew towards the other opposite shore.

Chapter 67

Unknown destiny

Drudan was outraged to see the waves fall in the sea.

'Demon planets, please kill them' he yelled.

But with the sound of lightening, darkness crept in the realm of evening. Drudan felt his energy sap.

'No demon planets, please don't go!' pleaded Drudan as the reddish tint began to disappear from the sky. The men in red fell on the ground and turned into red dust.

Drudan yelled 'No! My special force of red men'

In the meantime Leo regained some strength and secretly crept towards the shore. One by one, he began to pull Sussaina, Vivian and Lady Carol from the sea. They were partially conscious and fell on the shore.

Drudan saw them lying on the shore. Leo's back was towards him.

'I will kill them, saying this he raised his hand to pronounce the death spell.

Anika had reached the beach of Kanya Kumari, flying on the bird.

'Birdie fly towards Drudan! Sachinth when we are over Drudan's head, kick him on the head, while I will punch him on the stomach.'

Sachinth nodded and flung his right leg to hit Drudan who had just started pronouncing the death spell. Anika bent down and thumped him on the stomach.

Drudan fell on the shore. He fumed with anger and yelled 'You cockroach!' and raised his hand to pronounce a spell. Leo jumped up instantly and held Drudan.

Anika rushed towards Sussaina and held her. She gently stroked her head and whispered 'Mother!'

Sussaina hugged Anika and said 'We won!'

They heard some commotion nearby and turned to see. Drudan was lifelessly hanging in Leo's hand.

Sussaina looked up and saw the Moon. She joined her hands to thank the Moon for coming for their rescue.

She told Anika 'Destiny is in our hand. Never rely on stars because the will of a human can turn the universe for you!'

Drudan was instantly wrapped in chain and put behind the bars.

Anika sat before the Moon and said 'Dear Moon, please destroy the magical ability of this evil man.'

The Moon glowed brightly and sent its beam on Drudan. This evil man had used the Moon to kill Anika and destroy good in people. Now, it was turn of the Moon to destroy his magical abilities

Drudan screamed as the beam of the Moon began to scorch him. He fainted. His magical powers were taken away.

From the sea emerged few Penguins. They rushed towards Leo and said 'Our fellow penguins have safely taken Mashy away. Hope our doctor is able to cure him. Prince, the heat in this region will kill us. We cannot stay here longer. We have come to bid farewell. Please don't forget to call us when you need us'

Leo bid farewell to Penguins. As he turned, he heard a voice of a lady singing

'A true heart can call anyone
He may be in the sea or on the Sun
Call from the depth of your heart
With your loved ones you will never part'

'Mother!' whispered Leo in a state of surprise. Just then the voice faded.

Vivian Femina and Anika rescued the people captured in the prison. Anika saw her family from India and burst into tears. She cried aloud profusely seeing them. Radhika and Anika hugged each other and wept and wept.

Chapter 68

Don't ever let him sing!

A boat could be seen coming towards the shore.

Sussaina exclaimed 'My King Soto!' as the boat came closer. The head cook had requested some fishermen to help him carry King Soto till the coast of Kanya Kumari.

King Soto was unconscious. Sussaina rushed towards the boat. The head cook and some fishermen carried King Soto till the shores.

This was the best day in their lives after many years.

Femina hugged Sussaina and said 'Queen Sussaina, we have won!'

She looked around and said 'I will just come back in a minute'

'What happened?' asked Vivian

'I am looking for Romeo. He has really helped us in our war against Drudan.' She replied.

The mention of Romeo alerted Vivian as well. He rushed towards the palace and found Romeo lying on the floor.

'Is he dead?' exclaimed Femina, who had accompanied Vivian.

'I don't know' saying this Vivian touched Romeo. Romeo raised his head in pain.

'You are alive! I am so happy to see you!' said Femina

Romeo smiled and nodded. He wriggled slowly.

'Please don't get up. I will arrange for help' saying this, Vivian left the palace, trying to seek help from someone.

He returned with Lady Carol who bandaged Romeo's wound with some medicinal leaves.

Anika introduced her family to Sussaina. When Sussaina saw Radhika, she hugged her dearly and said 'What a pretty girl! Anika tells me how much you care for her'

'Yes, she is my dearest sister!' Anika said, clinging on Radhika.

Everyone assembled near the seashore. Drudan was bound in chains and tied to a tree nearby.

Drudan closed his eyes and mentally called out 'Mermie, I wish you were here to save me!'

Just then a storm erupted from the sea, a current of water gushed out and headed towards Drudan.

Vivian saw the wave and rushed towards Drudan and held me. Leo and Frederick joined him and together they held Drudan with all their might, stopping the waves to carry him.

The waves began to recede. While returning, the waves pulled Radhika with them.

A screaming voice came from the sea 'Anika, you have captured my husband, I am taking your dear sister away!'

Anika began to yell, but by then Radhika was lost in the sea.

This happened so suddenly that none got time to react.

Anika began to howl 'This has happened because of me! My poor sister is taken away in the sea'

Sussaina was comforting Anika's Indian mother when Venus descended and said 'Anika, don't lose hope. Find Pajaro and rescue your sister.' She said

'Pajaro? But she is dead!'

Venus smiled and said 'Death was her punishment for teaching magic to Drudan. Now his magic is gone. The Moon wanted a reason to take away his magic. Since he used the Moon against good, he loses his magic. Now when he has lost his magical abilities, find Pajaro!'

'My mother is alive?' Leo asked hopefully

Venus smiled and said 'Death was her punishment and life her destiny!'

'I am not able to understand' said Leo

'You have to find her. But before I leave, let me tell you, the mermaid is going to give birth to a son in six months from now. He will be ten times more evil than Drudan. Before he is born find Pajaro!' said Venus

'How is all this connected?' asked Anika

'That is for you to find. Remember, sometimes we have to struggle for a greater cause. ' smiled Venus

Venus waved goodbye to Anika and said 'Don't let the mermaid's son see your sister. Before he is born find Pajaro!'

Saying this Venus bid farewell to everyone, repeating very strange lines

'His son will be worse than him

Don't ever let him sing'

Book 3

Secrets of Zynpagua: Birth Of Mystery Child

The mermaid swims far away to Pacific Ocean and gives birth to a son. The mermaid realizes that her son had been blessed by the demon planets before they left. As soon as the son is born, he begins to sing and strange things begin to happen. She thus pledges to rescue Drudan and bring disaster for the world. She knows her son is now **The Evil one!**

Quiz

Dear Children,

Please answer these simple questions and send an email to me on Ilika.ranjan@gmail.com.

What is the special quality of the evil child?
Why could Anika's soul not leave her body when Leo drank magical water?
Which is the spell to reduce heights?
On what tree did the old eagle live?
What is the meaning of Senorita?
What is the name of Leo's mother?

A surprise gift is waiting for you!
Happy Reading
Lots of Love and Wishes,
Ilika